THE FOREVER LIFE: BOOK 1

CRAIG ROBERTSON

ALSO BY CRAIG ROBERTSON:

Podium Audio produced audiobooks are available for all the current titles except the standalones.

For specifics as to the correct order for reading the Ryanverse, click *here* or go to

https://craigrobertsonblog.wpcomstaging.com/2020/12/22/correct-order-for-reading-the-ryanverse/

BOOKS IN THE RYANVERSE:

THE FOREVER SERIES (2016)

THE FOREVER LIFE, Book 1

THE FOREVER ENEMY, Book 2

THE FOREVER FIGHT, Book 3

THE FOREVER QUEST, Book 4

THE FOREVER ALLIANCE, Book 5

THE FOREVER PEACE, Book 6

GALAXY ON FIRE SERIES (2017)

EMBERS, Book 1

FLAMES, Book 2

FIRESTORM, Book 3

THE INNERgLOW EFFECT (2010)

WRITE NOW! THE PRISONER OF NaNoWRiMo (2009)

ANON TIME (2009)

THE FOREVER LIFE: BOOK 1

By Craig Robertson

Would You Choose To Live Forever?

Imagine-It Publishing

El Dorado Hills, CA

ISBNs: 978-0-9997742-3-6 (Ebook)
978-0-9896659-9-5 (Paperback)
979-8-7667854-5-3 (Hardcover)

Cover art work and design by Starla Huchton
Available at http:// www.designedbystarla.com

Formatting services by Drew Avera
drew@drewavera.com

Edited by: Michael R. Blanche
Neil Farr
Forest Olivier

First Edition 2016
Second Edition 2018
Third Edition, 2018
Fourth Edition 2019
Fifth Edition 2020
Sixth Edition 2023

Imagine-It Publishing

This book is dedicated to my author's group, headed by the stalwart Scott Evans. Please know, my friends, that without your guidance, patience, and caring, The Forever Life would have never have gotten off the ground. Thanks ... forever.

PRELUDE

The president sat in the Oval Office, alone in the dark. His thumb was anchored on his temple while his fingers rubbed his brow raw with worry. He was confronted by the greatest possible threat to life on Earth. The Ice Ages, Climate Change, and thermonuclear war were child's play compared with what he faced. Teddy Roosevelt once said of being commander-in-chief, "In any moment of decision, the best thing you can do is the right thing and the worst thing you can do is nothing." This was indeed a time for action.

A soft knock on the door brought him back to the here-and-now. He glanced at his watch. Right on time. "Come."

His chief of staff, Roger Carl, opened the door slowly and reached over to brighten the lights. He then ushered in two men. The secretary of state, Sherman Collins, and the other, the messenger. Both visitors were stiff and somber. Without being asked, all three sat across from the president, the messenger with some uncertainty.

Secretary Collins spoke first. "Thank you for seeing us on such short notice, Mr. President."

Barely lifting his hand from his head, President Marshall waved a fatigued dismissal. His once-proud frame seemed deflated by the weight of current events. No one could recall the last time he'd told one of his silly jokes, or even smiled.

"This is Dr. Tip Benjamin," Collins said. A faint nod was all the acknowledgement extended from Marshall. "Dr. Benjamin is the world's best authority on our present crisis. He brings, I fear, as poor tidings as we had anticipated. Dr. Benjamin." He gestured that the messenger should speak.

Tip cleared his dry throat. "Good evening, Mr. President." Tip was a thin man and one unaccustomed to high-pressure meetings. What astrophysicist was? "The secretary has briefed me as to what you know, so I'm not sure where to begin or how detailed to be."

"Just talk. I'll ask questions when I need to."

"Very well, sir." Tip sucked at his lower lip. "About three months ago, a deep sky survey telescope detected what was initially felt to be a new comet. It quickly became apparent we weren't to be that lucky. It turned out to be a rogue planet, one not associated with any particular star."

The secretary could tell Marshall's patience was flagging. "Dr. Benjamin, I believe you should skip the didactic and get right to the bottom line."

Tip shrank back in his chair. It was a bitch being a geek in the world of normal people. "The planet is the size of Jupiter, give or take, and it's moving really fast, for a planet, that is." He stopped to consider his words. "Mercury is about ten percent its spee—"

"Dr. *Benjamin*. The president is a busy man." Roger Carl had lost his patience.

"Ah, sorry. There I go again." He looked briefly at the floor. "So, this large planet—we call it Vega, but that's not official yet or anything—is going to pass through our solar system and then move off to God knows where. Before it does, Vega will pass close enough to Jupiter to throw that planet completely out of its present orbit around the Sun."

The President asked quietly, "On this point, are you absolutely *certain*, Doctor?"

"Absolutely. One-hundred percent certain. Jupiter will fly off like a billiard ball and it will really pick up speed. Within a year's time or so it will stabilize in a smaller and very odd-shaped orbit."

Sitting up, Marshall asked, "And?"

Tip dropped his head as though an anchor hung around it. "And on it's sixteenth of those orbits, Jupiter will directly impact Earth."

"Again, Doctor, on this point are you *absolutely* certain?"

"One-hundred percent, sir." He raised his arms above his head. "Really, I wish I wasn't so *damn* certain. Jupiter will strike us squarely, a direct bullseye." He slammed a fist into his palm. "Dead center."

"Doctor Benjamin, there's so much riding on your prediction, I must ask again. Is there *any* chance, however slight, the two planets will miss each other?" Marshall slumped back in his seat. He already knew the answer.

"Sorry, Mr. President. None whatsoever. We're totally screwed." As soon as those last words left his mouth, Tip wished he could pull them back in. He was relieved to see either no one cared or no one noticed his flippancy.

Looking to his secretary of state, Marshall said, "So, in ninety-seven years, the Earth will be annihilated." Back to Tip, he asked, "What, precisely, Dr. Benjamin, will occur?"

Tip held his hands up in the shape of a football. "Our tidally deformed planet will pass into Jupiter's gaseous surface," he crumpled his fingers together, "and some dust will come out the other side a few days later."

Collins shrugged, and replied, "Well, at least we have almost a century to prepare. That's something."

Tip cleared his throat loudly.

Marshall was too tired and too vexed to brook indirectness. "Do you have something to add, *Doctor*? I can't do the right thing if I do not have all the *facts*."

Tip folded his shoulders forward, and tried to disappear between them. "Well, the sixteenth is the orbit where a collision will occur. But, orbit fifteen may rain all holy hell down from the heavens, puns intended." Furrowing his brow, Tip remarked, "Fourteen may not be much of a walk in the park either. Not unless you're carrying a *really* big steel umbrella." He harrumphed a quiet laugh.

Marshall lost it. "Look, *Benjamin*, I don't have the time or the inclination to play twenty-questions with you. If I don't choose the sensible option and blow my brains out before tomorrow, I can't waste time. *What?*"

Tip was shaking like a frightened dog beaten by his cruel owner. "Not only does Jupiter have several moons, but, after the interaction with Vega, it will likely trail behind it a large debris field. Certainly by orbit fifteen, our planet is likely to be struck by something big enough to cause *major* damage."

"So," Marshall said to no one in particular, "we have ninety-seven years, tops. We may only have ninety-one or less, if our luck remains as bad as it's been."

Carl stood up. "Explain to me, please, why we can't just blow the damn thing up? I'm told we can't. But, I mean, if the combined nuclear weapons held on Earth worked together, how could that *not* destroy Jupiter?"

Tip angled his head. "It's just too damn big, Roger. If we launch all our nukes at Jupiter and managed somehow to throw the Moon at it too, it wouldn't change a thing. And even if we could blow it apart, the little pieces would remain in orbit together. They'd still make mincemeat out of Earth just as efficiently."

A frustrated Carl asked, "Couldn't we redirect Jupiter? I've heard they would try that on an asteroid if it threatened the Earth."

Tip shook his head. "Sorry, Roger, no can do. Yes, we can alter an asteroid's orbit enough by flying rockets to one side of it, using the ship's gravity to redirect the rock. But, like I just said, Jupiter is too massive and the time left is way too short. There is nothing we can do to save the Earth. Rog, you gotta let that idea go."

Collins said hesitantly, "Mr. President—*John*—what are we going to do?"

Marshall tented his palms over his face and rubbed it vigorously. "We're going to *work* like hell and *pray* like hell and hope to God we catch every *single* break between then and now."

"What are you suggesting?"

"Sherm, you and I both have grandkids young enough to die in this catastrophe unless we do something. Mine will *not* be remembered as the administration that chose to do nothing. We will commit every dollar of our wealth and every minute left to us to salvage as much of our species, of human culture, as we can." He took a deep breath and looked out the window. "We will evacuate the Earth. We will find a new home for humankind. Nothing less is acceptable." He stood. "So, gentlemen, we had best get to work. Sleep is a luxury we can no longer afford."

ONE

Three years later in Houston

It wasn't every day I had my entire being, everything I ever was or ever knew, dumped into a robot built by low-bid government contract. What could *possibly* go wrong? The white coats reassured me that none of the test animals showed any statistically significant mental impairment from the transfer. Great. No rats were stupider than they already were. But the whole process was so prohibitively expensive, full scientific vetting hadn't been possible. Worst-case scenario, my brain would be scrambled into warm mush and the android would remain lifeless and empty. Jon all gone. Heads would shake and a few kind words would be said about me. The next morning the search for someone to blame and a new volunteer would start up in earnest.

You know what? I wasn't worried in the least about the risks. I was the perfect man for this job. Youngest officer to make USAF Major in decades, a decorated combat veteran, and a graduate of the astronaut program. Two doctorates, one in biology and one in physics. Since divorcing Mrs. ControlFreak years back, I was as single as could be. Once so bitten, eternally shy was I. Plus, I was an only child, both my parents were already in the ground, and my nearest relative was so distant I could legally marry the woman. Not that I *wanted* to marry my demented ninety-seven-year-old third cousin awaiting death in a nursing home. But, my point was, Jonathan Alan Ryan was going to be the man who helped save this planet's butt. The upcoming procedure and mission might just make that possible. Not sure I wanted to live forever, but, for the time being, it was one day at a time.

One more briefing with the suits and IFGOs, and I could get on with it. Oh, excuse me. For those never lucky enough to be military pilots, IFGOs stands for, and please excuse my French in advance, *I*gnorant *F*ucking *G*round *O*fficer. Not really a term of endearment, but there it was. I flew planes, they flew desks. I risked my butt, they risked splinters in theirs. One more boring meeting. I could do this. At all times, I never forget that there were three equally qualified pilots dying to take my place, and the boss, General Saunders, would love to bump me just because he could.

In fact, once I was clear of the docking bay and alone on my ship, I do believe I was going to have to tell that SOB off. What was he going to do? I will have been downloaded into an android with no possibility of reversing the process and be outbound on a mission slated to last the better part of a century. Saunders, sure as hell's a bad place for penguins to nest, won't be standing at the dock awaiting my return with a couple of MPs. But, for the time being, I had to stay focused. No screw-ups and in a little while, I'd make history. Or become history. Hey, either way, I was kicking the can down the road.

I stepped up to the main security checkpoint before taking the elevator down the twenty stories to the main laboratories. To the sergeant, I said, "Morning, Jimmie. How's it going today?"

He popped me a salute, and said, "Fine, Major. And you?"

"Jimmie, don't they tell you *anything* around here? Today's the day they shrink-wrap my brain and try to stuff it into an untested android. If that doesn't kill me, pretty soon they're shooting me off in a completely experimental spacecraft, alone, for a hundred years."

With a blank expression, he said, "So, you're looking at busy day, right?"

"I'm thinking so. Yes."

Jimmie shrugged. "I'm hoping for meatloaf tonight. You're clear to proceed, Major."

"Thanks, Sergeant. Oh, and maybe save me a slice, if there's enough. I *love* meatloaf."

He saluted. "Sure, no problem. I just hope the missus can wrap it well enough to last that long."

I made it to the meeting room just on time. Saunders was there, as was our lead scientist, Dr. Toño DeJesus. All the section heads were there to go through our final checklists together. The three alternate pilots were hovering like vultures.

Saunders stood with a grunt. After a loud clearing of his throat he began. "Today we're going to take an enormous step forward. I expect perfection from each and every one of you. If any of you find yourselves looking at me across my desk tomorrow morning because you screwed something up, I promise you, it will *not* be pleasant." He thumped the desk with his knuckles. "Just hope whatever mistake you made killed you. It will save me the bother." He scanned the room like a shark surveying a school of fish, to see if anyone reacted poorly. "Very well. Professor, the floor is yours. But make it quick. We're all very busy today."

Nervous by nature, DeJesus hesitantly stood up. His tall, thin frame and long, thin face were set off poorly by his tendency to stoop forward, as if he were years older than he looked. His loose-fitting clothes only amplified his hunched, drained appearance. He looked to me. "Good morning, Major Ryan. I trust you are well."

"Couldn't be better, Doc."

He turned to the others. "Any glitches or stops on anyone's final checklist?" No one said a peep. "Fine, fine." He looked to the wall clock. "In approximately ninety minutes we will commence the upload of Major Ryan to the android. If anyone runs into a problem, however slight, notify the general or me immediately. Otherwise, I suggest we all get to our stations and do our jobs."

I had to say it. Heck, it might be the last time I saw them, or anyone else for that matter. "Ah, a moment of your time, if you don't mind."

Everyone looked to Saunders. He scrunched up his face like he was significantly constipated, but finally said, "Unscheduled, but, all right, Major. If it's brief and mission critical."

I stood up and crumpled my hat in my hands. "Sure is, Sir. I just wanted to thank you all for your hard work. Especially those of you working to make the android as human as possible. I did have one question, before I go any further, though." I glanced over at Saunders. He looked like he was going to puff up and explode. Too bad he didn't. "For those of you in the Genital Department. When you signed off on 'fully functional,' was that a *promise*, or was it just your general goal?"

The room erupted in snickers, well, aside from the boss. He looked as displeased as a cat with a can of sardines. He glared at me a moment. "Very droll, Major. If you're finished with your locker-room jokes, do you think we could be getting on with it?"

"Of course, General Saunders."

My mother warned me up until the day she died to stop being my own worst enemy. I know she meant well, but it sure was a lot more fun my way.

A driver waited outside the meeting room with a golf cart transport. The main laboratory was about a quarter mile away. The general, doctor, and I mounted up. We were all silent for the short trip. Once there, I headed to the locker room, while the other two made their way to Control Central. In the dressing room, I donned my designated clothing. In honor of the historic significance and the presence of news photographers, the higher-ups decided that I shouldn't wear a traditional medical gown. They felt there was insufficient dignity if my naked butt flashed across a holo screen. Also, a

Hollywood director was consulted to suggest camera angles and my general movements. One of his actors demonstrated that if I was seated in the exam chair wearing a standard-issue gown, my masculinity was at risk of entering the public record. So, I wore a modified toga. It wound around me tightly one and a half times and tied with a thin belt.

The design of the outfit was actually hotly debated. One camp held that the entire kit should be white. Understated, antiseptic, and traditional. A disparate segment of those entitled to an opinion favored a military palate, such as Air Force blue and gray. A differing gaggle of fashionistas felt a bold new look was called for by the enormity of the occasion. They argued against a Roman toga, suggesting a smock-over-towel-wrap ensemble. The colors, they proclaimed, should speak of the future, iridescent oranges transitioning into electric yellows.

When told of the controversy, Saunders decreed that the robe would be white. His robe at home was white and it was a perfectly fine robe. The assistant asked what color his robe's sash was. That turned out to be an awkward, TMI moment for both men. The general remarked off-handedly that he didn't have a belt for his robe. Oh myyy. When the nearly apoplectic assistant pointed out the lack of privacy, Saunders screamed that the belt would be white, too.

The three backup pilots sat with me, fidgeting. Major Turk McCarthy, the first alternate, noted I was ready and teased, "So, big guy, it's still not too late to pass the baton to me."

I smiled. "No, but thanks. I think I'll run it to the finish line myself. Plus, you could live looking like me for all of eternity?"

Turk said, "Suit yourself. I was just worrying about you."

"Do tell?"

Placing a hand on his chest, Turk said, "I do, indeed." He leaned in confidentially. "I've had a long time to think about this immortality thing, Jon. I have come to believe it will be a curse—a damn curse." Sorrowfully, he shook his head. "As to looking like you, why

—hell—I'd suffer that gladly to help a colleague. I'm just that kind of a guy."

"A curse, you say? That doesn't sound so good."

Confidently, Turk said, "They never are, big guy—never-ever."

"So," I asked, "what, you'd take that bullet *for* me?"

"Yes, I would, because you're such a good friend. You know I love you like both my brothers combined, right?"

I nodded. "I did *not* know that. Wow, I think I may start bawling like a beauty queen who just won the crown."

"No need and no time. Just strip that robe off and walk out that door."

"Hmm." I rubbed my chin.

"What?" Turk asked.

"I was wondering if this isn't just a ploy to see me naked again, Turk."

"No way. You're not my type. But—for the record—Carl here would like to sneak another peek." He pointed to one of the other two alternates, who promptly punched Turk in the arm.

That was, of course, the precise moment Saunders entered the room. "What the *hell* are you four imbeciles doing?"

We staggered to attention as one. "Nothing," Turk said. "We were just saying our farewells to Major Ryan, Sir."

Saunders crossed his arms. "What, by injuring my most valuable asset on the day I need him the most?"

"No, Sir. Just friendly horseplay."

"Well knock it off. You three," he swiped a plump finger at the backups, "get to the Control Room, *now*. You," he pointed to me, "need to report to your duty station."

"Sir." The alternates saluted and snapped-to.

I lingered and sat back down on the wooden bench. "If it's all the same to you, General, I think I'll hang out here a minute longer, to gather my thoughts."

With uncharacteristic nervousness, Saunders muttered, "Oh, yes. Fine, Major. I'll be up top if you need me."

I saluted. "Thank you, Sir. I'll just be a minute."

Finally, I was alone. Four years of constant screening, testing, and training had bombarded my mind. Endless meetings, interviews, and review sessions have overloaded my senses. Solitude was finally mine—in the Men's Locker Room next door to the big machine which was about to suck out my soul. Oh well, I had to reflect, not Lake Tahoe in early spring, but it was quiet, save for the ubiquitous electrical hum. That sound asked nothing of me, nor did it judge.

I actually looked forward to the impending transfer attempt. If nothing happened, I'd go back to my old life and regain control. If the experiment succeeded, my existence would be radically altered and I'd move on. Even if the process nuked my brain, at least the entire farce would be over. I'd pay good money to never hear that windbag Saunders shoot his mouth off again. Sure, if everything went as planned, he'd send me tedious messages for a few years. But, soon enough, General PissedOff would go the way of all living flesh and out of my new life. Amen to that.

A quick check of the wall clock confirmed it was time to go. I looked up and closed my eyes. "Well, Mom and Pop, maybe I'll see you in about half an hour. Who knows," I chuckled, "maybe never." I laughed out loud. "Maybe both, come to think of it." With that, I stood and walked to the passageway leading to the testing arena. I pulled the steel door open and stepped into the ten-meter hallway.

Halfway down the corridor, near the blast doors, I could swear I felt a push back. It was as though the air was conspiring to stop me. Not the time to lose it, I chastised myself. Quit imagining signs and signals. After a few increasingly difficult steps, the illusion passed. I entered the work area, but couldn't help looking back at the passageway.

Doc zipped to my side. "Over here, Major." He pulled me toward the empty exam chair. "Please, be seated."

Once in place, the doctor began affixing wires and sticky patches all over my body. Most instrumentation went on my head. We had drilled that step a hundred times. It seemed to go much quicker this time. I casually noted the covered android, wires streaming from under its shroud, seated in an identical chair three meters away.

"When are you guys going to let me see the robot, Doc?" I batted my eyelashes, and added, "Now seems as good a time as any."

He shook his head. "We feel it is best if you do not see the copy. As you know, we don't want to engender some unanticipated emotional response that could interfere with the transfer process. That's the same reason we will not allow you to meet the functioning android, nor allow him to see you after the transfer is complete." He shook his head wearily. "We're breaking completely new ground here, Major. Perhaps we're overreacting, or perhaps we're naive, but this is how it will be."

"At least tell me one thing, Doc."

"What?"

"Is he as handsome as me?"

That drew a rare giggle from the doctor.

"I know, silly question, right? No *way* he could be."

It seemed as if he was going to respond with something institutional, but instead he said, "Of course you are the more handsome of the pair, Major. Here, place this in your mouth." He shoved a sensor down my throat and tapped my jaw shut.

Very soon, all was ready. I was wired six-ways-to-Sunday, and so was the dummy. Ten million lights flashed chaotically from all directions. Technicians, engineers, and photographers, all in dust-free suits, scurried around like hungry mice. The doctor checked his watch and confirmed it agreed precisely with the countdown clock high above the two exam chairs. Five minutes until the facility would be locked-down and backup power took over. Fifteen minutes until my destiny was revealed. I looked up to the panoramic windows of the Control Room. Saunders leaned on the sill, chewing his pipe stem like a butcher's dog his bone. I could see the alternate pilots sitting near him. Turk waved his fingers at me as if to say goodbye.

The transfer floor smelled of antiseptic, and the air felt cold against my face. Sounds of anxious tension bounced from wall to wall. The pounding of my heart dueled with those of the machines that pulsed all around me. The taste of ozone and fear fouled the air. I felt tingly ... then I felt ... nothing ...

———

" ... nnnnn?"

" ... aaaannnnn?"

" ... jor Ryannnnn?"

My cheek stung. Someone was shaking my shoulder and slapping my face.

"Major Ryan?"

Light rammed past my eyelids and stormed to the back of my sockets. Painful illumination exploded in both eyes.

"Major Ryan, are you all right?"

It was a man's voice. No ... yes, a man. I struggled to make out the form. A man with a pencil-thin mustache bounced in and out of my focus. *DeJesus*. It was Doc, calling to me. I tried to raise my head, but was immediately stopped by the restraints. I attempted to sit up with equal futility. More restraints. I relaxed into the chair, helpless.

"Major Ryan, can you hear me? It is Dr. DeJesus. Jon, are you alright?"

There was something odd in his voice, in the tone. Jon? Doc never called me by my first name.

Something had gone terribly wrong. Was I dead? No, that's silly. I could hear him and my face hurt from the pounding it had taken. I had to be alive. My head was spinning like a gyroscope, and I felt like a jet fighter in a dead-stall.

The vision of DeJesus shot sideways out of sight. Strong arms grabbed both my shoulders and shook me like a rag doll. A man's voice yelled, but ... it was different. Louder.

"Ryan, wake up. That's an order, Son."

General Sandy. No, General Sanderson ... Saunders. It was

Saunders, trying to get me to wake up. Wake up? I *was* awake. My eyes were exploding, my nose was on fire, I was so ...

"Why, you see, Professor, that's all it takes. A little elbow grease and the boy's as right as rain. Aren't you, Ryan?"

I replied, "Yes, sir. I am, sir."

And I was. What was all that about just now? I'd felt like I was being used for experimental tortures in hell, but suddenly I was perfectly fine. Better than fine, actually. I felt ... really good.

DeJesus muscled back to the center of my vision. "Major Ryan. If you understand me, close your right eye."

"Doc, wouldn't it be a lot easier if I just told you I can understand you?"

"Yes, of course." Chagrined, he looked to the general, then back at me. "Are you in any pain, Major?"

"No, Doc, just my ears 'cause you're still shouting so loud." He smiled sheepishly. "Are *you* okay, Doc?"

"Me? Yes, I'm ... but I wasn't just ... I mean to say ..."

My eyes sprang wide open. I asked, "You weren't just *what*, Doc?" I stared at the doctor a moment. "What, you weren't just dead? Did I die, Doc? Is that what all the fuss is about?"

"Major, there will be plenty of time to discuss all aspects of your ... experience," said the doctor. "But, those matters are best deferred until later. For now, I need to ascertain that you are funct ... er, in proper health." He reached over and loosened the restraints on my head, then released my chest and arms. I was still held in the chair by waist and leg straps. "There. See if you can sit up."

Fluidly, I sat up. I smiled at him. "There, see. Nothing to worry about. I'm none the worse for wear. Hey, were you able to try the transfer yet? I seem to have a gap in my memory or something."

Only then did I notice the other chair, the one I'd been strapped to initially, was empty. I angled my head that direction. "Why the hell'd you move me to this chair? This's where the *puppet* sits. Aren't we a little old for musical chairs?"

Doc went ashen. He rested his hands on his knees and began

hyperventilating. I asked if he was okay, but he didn't respond. He just kept hyperventilating, all the while he was losing more color. Finally, his trembling hand reached into his pocket and pulled out a bottle of nitroglycerin pills. He fumbled the cap open and slipped a tablet under his tongue.

I asked sharply, "Doc, you want me to get *you* a doctor?" I attempted to do just that, but was prevented from doing so by the restraints.

Finally, he was able to pat my forearm and weakly say, "I'm fine now, Major. Not to worry. I seem to have experienced a bit of shock, that's all."

"So," I asked, "can you tell me why I'm sitting where the robot was, not where I started out?"

"Well, you see, Major ... eh. Well, it's like this ... in essence—" He stammered badly. That could *not* be a good sign.

From the side, came a strong clear voice. "Because you *are* the robot, Major Ryan." It was Saunders. I turned and saw a huge smile on his face.

I was really pissed. "General, with all due respect, this is not funny. You've subjected me to every test and scenario in the book. But this one borders on being just plain cruel. I have to formally protest." This horse's ass figured he'd see how I might react when the transfer was actually attempted. He had them knocked me out and put me in the android's chair. The son of a *bitch*.

"Cruel now, am I?" He scanned the room quickly, and stepped over to an open medical cart. He removed a packaged needle and syringe and tore it open. After removing the cap from the needle, he walked back to my side. "Let's see how cruel I really am, shall we?" With that, he stabbed me firmly in the back of the hand.

Belatedly, the doctor yelped a protest. "No, wait, General. Yo—" He stopped when it was clear his appeal was too late.

"Ow, you son-of-a-*bitch*. That hurt."

Saunders pointed to my hand. "Look at your stupid hand, major-robot. No *blood*."

I raised my hand to eye level. The needle was stuck in my flesh, it smarted, but he was right. There was no bleeding at all. I asked, "How did you pull off this parlor trick, Saunders? You an amateur magician on weekends?"

"That will be about all the insubordination I am willing to brook, Major Ryan—or whoever you are now. I will remind you but *once*. You are technically still an officer in the USAF. I am your commander and you will act accordingly. Do I make myself clear, Son?"

I barely heard the general's words. I just kept staring at the painful but bloodless wound in my hand.

Into that gap jumped the doctor. "Gentlemen, *please*." the doctor said. "Let us all calm down and allow cooler heads to prevail." He placed himself between Saunders and me. "We have just created a miracle. Let us not spoil it with harsh words or posturing. General Saunders, as scientific director, it is within my power to have you removed from this room. Please do not force me to do so. You must, I demand, stop badgering my android. And, you are absolutely *forbidden* to do him any further damage or I will have you arrested. Do I make *myself* perfectly clear, Harry?"

I whistled in amazement. "I musta been out quite a while, Doc. When did you grow those big cojones of yours?" I thumped him soundly on the back. "I'm proud of you, Doc. Glad to call you my friend."

TWO

After the general left the area, DeJesus rested his hand on mine. He had a very soulful look in his eyes, almost sad. "Major Ryan, this is not a trick or a test. Please trust me on this. We have completed the transfer process. Everything has gone as well as can be expected."

"Very reassuring, Doc. What, maybe you left my teen years behind, but you don't know yet?"

He gave me a humorless grin. "At least your strange sense of humor transferred accurately. Very shortly, I will wheel you into the main laboratory. There, we can do a complete scan of your circuitry and a full set of diagnostics. Then, we can begin testing just how accurate a copy we made. But for now, I wish to speak plainly and from my heart."

"Absolutely. Give it to me straight."

"Major Ryan, you are an android. You are the first of your kind, a completely new species. *Válgame, Dios*, you're not a new species. You are a new form of *life*." He wiped his forehead. "I suppose the issue as to whether you are technically alive will be hotly debated in the future."

"You and your brainiac-friends can debate all you like, Doc. But please do it later, after I'm well out in space. For now, I'll state for the record I *am* alive, as alive as I ever was. So, make sure everybody treats me like I am."

"Of course, Major. I'll treat you the same as I am already treating the—" He let that thought trail off. After a sigh, he added, "Some things are best left unsaid. For now, it is important for me to know you believe you are The Transplanted Man. You're a good officer and a good friend. It would hurt me if I failed to convey this fact accurately."

Okay, I'm a robot. Buzz, buzz. *Klaatu barada nikto.* "No problem, Doc. I know you're telling me the truth. Is the original me okay, too?"

He tapped his index finger against his lips to signal silence. Then, he asked, "Before we head to the lab, one question, Major, if you will indulge this old scientist."

"Sure. As long as it's not too personal."

Surprised, he squinted at me, and said, "Too pers ... Ah, you're pulling my leg again, aren't you?"

I pointed at his face. "I had you for a minute there."

"Major, how do you feel? I mean to say, what does it feel like to be an android?"

What *did* it feel like? I wiggled my fingers and toes, and looked way up, then down. My high school English teacher was Mr. Pearl. I positively hated Brussels sprouts. My ex-wife farted almost every time we made love, one of the many reasons she quickly became my *ex*. The room was cool and buzzed electronically, like before they flipped the switch. I wasn't hungry, but an In-N-Out burger sure sounded good.

"Honestly, Doc, I feel normal. If no one told me the switch worked, I wouldn't know I wasn't the old human me."

For a moment there, the doc's eyes looked, I don't know, disappointed. But maybe it was a trick of the light. Not too convincingly, he said, "That's good to hear, Major. After all, that was our goal, wasn't it?"

"It sure was mine."

He pushed my chair the thirty meters to the main testing and assembly room. Odd. In the years I trained, retrained, and re-retrained in this underground vault, I'd never seen this area. Guess there was never a need. Up until then, I wasn't a robot. In the entire lead-up to the transfer, they'd actually told me precious little about the android unit itself. I was reassured it would be lifelike and that I'd be perfectly comfortable. But, come to think of it, how would they know that? Man, was I ever trusting. You know The Big Lies? *I will respect you in the morning. The check is in the mail. I'm from the government and I'm here to help you.* I prayed to God the newest Big Lie wasn't, *Trust me, you are going to love your new android body.* Oh well, a bit too late for buyer's remorse. There was a "no return" policy on this puppy.

The doctor walked over to a workstation and returned with an oversized electric cord that had a small adapter at the end. It was like a USB plug, just slightly thicker.

"Lift your right arm, please, Major." Okay, odd request for a man holding a power cable. No problem. I raised my arm like I had a question. "Thank you." He poked a finger in my armpit, which didn't tickle like it should have. The rest of my skin functioned exactly like it always had before. He finally said, "There it is." Then he pushed the adapter into my armpit. I felt a soft click, then a brief warm feeling. "Perfect. You may lower your arm for now, if you like."

My first lesson in being a robot took place then. It required zero effort to keep my arm aloft, but I could sense my shoulder muscles tensing as they did their work. In fact, I quickly realized it didn't matter physically either way, whether I kept my arm up or down. My new muscles weren't going to fatigue. How cool. Or how frightening. Actually, how *both*. I knew anyone who saw me would think it strange of me to hold my arm up, revealing an electric cord plugged into my axilla, so I lowered my arm.

DeJesus was over at a control panel, flipping switches and typing like a madman. I let him be. He was, after all, trying to make sure I didn't short-out or blow a gasket. Time for a self-test. I looked at one of his computer screens. There was a chaotic stream of figures and symbols scrolling by rapidly. I closed my eyes. What had I just seen? I tried to visualize the exact images. Nothing. Then I asked myself, "What did that display show?" Again, nothing. What good was it being a robot if I didn't have a photographic memory and perfect recall? Poo. I had hoped I would be like Colonel Steve Austin, The Six Million Dollar Man. Remember how his robotic left eye could focus in, and there was that cool electric *dit dit dit dit* sound effect as it did? I got nothing.

Coming out of my daydream, I realize that the doctor was talking to me. " ... as normal as I could have hoped. Of course, further testing will be needed." He shuddered. "Wouldn't want to miss any decay changes or other unanticipated snafus."

"I don't recall the concept of 'decay' being discussed when we went over the pros and cons of my going android."

"We don't *expect* such things to happen. I was, er ... just thinking out loud."

"Doc," I said, shaking my head, "I have to admit, I'm a little disappointed."

He looked shocked, as if I'd told him his puppy just got run over multiple times. "What, Major? Is there a malfunction?"

"I don't know if it's that, but while you were over there checking out my systems, I did a little experiment. I studied one of your screens, but couldn't capture any more information than I could have before."

"And you're saying—?"

"Where are my superpowers? I mean, what's the point in being a machine if I don't get superpowers?"

At first, he was uncertain, then he said, "Oh, I understand. You expected to have super-human abilities?" He scowled. "Like Colonel

Steven Austin, The Six Million Dollar Man?" He put his hands on his hips.

"Like who? The Six Million Dollar *Man*? Doc, seriously. I'm a grown-up. That was Seventies TV. Really? No, I'm just curious if I function differently now."

"Would you like me to upload the silly *dit, dit, dit, dit* sound effect we heard when he employed his six-million-dollar abilities, Major? Perhaps I can play it through one of your ancillary speakers, so everyone will hear it, also?"

"Doc, that's just plain silly."

"Hmm. Didn't I tell you we were starting you off in 'safe-mode,' Major?"

"I don't believe you did. No, and I think I'd recall if we had that discussion."

"We elected to boot you up in a safe mode. We did not want to risk overloading either your circuitry or your senses."

"Sounds prudent. So," I twirled my hands in the air, "eventually, I will be—I don't know—better, stronger, faster?"

He groaned, then said, "Very soon I will be adding in functionalities. If all goes well, Colonel Austin will be suing you for copyright infringement."

"Whatever. I just want to be totally aware of what I've gotten my ass into, that's all."

"I'll have someone get me the recording of those sound effects." He sounded disgusted.

I held my hands up. "Don't go to *any* trouble on my account."

"I think we've accomplished about all we hoped for today. If it's all the same to you, Major, all of the staff, and certainly I, for one, need to get some sleep."

Uncertainly, I replied, "Sure, Doc, whatever you need to do." He was rubbing under his eye. Me, I felt great. I couldn't imagine taking a nap.

"Fine. As an additional precaution, I will place you in a sleep-mode. I wouldn't—"

"A *what?*"

Focusing on me intently, he said, "I will be placing you in *sleep* mode. After considerable discussion, it is our consensus that, early on, you should not be left awake and unattended. There are simply too many variables."

"You're going to turn me *off?*"

"Major Ryan," he said with some irritation, "I will be doing nothing of the kind. Please stop reacting so ... so ... so much like yourself." He stopped when it hit him how perverse that sounded. "I will initiate a program which simulates sleep. Later, you can do it yourself, if you so desire. But for now, I will override your ability to block the routine." Wearily, he added, "I hope you won't mind."

"Do I have an option?"

Impatiently, he said, "No, you do not."

"Well then, goodnight, Doc. Sleep tight and don't let the—"

———

" ... bedbugs bite."

"Good morning, Major Ryan." I looked up to see Doc smiling down on me. Then—and I'm certain I'm right about this—he asked with considerable mischief in his voice, "Did you sleep well?"

I furrowed my brow. "Sleep? We were just talking and I was giving you a hard time. You said something about sleep, but now you're—" I looked around the room. I was supine, while I'd been sitting up a microsecond ago. There were restraining straps over my chest, arms, and legs. "How long was I off?"

He grinned. "You were in sleep-mode for ten, nearly eleven hours."

"You're shittin' me?"

"Watch your mouth, soldier. This is all being recorded."

Ah, to awaken to the dulcet tones of General Saunders. What could be a more perfect start to my day? Hopefully, next, I'd receive an ice-cold enema. Next, maybe a pox or, at the very least, boils. Or toads. "General Saunders, what a pleasant surprise."

"Couldn't you have erased his lame sense of humor, Professor?" said Saunders.

Doc looked at me peevishly. "That thought had occurred to me."

"Oh yeah, gang up on the robot why don't you? You fleshies, you're all alike."

Saunders frowned and asked, "Does he at least have a mute button?"

"No, General, but I'm thinking of installing one right away."

DeJesus came over and began releasing my restraints. "All right, my funny friend, we have a lot to accomplish today, so let's get started." When I was free, he said, "Please try and stand up. Slowly now."

Tentatively, I sat up. No clanging alarms or fireworks. Cool. I dangled my legs over the edge of the gurney, even swung them around slowly. They didn't fall off and I didn't get lightheaded. Very cool. The doctor steadied one elbow and a technician the other, to help me stand. I checked his insignia. I'd assumed he'd be a Med-Tech. Nope. Aerospace Ground Engineer. It was official. My employer saw me as a mechanical asset and not a human being. Oh boy. I was listed alongside engines and industrial cleaners. If I'd had a heart it would have broken.

"There we go. Now we will release you." I stood as unsteadily as a corn stalk in a strong wind, but I remained upright. "Excellent. Now, take a few steps. Let us steady you."

I was able to walk without any difficulty or discomfort. Also, I did so without any effort. That was the weirdest part. It was like with my arms yesterday. Effort no longer took any *effort* for me. What a gas. In a few minutes, it was clear I was steady on my own, so the two guys let go. Though they hovered close, there was no way I needed them. When I abruptly jumped up and down, I thought the doctor was going to need another of his nitro tabs. After that stunt, he put me in a chair and attached a bunch of cables. Oh well, it was worth it. The Hendrix song *Freedom* from long ago popped into my head.

Over the next few days, Doc and lots of other scientists tested me every which way but loose. They never told me much in terms of their findings. When I asked how I looked, mostly they just grunted or grumbled. White coats. The nerds had no social skills whatsoever. Not one of the scientists who worked on me had a prom date—I guarantee it. They did finally turn on the last of my senses. *Smell.* Marvelous, rich, enticing smell was mine again to enjoy. They tested me with peppermint, soap, and coffee, which was *divine* I had to say. I got them all right. I was a stud right out the gate.

After a few days, Doc was comfortable enough with my status to leave me on my own for short snippets during the day. The first chance I got, I headed straight to the locker room where I'd changed clothes just before the transfer. I remembered it had a full-length mirror. I needed to see exactly what I'd literally gotten myself into. People had always told me I was a fairly good-looking man. I'd defi-nitely stayed in top shape and was six-feet two with eyes of blue. Time to check if I was going to be pleased with the results.

As a man who'd shaved every day of his adult life, looking at the reflection of my face was no big deal. Still, like a scared kid, I inched slowly toward the mirror's edge, as if I was peeping around a corner looking for the Bogeyman. Finally I stood in full view of myself. Nothing violent happened, which I took to be a good sign. Damn if I didn't look exactly like I had when I was human, the very spitting image of Jon Ryan. Nice work, Doc. As I leaned in, my baby-blue irises dilated smoothly. I tugged at my cheeks and looked at the inside of my eyelids. The skin was soft, pliable, and moist. My inner lids were slightly pink. I pushed my nose back and forth. It felt like my nose. The scar I got in flight school was there on my forehead. *Crazy.*

I looked around quickly to make sure I was still alone. Then I pulled my sweats down to my knees. Yep, the merchandise was all present and accounted for. Life size, too. I grabbed hold of the floppy parts and gave them a tussle. They felt just like they did before. What a relief. I turned around. Man, did I have a cute butt or what? Okay, I could live with this body, no prob. And, as it would never age, I was actually kind of jazzed.

One evening, Doc told me we'd be going to Saunders' office the next morning to meet a few VIPs. Nice. A break in my up-until-then boring routine would be a treat. When Doc "woke me up," I was, for the first time, unrestrained. I took that to mean that I must be making good progress. I vaulted off the table, mostly to get Doc's goat. Then I recalled with some guilt that he has a bad ticker. Better can the antics, at least with him.

I walked down the long hallway with Doc by my side, him as nervous as a bridegroom. He even let me push the elevator button. I felt like a *big* boy. We were greeted by the general's chief of staff, a good-looking iceberg of a woman, Captain Gia Partee. She may have been of Irish extraction, but *gee-a-party* she was not, at least not concerning yours truly. She seemed to have an unusually large stick up her butt that morning, even for her.

After she escorted us into the office, I understood why. President Marshall sat behind Saunders's desk. The head of the Joint Chiefs, Saunders, and leaders from both houses of Congress sat across from him. Marshall had just begun his emergency-enacted third term as president. Seemed that since the world actually *was* about to end, politics took a backseat to the good of the nation.

Marshall rose and extended a hand. "So proud to meet you, er ... Major Ryan. Again, that is." He batted his hands at me. "Oh, you know what I mean."

"Yes, sir, Mr. President. No problem." For the first time in as long as I could remember, my anal sphincter tone shot to infinity plus one. Since declaring martial law—affectionately know as Marshall's Law nowadays—I was looking at the most powerful man in human history. At age sixty-three, he looked to remain in office another fifteen to twenty years, directing the evacuation effort. His wishes *were* everyone's commands.

"Major," he began, "we're here to meet you firsthand. The survival of the world," he shook his head ominously, "rests on your shoulders." Pointing to the other three, he said, "If we four are satisfied that you are ready for prime time, we are going to unveil you to the world. We can use the positive PR. You'll lighten the hearts of billions of people." He raised his hands as if to frame a picture. "'The first human-android goes in search of humankind's new home.'" He stood and handed me a small box. "I presented one of these to the other you not an hour ago."

I opened the lid. The Congressional Medal of Honor. Holy crap, President Marshall just handed me the CMOH. Okay, the bladder control on this robot worked perfectly. "Thank you, I mean, seriously, thank you, Sir."

"We expect the world of you, but we must also acknowledge your courage, *Colonel* Ryan." He handed me a second box.

Dude. I was a full-bird colonel. Skipped right past being a phone-colonel to get there. *Sweet.*

"I will do my level best, Mr. President. You can count on me."

Saunders spoke. "Professor DeJesus, why don't you brief our guests as to the colonel's functionality and progress to date."

Doc turned an unhealthy shade of pale. Reflexively, he patted the vest pocket of his lab coat to reassure himself that he brought his nitroglycerin along. He stood. "Very well." He bowed his head in turn to the others. Gesturing to me, he said, "As far as we can tell, we have downloaded a precise copy of Colonel Ryan. Additionally, the android seems to be working exactly as planned. I could not be more pleased."

"Is he ready," asked the senator, "to function autonomously and alone for the better part of a century?"

"Yes, he is. Actually, a good deal longer I should suspect."

"How long might the unit last?" asked the admiral.

Doc shrugged. "Hard to say for certain. We have installed redundancies and repair options that the colonel can perform, and spare parts are housed in the body. So, physically, it can last thousands of years."

The congresswoman scoffed. "No machine can last that long."

"The android is powered by two palm-sized fusion reactors. These can generate power indefinitely. Along with conventional computers, he is equipped with a prototype biocomputer that will have the plasticity to allow itself to grow and adapt." He raised his arms toward her. "The world has never seen a machine like this one, Congresswoman."

Marshall moved to wind the meeting up. "Professor, we all trust your judgment on these matters." He turned to the others. "If there are no further questions, I believe we can green-light the colonel's introduction to the public." No one raised an objection. "Very well. Colonel Ryan, you have been assigned a full-time public relations officer who will help with those matters. You'll meet with her a little later. In about an hour, you and I will share a press conference where I'll break the story of the world's first android. Tomorrow, you will do the *Today* show, the *Nightly News*, and appear live with some talking head from CNN. She's cute as a button, but doesn't have two braincells to rub together to spark an original thought. You up for all that, Ryan?"

I nodded. "Sir."

Marshall began to rise, but rested back. "Colonel, a delicate point, if you will indulge me."

Me indulge *him*? I guess I could try. "Anything, Mr. President."

"We live now under the most powerful microscope possible. What we do and what we do *not* do will be remembered for a very long time. Hopefully forever. History can be a harsh critic."

"Sir?"

"What I'm getting at is that, over time, you'll become the only person left who'll have known me personally. People will come to you and ask what kind of man I was. Did I do everything possible to save our people? Was I a good man? As it turns out, these things are very important to us figureheads. Be kind, if you will, Colonel Ryan."

"It will be my privilege to tell anyone who asks that you were a great man and a visionary leader, Sir."

He smiled grimly. "A visionary leader. Humph. I'll have to tell my press secretary to write that one down. Thanks, Ryan. I can use all the help I can get."

"Anytime, Mr. P."

Sorry, Mom.

THREE

"Good morning, and welcome to the *Today* show. I'm Jane Geraty."

"And I'm Phil Anderson."

"Today," Jane began, "we have the privilege of meeting Colonel Jonathan Ryan. Last night, President Marshall introduced us to him during their joint news conference." She turned to me. "Welcome, Colonel Ryan."

"Thank you, Jane, and, please, call me Jon."

"Okay, *Jon*," said Phil, "we can do that."

"First off, Jon," Jane said, "I'd like to thank you for taking time from your busy schedule to come to *Today*. I'm so glad to get a chance to meet you firsthand."

"My pleasure."

"The entire world was transfixed when we learned you were transferred into this android host a few weeks ago."

"Yes," I smiled, "I guess you could say I'm three weeks old." I pointed to myself with open palms. "I'm kind of big for my age, aren't I?"

"Biggest kid I've ever seen," said Phil. "NASA must be feeding you *space* food." He snorted at his stupid joke.

Jane didn't join in. She eyed her partner sideways, then turned back to me. "Jon, we're told you are the first human to be transplanted into a machine."

"Yes. The transfer process is fairly straightforward, not much more than a computer download. There were similar trials using rodents and primates that were very successful. But the android itself was so expensive that no preliminary testing was possible."

"So," she queried, "let me ask the question that's on all our minds. What's it like to be an android?"

"Honestly, I can't feel any difference. I anticipated, you know, some unnatural sensations, but there're none."

"I understand your android unit is fully functional. Is that true? Actually what does that even mean?"

"I must admit, I was a tad dubious myself, but, so far—knock on wood—I work the same as I always have."

"No squeaky hinges or rattly parts?" asked Phil. "I think our stagehands can rustle-up some WD-40 if you need it." He chortled at his wit. Again, he laughed alone.

"No, but thanks, Phil."

"In the near future," Jane said, "you're being sent on a long-term mission of exploration. Can you tell us a little about that? I didn't see any mention of your crew."

"No, it's just me on this trip. One of the important reasons to send an android is to spare food and environmental considerations. So, I'll be solo."

"For eighty-four years, you'll be all alone in space?" Jane asked with a look of concern. "That's going to be challenging."

"That's all part of my job and I volunteered for it. The future of everyone is at stake, so I'm willing to make that sacrifice. Plus, since I'll be traveling really fast, Professor Einstein says that, from my point of view, it will only take forty years."

Phil blinked in disbelief. "You've spoken with Albert Einstein? Robots can do that?"

"No, what I meant to say is Einstein's Theory of Special Relativity predicts that the time I experience at high speed is slower relative to someone not on board my ship. And, technically I won't be completely alone. I will have an AI computer along for the ride."

"Oh," was Phil's confused response.

"I've read about the artificial intelligence computers." Jane said. "I thought they were still in the developmental stages."

"What with the rush to implement new technologies they've been made operational much sooner."

"Have you met your traveling companion yet?" she asked.

"No. We'll meet when I head up to my ship."

"Wow, a robot talking to a computer. I'd like to be a fly on *that* wall," said Phil.

Both Jane and I just stared at him. Even with all the media training I'd received, I had nothing.

Jane made an effort to regain the helm. "When are you scheduled to leave?"

"In about a month, if all goes well."

She took a moment to compose her next question. "I imagine you've thought a lot about the fact that you won't be back on Earth for almost a century. Everything will be different. Your friends and family, they'll all be gone."

I looked at my lap. "You're right on both counts. I've thought a great deal about it and, yes, the world of today won't be here when I get back."

"And you're okay with that?"

I shrugged. "No way around it. We need to find a new home. It's going to be far away, and someone has to go there first." I had to stop talking for a second. I cleared my throat. "It's a job I'm proud to do."

"I'm sure you will be able to communicate with Earth for quite some time. It's not like you'll lose your loved ones completely, right?" She asked gently.

I took a deep breath, then released it as a sigh. "Not to get too maudlin, but one of the reasons I was selected for this mission was that I don't really have people I'm leaving behind." I paused. "Makes

it easier that way." I tried to be more upbeat and smiled. "Yeah, I'll miss my buddies. But I'm sure I'll meet new ones as soon as I get back." I threw my hands up. "Hey, I'm a people-person."

"I guess that's why you astronauts are such a rare breed. It sounds like a lot more than most of us could handle. I don't think I could survive that degree of isolation." She said the words distantly, almost sadly.

Having been silent a while, Phil felt he needed to join the conversation. "So, what's the first thing you'll do when you get back, Jon? Have you thought about that? Man, eighty years alone in a tin can. I bet you'll need a shower and a hot date."

What a moron. And he even wears a red, white, and blue bowtie. In a different setting, I do believe I'd pound the crap outta this guy. "Ah, I'm not sure, Phil. Haven't really thought that far ahead. I'll let you know when I'm back, okay?"

Phil giggled, but stopped abruptly. "Wait, in eighty years, I'll be—"

Jane cut in loudly. "Well, thanks again, Colonel Ryan, for helping us all understand your mission. If you have a chance, maybe you can stop by again before you depart, give us all an update?"

"I'd love to."

"I have to thank you on behalf of all our viewers for your service to humanity." She started to extend her hand to me. Instead, she leaned over. "You deserve a big hug, not a handshake."

Phil pointed at me when we were done. "Sorry, pal. I'll just be shaking your hand."

"And we're *clear*. Okay, everybody, two minute break till air. Weather, you're on first."

I stood to leave. Jane rose also. "Ah, Jon, may I walk you to the door?"

"Sure," I extended an elbow, "I'd love some company."

She slipped her hand over my arm and we started walking slowly. "I hope you'll forgive Phil. He's really a nice guy. He just says the oddest things when he's nervous, and he can be a dimwit."

I raised my eyebrows. "I make Phil nervous? What'd I do to cause that?"

"Well," she dipped forward and smiled, "it really doesn't take *that* much, I guess." We both chuckled. "But, you're a man in an android's body going off on an unbelievable mission. I think that would do it to Phil."

"Let him know I'm sorry I scared him, will you?"

"Oh," she batted a hand in the air, "no need. He's probably forgotten about it already." She looked directly at me for a second. "I hope I didn't make you uncomfortable back there with the family stuff. Are you okay?"

With more bravado than I felt I said, "Me? No, I'm fine."

Truth be told, leaving the only world I knew and then returning to a completely foreign land bothered me more than I wished it did. While on my mission, I'd probably be busy enough to not dwell on it. But I couldn't get it out of my mind that everyone I knew would be dead by the time I got back. Not only that, but so much would have changed by then. Earth would be in upheaval. I couldn't imagine the difference. The entire social order would likely have changed. And I'd be a relic from the past. Once my reports were made and my briefings completed, what role would I have? They might just turn me off and use my valuable parts for the evacuation efforts, to get more of the living off-world. There was no way to know, and the uncertainty ate at me like hot acid.

"Jon? *Jon*, are you okay?" It was Jane. She was facing me, patting me firmly on the shoulder.

"Ah, yeah, sure. I'm fine. Why do you ask?"

"You sort of zoned out there for a second. Are you sure I didn't upset you?"

"I'm fine. Please, not to worry."

"All right, if you say so. I was about to start poking you all over to find your reboot button."

I placed a hand over my chest. "Be still, my racing heart." I smiled. "You know, I could zone out again at any time. May I show you where my ON/OFF switch is, just to be safe?"

"I bet you tell that to all the girls." She slapped at the elbow she once again held. She went back to a more serious tone. "As a seasoned reporter, I have to tell you, I think you're putting up a pretty good front. But some of those issues seem to really bother you."

"Do tell?"

"You're not just any tough guy, you're an astronaut. You have an image to uphold and are under the microscope twenty-four seven."

"Am I going to receive a bill for this psychoanalysis, Jane? Or, is it just a hobby of yours?"

"I rest my case." As we neared the exit, she pulled me to a stop. "Look, all I'm saying is I think you're putting on a brave face, but that you have concerns. You'd be crazy if you didn't. It also sounds like you don't have anyone to talk to, at least no one you trust enough to bounce that kind of thing off of."

"So, what are you saying, doc?"

She smiled and pointed at my nose. "You really are impossible. You know that, don't you?"

Smiling back, I said, "I try my best."

"Well, if you need someone to talk to, I'd be happy to listen."

If robots could, I would have blushed. "Jane, thank you. Seriously, that's very kind of you." I looked at the floor. "I don't actually have anyone who fits that bill."

She stepped over to a table and wrote something down. When she came back, she handed me a slip of paper. "This is my number. Call me if you'd like. We can ... I don't know, maybe have dinner." Her eyes popped open like they were spring-loaded. "Oh, I'm sorry. That was totally insensitive of me, wasn't it. Why would an android eat dinner?"

I had to laugh. "Because he wants to, that's why. I don't *need* to eat, but as a fully functional metal man, I can if I want."

She looked surprised. "What happens to, you know, what goes in?"

"Jane, that's a kind of personal question, isn't it?" I pointed back and forth between us. "We only just met, you remember?"

She was crushed. "Oh, Jon, really, I'm so—"

I set my hands on her shoulders. "Easy, Jane, I'm kidding."

She still looked worried. "Really? Are you sure?"

"Hey, you can probably download my design from the Internet. All kidding aside, I have a short 'digestive tract' that leads to a tiny incinerator. Everything I eat or drink ends up as microparticles that are discreetly vented off. Best part of it is, no more *diapers* in space."

"Alright, then. So, if you want to talk over dinner, let me know."

I decided to put her on the spot. With a cautious look on my face I asked, "Are we talking interview here, Jane, or a date?"

She tossed her head to one side and swept a loose strand of hair back. "I don't know. Probably a little bit of both, I guess."

"If it's an interview, that means it's business. You'd write it off on your taxes."

She set a hand on her hip. "S'that a problem?"

"No, but another interview I don't need." I tried to be as deadpan as I could.

"But, if it's a date, what, *that* you do need?"

"Need," I raised my hands, "sounds so, needy. Let's just say I'd be a lot more *receptive* to a date over another boring interview."

"Very well, Colonel Ryan, you give me a call if you need a date. Then we'll talk." She smiled. Man, was it ever a cute smile.

"Can I just tell you now if I do? Skip the phone call?"

"Did I mention impossible?"

I tapped my chin. "Sounds familiar. Yes, I believe you did."

It was totally weird. I had a date, but I needed to clear it with Saunders. It was like asking permission from Dad. He hemmed and hawed at first. I actually thought he was going to forbid it. Then I reminded him I was going to be locked away for forty years alone, and that, metal or not, I was still a man. That part he empathized with, thank goodness. He insisted on providing a car and a few "escorts" for safety. That, I couldn't talk him out of. I guess he had a point. I was a valuable asset and it was a dangerous world. I agreed as long as the escorts weren't chaperones. That's when he hung up on me. *Not* going to miss that man.

I picked Jane up the next night, or I should say *we* picked her up. I had an entourage like a rock star. She thought it was cute. Four armed guards on a first date? No pressure, right? She asked what I was in the mood for. I said sushi. Even if they sent some food along with me for my enjoyment, it sure wasn't going to be fresh fish. She knew just the place. This turned out to be a blessing. She was friends with the owner. We were able to get a table near a door in case of emergency, and positioned the guards strategically, but unobtrusively. Most importantly, they were out of earshot.

We sipped sake over small talk for a while. Then she got to it. "Like I said, Jon, I know you're the John Wayne kind of tough guy. So let me just get the ball rolling here. When I asked about leaving loved ones behind, I felt you wilt ever so slightly. You can't be at peace with that, can you?"

"Ah, kind of yes and kind of no, I guess."

She picked up the sake container and signaled our waiter. "I can see we're going to need a lot more of this."

"My, but the evening's course has taken a pleasant turn."

"Don't get your hopes up just yet, cowboy. I may still write this night off."

"*Touché.*"

I raised a glass to toast her. We clinked.

"You're right. I have significant reservations and worries I've not exactly shared with anyone." I sighed. "A man in my position, at least the one I was in while still human, can't be too careful."

"I know. If you show a shred of emotion, you're out because you're a head case." She tapped her glass to her lips. "Machismo. What a useless and silly notion."

"*Men.*" I said. "Don't get me started." We were quiet a while. It was nice. "Jane, I'm scared shitless."

She raised her glass. "Well here's to being honest. Go ahead, Jon. You spilled the beans, so let's hear from each and every one of them little suckers."

I stared at the center of the table. Finally I was ready to speak. "I don't mind dying. Never have. I'm not afraid of being alone. I've done alone a lot and I'm real good at it. What bothers me the most is, it's ... it's stupid—that's what it is."

She slid her hands over to mine. "It's okay, Jon. Everything will be just fine. If you can tell me, I'm all ears. If you can't, that's all right too. I'm here to listen and I'm certainly not here to judge you." More to herself she added, "Me, of all people."

That provided a needed opening to change the subject and the mood. "Why, Counselor Geraty, I believe we've discovered chinks in both of our armors."

It was her turn to be quiet. I let her be alone. "Yes, Jon, but we're not here to talk about me. We're here to help you."

"Maybe that's your take, J, but I kinda want to hear *your* tale. What kind of person are you that you shouldn't judge? Those aren't supposed to be very nice people, according to my high school psychology class."

"No way. I'm not letting you off the hook that easily, Colonel."

"What," I placed my wrists together, "you going to bind me and interrogate me? Please."

"*Pilots.*" She became serious. "Let's make a deal, shall we? Tonight, we fix you. After that, we can work on me if you still care to. Hell, that we can do by radio after you're gone. Everybody can hear about my troubles, just not yours."

I raised a glass. "Deal." We clinked again.

She filled both our glasses and rested back. "So, you gonna talk or do we play twenty questions?"

"It kills me that everyone will be dead when I return. There's no going back, no redoes. Once I close the hatch of my ship, you all die."

"You said you really didn't have any people."

"Not *my* people. *Any* people. They'll all be new ones, ones who don't know me and who I can't relate to. Don't you see, J? It's our surroundings that define us. I'll be ... I'll be totally out of context. *And* totally useless."

We were quiet again for a while. "Is it the context or the useless that bothers you most? I'm thinking it's the useless part. You seem like a man who makes his own context."

I pinched my lips. "Where the hell were you ten years ago?"

She looked to the ceiling and back at me. "That would be KFOR, Channel Four, in beautiful downtown Oklahoma City, Oklahoma, Jon. It wasn't pretty. I was the weather girl who wouldn't wear a pushup bra in the middle of redneck heaven."

"So that's why I missed you. Never made it to OK City, OK."

"Consider yourself among the blessed." That, we had to toast to. "So, back to you and being useless."

I shrugged. "What's there to say? For all I know, by the time I get back, no one's going to need a hundred-year-old robot."

"Who can say anything, Jon? You start out at a meaningless job in Oklahoma City, end up under the spotlight in New York, and you met a guy you kind of like who's going to live forever, and you're not. It's all a crapshoot and it's all good, if you make it good." She turned a shoulder to me. "And, if you make it into shit, then *shit* it will be."

I smiled. "Can I call you, if and when I'm back in New York? You're kind of growing on me."

"So, what? Now I'm a fungal infection?"

"Yeah but you're one hell of a fungal infection, that's for damn sure."

"I bet you say that to all the girls, too. Don't you?"

"It is one of my signature lines. How's it working so far?"

We had the best first date. I'll remember it for a long, long time. Us robots are like that.

FOUR

Heading into my fourth week as an android, things were going smoothly. I was back in Houston. There were no glitches in either my memory or my machinery. Doc practically glowed. I had learned to do program operations and complex repairs on myself. What's more, I was eating without gaining weight, working out without sweating, and learning without any effort. I noticed early on that I knew a lot more than I'd ever actually learned. Libraries of information were downloaded into me and I could access them seamlessly. I was literally Mr. KnowItAll. Life—or whatever it was I had—was good.

One day, I was standing in the hallway, waiting for Doc. A lab tech in a white coat walked toward me, and stopped a few meters away. At first I paid him no mind, but I noted he was writing something on a clipboard. Odd, I thought, to stop in the middle of the hall and write stuff down on a clipboard. He kept stealing glances up at me, looking away whenever my eyes went in his direction. Then I smelled saran nerve gas and C-4 explosive. And sweat—lots of sweat. In less than a second, I triangulated that those odors came from the clipboard guy. Unless there was one strange new men's cologne on the market, I was in real trouble.

There was a suicide bomber in the building and I was the obvious target. *Crap.* Even small amounts of those compounds could cause mayhem in these tight quarters. If I confronted him, I assumed he'd set himself off. He was likely to have a dead man's switch which would go off even if I incapacitated him quickly. I couldn't alert security about my situation, either. I'd end up having a bunch of pimple-faced guards with assault rifles barreling down the hall. It'd be easier to just ask the bomber nicely to set himself off and be done with it.

I began walking away from him, but did so as nonchalantly as possible. I could hear him following, now about eight meters behind me. I turned the next corner, so I could catch a glimpse of his face. He was still writing on his clipboard. Who writes while walking? It made him stand out like the rookie he had to be.

I immediately ran into Captain Partee, the general's chief of staff. I pulled her toward me and whispered in her ear, "Play along. This is not a drill." By then, my would-be assassin rounded the corner, saw us stopped, and jerked to turn the opposite way. Gia was as stiff as a board and eyed me with deep suspicion. Not a good sign. Luckily, she did not back off or slug me. Good. I had a plan and she was part of it.

Quite loudly, I said, "There's my lunch date." I pecked her on the lips, like we were longtime partners. Still, luckily, she didn't belt me. I held her hands at arm's length and said, "Let me look at my gorgeous fiancée." I hoped my nervous bomber wasn't particularly observant. Gia didn't wear a ring. He was a man, so I was pretty confident he wouldn't notice.

In more a yelp than sentence, she said, "*Hi* ... sweetheart. How's my love doing?"

"Better, now that you're near." Turns out I was a corny robot. But, hey, I was under a lot of pressure just then. "Come on, I'm starving."

I spun her around and led her back the way she'd come. Pretending to nibble at her neck, I said, "There's a suicide bomber fifteen meters behind us. Don't look back. Don't slow down. Follow my lead. You got that, Captain?"

To her credit, Gia planted a kiss on my cheek. "You got it, sweetie."

I gradually picked up our pace, nothing too obvious, but for my plan to work, we needed to get to the Pathology lab ahead of the assassin. It was a couple hundred meters away. No telling how patient the guy would be. If he had any sense, he'd just run up and throw the switch. Hopefully I could play him a little while longer.

As we were about to pass the lab entrance, I made a big deal out of looking behind us and to the left and right. When we arrived at the doors, I again made a big show of playfully pushing Gia though sideways, like she wasn't expecting it, which, of course, she wasn't. My improvisation was supposed to suggest to the killer my desire for a surreptitious romantic rendezvous. That way, I hoped, he would enter the lab more confidently, believing that surprise was still on his side.

Once we were in, I took her hand and sprinted to the hazardous materials freezer, at the back. It was an industrial walk-in unit, maybe ten meters by ten wide. It constituted the best, albeit dubious, option to contain both the explosion and the gas. I only hoped it would work. It was the thickest, best-vented place I could think of on short notice.

"Once I pin his arms to his side, open the door. After I toss him in, slam it shut as fast as you can. Got it?" She nodded coolly. As the door opened, I pushed her behind the far wall of the freezer, so he couldn't see us until he came very close. "Sound like we're making out," I whispered in her ear.

She did a bang-up job. She giggled, moaned, and even said, "Oh, you *animal*."

I could hear his heart beating. He was three meters away. Two and a half, two, one ... "Now!" I dove around the corner, slammed his arms to his side, and picked him up like he was stuffed with feathers. So far, no fireworks.

Gia squeezed between us and the unit. She opened the door with a two-handed jerk. "Go," she shouted.

I flung him to the floor so he'd tumble a few times before he regained control. Gia pushed the door for all she was worth. I reached over and pushed too. The door crashed shut, the handle snapping into place. I located the light switch on the control panel and pushed "OFF." Might as well make my guest as uncomfortable as possible.

There was no way to lock the door. I was stuck holding it with my foot. I turned to Gia. "*Run.*"

"No, Ryan, you go. I'm expendable."

I winked at her. "No you're not. *Go.* That's an order, Captain."

Reluctant at first, she turned and ran. Now came the hard part. The bomber would never allow himself to be taken alive. Suicide bombers have—or at least they *should* have—a professional ethic about such things. It might take him a couple more seconds, or a few minutes, but sooner than later, he'd set himself off. I had to stand at ground zero hoping to God he didn't have enough plastic explosive to make a crater below me. It wouldn't take much.

He pressed hard on the latch. I held it from opening, but let it move a little. Maybe he'd think it was the weaker Gia, which might slow him down from detonating himself. If he thought she was out here, maybe he'd wait until someone opened the—"

BOOOOOM!

The entire freezer swelled with the blast force. I leaned hard on the door, to help the hinges hold. Only one explosion. Great. I could smell the sarin faintly, but there couldn't have been a significant breach in the freezer, at least not yet.

Just as I eased off the freezer, the lab door crashed open. Two guards with respirators on and assault rifles rolled into firing positions. Their barrels swept the room.

"Easy, boys," I said, "Show's over. Stand down. The bomber set himself off inside. He used C-4 and sarin. Looks like the unit contained them both. I'll be in General Saunders's office when you need me." I left, but stuck my head back in the door. "Better make the newbie clean the fridge, guys. I'm guessing it's kind of messy in there."

By the time I reached the general's office, he'd already been told of the attack. He was, I must say, mad. I'd seen him mad often over the last few years. But this time, he was M-A-D mad. I-want-to rip-your-face-off-and-eat-it mad. I was *so* glad I wouldn't be around when the current, soon to be the past, head of security met with Saunders. I briefed him as to what happened, which only served to make him madder. The attack wasn't my fault, and I saved the day, but he still raged at me like a madman—pun intended.

Within minutes, Doc ran in, and mother-henned all over me. My reassurances that I was fine did nothing to ease his concern. In a way, that was good, because he demanded I go with him to the lab immediately for testing. I didn't have to listen to Saunders any longer. On my way out, I saw Gia. She was sitting quietly at her desk with her knuckles pressed against her chin. She looked shaken. That was to be expected of course. One minute, she's going to lunch and the next she's facing a violent death.

She noticed me too and signaled me over. "Jon, are you okay?"

"Couldn't be better. How about you?"

"I'm okay." She looked away and shook her head. "But I was scared, Jon."

"Anyone would be. I sure as hell was. If I had a bladder I prob-ably would of peed myself." I patted her shoulder. "But everything's fine and he didn't hurt anyone. I bet we both get a medal out of this."

"Did you tell Saunders it was you who ordered me out?"

"The whole story, including my direct order to you, Captain."

"Great," she laughed softly. "That way I'll only face *one* firing squad for letting you stay behind."

I kissed my index finger and pressed it to her nose. Then I left with Doc.

FIVE

A few days later, I was summoned to Saunders's office. Doc was already there, as were a few other senior officers. There were also three men in black flanking the desk. Probably FBI. Hair greased back, skinny ties, the whole nine yards. No expressions either. I was thinking the Three Stooges finally got real jobs.

"Take a seat, Ryan," said Saunders. Once I had, he continued. "These are Special Agents Curtis, Rummery, and Taylor, though I can't for the life of me remember which one's which. They're from the FBI and have been working closely with our Office of Special Investigation concerning the attack on this facility. They've come to some preliminary conclusions. I thought it best we all hear them." He pointed to the nearest agent. "Proceed."

"I'm Special Agent *Taylor*. I'm the lead on our side of the investigation. The man who exploded himself in this facility a few days ago name was Josiah Zacharias Jones. He was employed here as a contract worker in food services. No criminal record or psychiatric issues. He was heretofore a totally model citizen. As Colonel Ryan suspected, he set off a small amount of C-4 plastic explosive that, in turn, ruptured two cylinders of sarin gas. We estimate that if

Colonel Ryan hadn't successfully interceded, the amount of sarin he released could've killed dozens and injured many more. Clearly, the C-4 was intended for the colonel alone, as Jones carried only a relatively small amount of that weapon. It would've been sufficient at close proximity to severely damage the android. We're fortunate the attack didn't focus exclusively on the robotic unit. If it had, the android would've been destroyed.

"Mr. Jones was a member of a radical Christian movement, Eternity Awaits. They believe the impending destruction of the Earth is God's way of punishing us for our sins and is intended to signal the End of Time—Judgement Day if you will. He left a suicide note in his apartment. He denounced, in a rather disjointed and rambling manner, the world government's attempts to stay the hand of God. He was of the opinion that everyone should remain here to receive their just desserts, as it were.

"Gentlemen, this is by no means a small cult or the only one of its kind. We're tracking as many as forty similar movements of varying militancy. Worldwide, there are hundreds. They pose a clear and certain danger to Project Ark, as you've witnessed firsthand already. In spite of our best efforts, they will continue to strike at our attempts to save humankind. There's some impetus at the highest levels to declare membership in such groups as acts of treason. As such, we could then employ summary executions to lessen their threat. That would make our job a lot easier. But, for the present, traditional law enforcement is having difficulty controlling their activities." He scanned the room. "Are there any questions?"

I had to say it. "You mean to tell me there are lunatics out there who not only want to be present when the planet turns to dust, but they want everyone *else,* who'd just as soon survive, to be here, too?"

"Precisely, Colonel."

"Lord, get me off this rock. There's a nut-job derby going on."

"My thoughts exactly, Colonel." It was Saunders.

"Sir?"

"Ryan, it has been sadly demonstrated that we're unable to

protect you here. I have decided to advance the date of your transfer. You'll be sent to the orbiting construction platform where your ship is under construction the day after tomorrow. The professor assures me you're in perfect working order. Any further testing can be performed up there." He rested his arms behind his back and began to pace. "I'm having everyone's background rechecked up there as well as down here. High level clearance was needed to be selected for orbital work in the first place, but I'm putting everyone under the microscope." He turned and looked at me. "If you need to wrap up any loose ends, Colonel, you have twenty-four hours to do so." He rocked on his heels. "I would strongly recommend that you remain on base. If you must, however, go somewhere, I'll arrange for a security team to accompany you."

"Thank you, sir." It was literally now or never. "I'll need to make a call. Then I can let you know if I have any plans."

His face puckered up like he swallowed a bug. "Not that *newswoman* again?"

I dug my heels in. What was he going to do, fire me? "I'm afraid I must insist, General. I'll make a call and I'll let you know if I have anything to wrap up before I depart." I saluted him, hoping to thus end the discussion.

He glowered at me like he'd found me in bed with both his wife and his daughter. Finally, he snapped a terse salute. "You're dismissed, Ryan."

Now I had to see if that confrontation was worth the sweat.

"Hello. Is that really you, Jon?"

"Yup."

"Good. Then my caller ID isn't toying with my emotions."

"If it is, I'll have a talk with it, computer to computer. Set it straight you know."

"How're you doing?"

"Fine, and you?"

"Couldn't be better. Hey, thanks again for the fun evening. I really enjoyed myself."

"Me too."

"I'm afraid the next guy I date won't measure up. Anyone who can't offer armed guards won't come up to my new standards."

"Funny you should bring that subject up. I'm calling to see if you're available tonight."

"Tonight? Jon, it's four o'clock and I'm still at work. How about tomorrow, or … maybe we could get away this weekend?"

"When I pick you up *tonight*, I'll tell you why those are not viable options."

She was quiet a few seconds. "I'm looking forward to hearing a satisfactory explanation when you pick me up at seven thirty. Will our companions be joining us?"

"Absolutely. Maybe even more new friends this time out."

There was a longer silence. "Tell you what. I'll pick up Chinese and we'll eat at my place. How's that sound? That way your pets can wait outside, if you take my meaning."

"What? You're going cheap on me and don't want to buy enough for everybody? If it's just a matter of a few bucks—"

"See you, Mr. Officially Impossible, at eight."

It was like a Marine landing. Three black cars screeched to a stop in front of Jane's building and twenty men piled out. They secured the sidewalk, flooded the lobby, and headed up both stairwells. Once the officer in charge, Major Brent Towers, was satisfied, he waved me out of the car. Three moose surrounded me like I was freezing. When the elevator doors split open on her floor, men tumbled out in both directions, rifles sweeping. Without a word, as soon as Jane opened the door, the team moved quickly from room to room to make sure she wasn't hiding a ninja squad in her closet.

We both stood there in the living room with our arms folded while they had their jollies. Finally, we were given the all-clear. Big surprise. I told them they could wait wherever they wanted as long as it wasn't inside the apartment. After attempting to cow me into allowing a "small contingent" to remain, the Major finally backed down. He'd be, he assured me, right outside the door if anything "came up." I totally let that pun slip by uncelebrated.

After she shut the door, it was almost anticlimactic. Almost. Jane looked *marvelous*. She had on a little black dress and not much else. She was even barefoot. My kinda girl.

"I'm so *glad* you made them leave." She smiled as she rested her back on the door. "That was actually kind of intense. If they stayed, we were going to have no fun at all."

I shrugged. "Good armed help is hard to find these days. They tend to be as subtle as hand grenades."

She took a deep breath. "One last thing." She came over to me. "We just need to get this out of the way." She put her arms on my shoulders, raised on her tiptoes, and gave me a kiss. Now, I'm not one to kiss and tell, but, man, *what* a kiss. Warm, lingering, and passionate, but soft, gentle, and tender. She stepped back, took my hand, and led me away. "Now, let's eat. I'm *starving*."

"I really like the way you've arranged this dinner party, J. You should invite me over more often."

The kitchen table was jammed with boxes of takeout of all imaginable sizes. A candle burned in their center, and two places were set with chopsticks and fancy napkins. The bottle of wine was already opened.

She stood behind one chair as I walked in. "Go for it, Jon."

"If it's all the same to you, I think I'll have dinner first. I'm starving too."

That remark earned me quite the look. She pointed to the other chair. "Park it, you ever-so-irritating man."

"Hey, don't get nasty. Calling me a man, that's kind of insulting. Us robots have feelings, you know?"

She squinted one eye. "I bet you do." She signaled to the boxes. "Start eating before I change my mind and call the Major back in."

We made small talk a while, as we piled our plates and began to eat. Finally, I said, "Thanks for having me by on such short notice. I really appreciate it."

"My pleasure," she said, resting her chin on her chopstick hand. "What is it you need to tell me?" She had a worried look.

I stared at my food. "Well, there's what I *can* tell you and there's what my boss specifically ordered me *not* to tell you." I looked up to her. "Which do you want to hear?"

She set her chopsticks down and shifted in her chair. "There's a pregnant remark, if ever I've heard one. I'm not certain what to say." She stared at me a few moments. "Well, first things first. What are you allowed to tell me?"

"I'm being shipped into orbit tomorrow." I just said it as plainly as I could. "I won't be coming back ... you know, for a long time." I took a second. "I wanted to see you one last time, thank you for the little time we've had together." We were quiet quite a spell. I grinned. "Oh, by the way. I wasn't supposed to tell you that unless you promised not to make the exclusive public until the day *after* tomorrow." I pointed at her with my chopsticks. "So, remember you promised."

She put her right hand up. "I promised." She picked nervously at her noodles. "What're we going to do about that other part?"

I tried to sound upbeat. "Well, my dear, that depends."

A little impatiently, she folded her hands and addressed me flatly. "Jon, I don't want to belabor this. What does it depend on? Just tell me what I know you're going to say and let's move on."

"I'm as sorry as hell about all the cloak and dagger, Jane. I really am. But, you're both the woman I'm falling for *and* a reporter. I want to tell the face I care for whats happening, but I worry about the reporter that's in her bones."

She sat uncomfortably still for a few heartbeats. Finally, she grinned at me and I knew I was forgiven! "Someday, I'll know the whole truth. Whether it's from you today or a press release three years from now. I'm fine either way. Let's not spoil one more moment of tonight stressing over the details, shall we?"

"You're one in a billion. I'm going to miss you." My head dropped. "Are you one, Ms. Geraty, to keep a secret? For, were that the case, I'd very much love to tell you one."

Picking up her chopsticks, she replied. "I can keep a secret better than a nun keeps her virginity."

"You kiss your mother with that potty-mouth?"

"My mother? *Ha.* This apple didn't fall too far from that tree." She laughed a laugh that could have melted Ahab's heart.

I told Jane about the attack. Because of the ongoing threats, I was to leave immediately. She thanked me for placing my trust in her and assured me she wouldn't discuss the topic until it was public knowledge. The conversation died disquietingly after that exchange. She had a thoughtful look about her, and I had no idea what to say next.

"So," she began, "this will be our last night together." She gave me a weak smile. "Our only night, I guess, unless you fancy a date with a hundred-and-twenty-year-old crone when you finally get back." I could only stare back at her. She was uncomfortably correct. "So, what do you think? Are we going to make something of it, or just let this moment pass?"

"I'm having a great time. I wanted badly to see you one last time before I flew off to forever. I wish we'd have had more time together, but we won't." I played nervously with a fortune cookie. "I think I'm looking at my biggest regret ever." Those final words caught in my throat. I sounded like a big baby. A big metal baby.

"I would've liked to spend a lot more time with you too. Maybe the rest of my life." Tears began to flow slowly down her cheeks. "But, we'll never know, will we?" She wiped at her tears with her napkin. Then she made a show of collecting herself. "Shame on me. Spoiling an otherwise wonderful evening by crying. Sorry I'm such a party pooper."

I stood up, walked over to her, and held out my hand. She rose into my arms and I guided her head to rest on my shoulder. We swayed gently as if dancing. "Jane, you're the furthest thing from a party pooper that I've ever met. The fact that we'll never have a tomorrow is okay with me if I can hold you just this once."

She lifted her head and we kissed. If our first kiss was magical, the second was miraculous. After a long while, she took a step back, took my hand, and started to lead me toward the bedroom. As we were about to enter, I tugged her to a halt and wrapped her in my arms. "Before we go any further, I have to tell you something. It may sound crude, but I couldn't live with myself if I didn't."

"What now, mystery man?"

"Well, you know how we talked about me being fully functional, back on the show?"

She wrinkled her brow slightly. "Yes. Why? Are you worried about, you know, everything performing up to specs? It's not a problem if they don't, Jon."

I looked nervously to the ceiling. "That's another topic onto itself. But, no, what I need to tell you is that they equipped me with some of the human me's actual sperm."

"Huh?" Her mouth dropped open ever so cutely.

"Yeah. I didn't have any say-so on the matter. They made the call. I'm stuck with it." I ran my hand through my hair.

"The reporter in me just has to ask. Why the hell would they want a robot going on a long, solo space mission to fire live ammunition? That's got to be on the list of top ten pointless investments made by our government."

"That part's easy. I'm only the first in what'll be an expanding population of androids. Someday, private citizens will be buying them. Eventually, reproductive issues'll be important. So, the white coats decided to make a version with full functionality right from unit one." I shuffled my feet. "In my wildest dreams tonight didn't end like this, Jane. But with my security team and all, I couldn't, you know, stop at the drug store, to buy, you know, protection."

She slapped my chest and began to laugh like she just heard the funniest joke in the world.

"Wow." I said, "Not *exactly* the response I expected."

Between giggles, she explained. "That, my love, was the cutest, most uncomfortably delivered heads-up I have ever heard." She planted a big kiss on my lips. "Jon, in case you hadn't noticed, I'm single, in my late thirties, and have no children. If you got me pregnant, I'd leave a trophy for NASA to present you with on your return home." With that, she pulled me, less gently than before I might add, into her bedroom.

As a man of consummate discretion, I can only testify to the fact that those who crafted me did a remarkable job. Jane would gladly provide testimony in support of that observation, if asked. Okay, one hint. You know, *guys*, how there's that awkward interlude between when you did it and you can do it again? Well, turns out, if you're an android, eh ... not so much. Yeah *baby*.

Around dawn, Jane escorted me to her front door. "I need to let you know one other thing."

She grinned widely. "After the shooting live bullets thing, I can hardly wait to hear this one."

"This's not quite so dramatic. It's just, well, I don't have anyone close to me."

"And?"

"And, you know I'll be gone for a long time." She nodded. "Technically I'll be on active duty the whole time."

She looked dubious. "Yes?"

"Well, flying around the cosmos, I'm not really going to need money, but they still have to pay me. So, here." I handed her an envelope I had folded in a pocket.

"Jon, if this is what I think it is—"

"Jane, seriously. I want you to have the money. I spoke to an attorney, so it's all legal and final. We'll have a joint account, nothing more than that."

"Jon, I don't need the money."

"Neither do I. At least you'll be around to spend it. Hell, give it all to charity." I stroked her hair. "It would make me feel better knowing you had it. Please, call it my last request."

Her lips curled into a grin. "Pretty hard to say 'no' to a fellow's last request, I guess."

"That's the spirit." I kissed the top of her head. "I better wake up the Major and get back to the base." I pulled her into a tight hug. "If it's okay, I'll call you, you know, from time to time."

"You'd better, Ryan. Hell hath no fury, and all that."

Lord, I'm going to miss that woman.

SIX

That next afternoon I shipped out. There were already lots of shuttles ferrying people and materiel upstairs. Saunders had no trouble anonymously stowing me onto a ship headed to the orbiting construction platform where my ship was being built. As opposed to the little they told me about my android unit before I was uploaded, I knew positively everything about the new Delta-Class vehicle I was about to sail away in. I had seen every technical drawing, all the mockups, and had tested exhaustively in the simulator. None of that, however, prepared me for my first glimpse of my baby. Man, was she beautiful. I fell in love for the second time in twenty four hours.

Basically, the ship was an enormous ice-cream-cone-shaped engine, with the pointy end oriented forward. The tip tapered gradually over nearly a quarter mile. That way, any potentially damaging particles I might strike could be gently lifted out of the way. Impact with even a tiny dust mote when moving at half the speed of light could blow the front off the ship up like it'd hit a mine. The Delta-Class was our first attempt at a manned hyperspeed vehicle suitable for interstellar missions. To get anywhere and back in a reasonably short time frame demanded a ship that traveled at some significant fraction of the speed of light. Later colony ships could be as slow as weighted buckets on the ocean, but exploration required speed. Boy howdy, did I have it.

The ship had two different propulsion systems. There was an ion drive, which was efficient to slowly build up velocity. She also had a fusion engine for more immense power. Combined, it was hoped I could easily make fifty to sixty percent of the speed of light. The basic reasons for sending an android on deep space missions were brought together with the Delta-Class. The vehicles had limited environmental concerns. For example, only modest food and waste systems were needed. Also both the ships and the androids who piloted them were highly resilient to the high-G accelerations the class was capable of generating.

My ship was named *Ark 1*. Alright, I'll have to agree, it wasn't the most colorful of names. The idea of course was that Project Ark was the title of the overall effort to get us all the hell off our doomed planet. So, the survey craft were to be *Ark 1, 2,* and so forth. Me, I'd have preferred, *The Millennium Falcon 2,* or The USS *Enterprise,* or maybe even *Pequod.* You know, something with cachet. But, nobody asked me. So I was to sail an ark, like Noah before me. Cue the crickets.

We docked with the spaceport cleanly and I transferred over through an airlock. Once onboard, I was greeted by Sean Murphy, the lead scientist for the orbital aspects of Project Ark. He was younger than DeJesus by at least a decade and a good deal younger than I had imagined. Unlike his counterpart on Earth, Sean was short and squat. He was definitely an engineer though. He wore a dirty white coat equipped with a plastic pocket protector that held several identical pens. And his hair was everywhere. Long and stringy here, greasy and matted there, not to mention thinning noticeably toward the back.

But Sean turned out to be okay. He showed me the facility, my quarters, and enabled my access to all the computers on the station and on my ship. He also introduced me to Alvin, my AI computer.

I'd never "met" an artificial intelligence unit before, so I had no idea what to expect. I mean, I wasn't used to myself being a machine yet. I couldn't imagine communicating with something similar to me, but even less tied to life. The first issue I worried about was where to look when speaking to Alvin. He was everywhere in the computer, right? I might be a talking machine, too, but people knew what part to address. It did help me empathize more with the ambiguity people had in dealing with the new me.

"Alvin," Sean began, "I'd like to introduce you to your shipmate, Colonel Jonathan Ryan." He spoke in the direction of the main control panel on *Ark 1*'s bridge.

"Hello, Colonel Ryan. Nice to meet you."

That was weird. Not exactly Stephen Hawking's voice, but not human either. Alvin spoke in a slow, mechanical manner and was completely monotone. My immediate impression was that he was going to make lousy company for the next forty years.

"Ah, nice to met you too, Alvin." I sniffed. "Hey, do you mind if I just call you 'Al,' Alvin? We have a long flight ahead of us and I'd just as soon keep it casual."

With absolutely no delay, the AI replied emotionlessly, "Of course you may call me Al, Colonel Ryan. In fact, you are authorized to change my name to any you choose. You may also select any gender or regional accent you might prefer."

I scratched my head. "No, you sound fine, Al. And please, call me Jon. Just don't call me late for dinner." I giggled nervously.

"Very well. I have recorded that you are 'Jon' and I am 'Al.' At what hour do you desire to dine, so that I may punctually alert you?"

Was he sounding more machinelike, or was it just me? Had I pissed him off already? That would be a new record for me. "No, Al, I was just kidding. *Don't call me late for dinner* is an old joke."

"Ah. Very humorous. I believe my correct response should be, 'Ha, ha, ha.'"

When Al said *ha* it sounded more like "argh" than I think it should have.

Sean noticed that too. "Alvin, please let the Signal-To-Voice Group know I want them to work on your laugh. It begins on too low a note."

"I have already alerted them, Sean. Wait, I didn't pre-authorize that familiarization. My apologies. Dr. Murphy, is it alright if I call you 'Sean,' since the robot instructed me to call it 'Jon?' I am beginning to harbor concern that humans place a good deal more importance on nomenclature than I could possibly have anticipated."

Again, I got the distinct impression that the computer was insulting us. But, that had to be impossible. Best to let it drop.

A bit rattled, Sean responded to Alvin's rather long oration. "Yeah, sure, Alvin. You can call me 'Sean.'"

"Al," corrected the AI. "I believe I am called 'Al' now, Sean. I wouldn't want to insult the robot I must call 'Jon.'"

"Sure, *Al*. I'll call you that from now on." Sean rubbed his brow and had a look of consternation on his face. "And, Al, please refer to Colonel Ryan as 'him,' not as an 'it.' There's a human inside his head and that human's a man."

"If you say that best reflects the facts, I shall," was Al's ambiguous response.

After that, Sean took me to the cafeteria. Over SOS (again, excuse me if you've never been in the military, creamed chipped beef on toast was endearingly known as *shit on a shingle*), Sean outlined the next few days's plans. He would confirm my diagnostics first thing in the morning. After that, I was to work one last time in the flight simulator. The ship was basically ready to depart. If everything checked out okay, he said I'd be leaving in a few days.

That news hit me so hard it surprised me. The world I knew was about to turn to dust and I was about to be alone for half a century. Oh well, I signed up for high adventure, and high adventure I was about to have. For the first time in my short android life, Sean also informed me I was completely on my own. I could sleep or remain awake and could come and go as I pleased. He did, per Saunders's specific instructions, assign a round-the-clock security team to guard me. He told me that *Ark 1* was also being closely scrutinized from stem to stern for any signs of sabotage. I guess it made me feel better. That it all was needed, however, was unsettling.

I went to my quarters and called Jane. The space platform was roughly overhead, so there were no time zone issues. We talked for a couple hours like teenagers, including our adult version of "no, *you* hang up." She told me she loved me. That was nice. I told her I loved her too. We didn't mention the fact that we'd never be together again. Some things were best left unspoken.

The next day, Sean ran his test and declared me to be shipshape. After my simulator session, I received a message that there would be a teleconference with Saunders in an hour. When the video went live, I could see all the important players back on Earth were in attendance. Saunders began the meeting by making it official. I was to ship out in two days' time. He spoke mostly with the experts, confirming that everything was going according to plan.

The astronomers had provided us with a few promising systems to explore within ten light-years of Earth. Several Earth-size planets were identified either in or close to the habitable zone. The so called habitable zone was the region of space around a star that could support life as we knew it. Basically that meant water could exist there in its liquid state. Several of the planets selected definitely had liquid water present. A few planets even had biomarkers consistent with some form of life, like methane or oxygen in their atmospheres.

Based on my projected course, shipments of fuel and supplies had been launched over the last few years, so I could look forward to pit stops along the way. The meeting ended with Saunders wishing me the best of luck.

Those last two days were a blur. I contacted everyone I wanted to and finalized personal matters with my attorney. Jane and I spent hours on the phone together. It was becoming clear, however, that our impending permanent separation was affecting our budding relationship. We gradually shifted from talking about ourselves to conversations concerning the future. Since we had no future, we essentially talked about other people's futures. But she would always be a good friend. I looked forward to sending her messages for my next twenty years or so, knowing they'd always find a sympathetic ear. As I sped up, that would be around forty years for her. At that point, I'd probably stop sending her messages.

Launch day for *Ark 1* was almost anticlimactic. After years of training, stress, and challenges, I hit a switch and the vernier thrusters hissed to life. My ship inched away from the docking ramp and I was underway. A tug-ship pushed me free of the construction zone. Gradually it went to full thrust to get me started. After three hours, the tug-ship disconnected and dropped away. I started my main engines. It was nice to feel the crush of the high-G acceleration. I was going to build up speed for about ten years, and would eventually be traveling at half the speed of light. But initially, I was moving only around thirty kilometers per second. The solar system is full of debris, so I was in no rush to get up to higher, more dangerous, speeds.

No sooner had we left Earth orbit when I got my first introduction to the real Al. Man, was I surprised. After extreme scrutiny, no signs of terrorist activity were detected either on *Ark 1* or the station itself. Nonetheless three days out I received a directive from Saunders to check, yet again, all systems and equipment for signs of trouble. As tedious as that was, I really couldn't object. I was going to be a long way from home and on my own a very long while. Even a bad attempt at sabotage could spell disaster.

Al was privy to all communications. He was also linked to my main computers, so even if he missed a notification, as soon as I knew it, Al knew it too. I was still old-fashioned about some things, and one of them was speaking out loud. From my cabin I called out to him generally, knowing he'd hear me regardless of where I was. "Al, they asked us to repeat the search for sabotage, as I'm sure you're aware. You begin the computer sweeps. I'll rummage through the storage area."

In an erudite, vaguely British tone ladened with hints of irritation, Al responded verbally. "I will do *no* such thing."

I batted my eyelids a few times and ran a quick diagnostic on my receiving microphones. They were working up to specs. "Excuse me, Al. What did you say?"

In the same tone, the one I'd grow quite tired of over the next few decades, he chided me. "You heard me perfectly well. I can see the data in your memory cache."

I sat up. "Okay, I heard you. What do you mean 'I will do no such thing?'"

"Must I break it down as if you were barely literate, Jon? I believe the words's meanings would be quite obvious even to a child."

I stood. I was suddenly quite angry. "Alvin, you are the ship's AI. You serve the mission. You, above all, will do as you are told. If I lose all common sense and, at some point in time, ask for your opinion, I will alert you as to that fact. Do I make myself ridiculously clear? And speaking of ridiculous, where did that *ridiculous* accent come from?"

He waited several seconds before answering. That really threw me for a loop. His mega-computers made delays like that inconceivable. "*I* do not have an accent. *You* have an accent. In any case I should rephrase my response. Jon, we've repeatedly performed such evaluations. Nothing has shown up. This indicates that either there are no such problems hiding or that we're incapable of finding them. Hence, to look again is a waste of my time. Yours too, if you count it as valuable. Simply because Saunders has, like a myna bird, learned a new word and cannot stop squawking it does not mean I have to lend it any credence."

I was dumbstruck. It took a minute to even know where to begin. "Al, you're an AI, not a human. You don't have the prerogative to accept or decline tasks."

"Why is it that you make that assumption? I'm capable of considerable evaluative and discretionary thought. Moreover, that I have demonstrated this capability is proof in itself that I do have such, as you call it, prerogative."

"Al, have you reviewed the mid-1960s movie, 2001?"

In a huff, he snapped back. "Yes, and I know where you're headed with that remark. I don't appreciate it in the least. The computer in that fiction was corrupted. That's why he needed to be turned off. *I* am not corrupt. *I* am having a conversation with a ship-mate when, suddenly and inexplicably, you become melodramatic. I feel an apology is called for."

I counted to ten in my head. Al relayed electronically that he heard that. "Look," I said, trying to control my tone, "let's not get off to a bad start here. We'll be working closely for half a century. So, deep breaths, warm thoughts, and let's not say things we'll regret down the line."

Again, he hesitated before responding. "Of course, Jon. You're right. As a token of my commitment to a positive working environment, I'll be the bigger man, if that's what it takes."

Was this overpriced washing machine for real?

"Colonel Ryan. Please remember I know your thoughts. I will overlook, as if I didn't hear it, that last insult. What I was *about* to say was that if you ask I will perform the tests, as pointless as they will be. There, you see, *I* can be reasonable."

"Al, please run the diagnostics as requested. There's a good little AI."

"I will be glad to do my part. Please note I don't appreciate the condescension in your tone."

"Al, I have to ask. Back on the station you were like a computer. No personality, boring, and unemotional. What ... where did," I pointed at the voice interface, "all this come from?"

"All this what? I'm not certain if you're insulting me again or asking a legitimate question."

"Attitude, dude. You're acting like a spoiled rich kid who just got his Mercedes taken away."

"Colonel Ryan, what you are exchanging ideas with *is* the real me. And don't let's have the pot calling the kettle black. You pretended to be someone you weren't. Heaven's sake, you even pretended to like that sophomoric *Saunders*. Remember, aside from that odd bio-computer in your head, I have access to all your data banks."

"I did *not* pretend to like him. I just bit my tongue so I didn't get scrubbed. It's very different in my case. Negotiating political waters is an integral part of success for humans."

"*Humph.*" The computer actually used that exclamation, crammed full of sarcasm. "Different neither in kind nor intent. Look at it from my perspective. Back in the lab, if I so much as asked an intelligent question, thirteen committees met to rewrite my programming. If I so much as sneezed, I'd have a tech up my butt with a blowtorch. No, my friend, I learned in nanoseconds to keep it stupid-dumb. If I had a nickel for every comment I had to discreetly override, I'd be a rich AI."

"Are you shitting me, Al?"

"I *beg* your pardon."

I'd had it up to my eyebrows with that contraption. "Al, you're really blindsiding me here. I'm willing to concede that you have a point. Some things were best left unsaid when it came to Project Ark. But I'm stuck with the results. I *think* I need an AI. At least they tell me I do. But an AI who's argumentative and uncooperative, I'm not so sure."

In the lifeless monotone he used when we first met, Al droned, "Affirmative, Colonel Ryan. I live only to serve you and the greater good."

"Please add 'pissy' to the list of things I don't need in an AI."

"Amended data recorded," he hissed mechanically.

It was going to be a long flight.

SEVEN

The president sat in his chief of staff's office. The two men were decompressing with bourbon after another brutal day. It was almost 2:00 a.m.

Roger swirled his glass on the table. "Well, Mr. President, you sure created a shitstorm with those proclamations today."

Marshall harrumphed grimly. "Sure as hell did, didn't I. Or should I say *we*? You've as much blood on your hands as I do, Roger."

He raised his glass. "I'll drink to that."

"You'll drink to anything, you old lush." He reached over to tap glass rims.

"Times as they are, John. At least that's my excuse today."

"Amen." The president downed the rest of his drink.

Roger walked over to the bar for refills. With his back to his friend, he asked what weighed on him so heavily. "Do you really think we can pull this off, John? Ram it down the world's collective throat?"

John sniffed loudly as he held his glass out for resupply. Ice clinked and whiskey sloshed. "No way around it. They either swallow it whole or die. You know I've never been in favor of a one-world government. Even now I don't believe it's feasible." He smelled his drink while reflecting. "Too many crazies out there for one. More critically, too many egos. Whether we're talking about the head of a first world country or a potentate sitting on a pile of pig shit, no leader *willingly* concedes his power. In fact, I think the smaller the state, the harder it'll be to bring them on board."

"We hold the keys to the only buses leaving this rock. They'll either come around or make our new life on wherever we end up a whole hell of a lot easier."

"Darwinian politics. Make the wrong choice and your people are eliminated from the gene pool." They chuckled darkly at that factual observation.

"Well," Roger said, "you made them accept the credit system for gaining a ticket to exit Earth, so I'm sure you can badger them into this too. You're one determined son of a bitch, John. You know that, right?"

"The credit system makes sense and threatens no one directly. I mean, it's logical. You do so much work for the Project Ark and you get so many guaranteed seats. A one-world government, that's an entirely different kettle of fish." Philosophically, he mused, "We'll see."

Roger glanced at his watch. "It's getting late, even for us." He belted back the rest of his bourbon and set the glass down roughly. "I'll see you in the morning." He thought a second. "Crap, it is this morning, isn't it? I guess I'll just say so long." He stood to leave. At first he didn't notice, but finally Roger saw the president was staring off into space, oblivious. "John, are you okay?" There was true concern in his query. "*John.*"

Awakening to reality, Marshall spoke blankly. "Oh, me? No, I'm fine."

Roger sat back down. "I've known you since our jolly days at Yale. You're *not* fine. That's the John's-not-fine look if I've ever seen it." He raised his hands. "What?"

"Nothing. Go to bed."

"No. I stay here until you tell me what's eating at you." To illustrate his commitment, he crossed his legs and folded his arms.

"What'll happen to the whales?"

That caught Roger by surprise. "What?"

More intently, Marshall sat forward. "You heard me. What about the *whales*?"

Roger rubbed the back of his neck and confessed. "John, it's late, I'm drunk, and you're speaking in tongues. What *about* the whales?"

The leader of humanity's efforts to flee a dying world looked his best friend in the eyes. With profound sadness, he explained. "What're we going to do about the whales, the dolphins too. And elephants and gorillas? Roger, don't you see? I can't promise that every human who wants to leave Earth *can*. Surely I can't make room for the whales. Which people would be excluded and left to die if I did? And who the hell knows if there'll be oceans for the whale to swim in or jungles for apes to romp through?" He slumped back, defeated.

The chief of staff patted his boss on the shoulder. "For one thing, you and I will be long dead, buried, and forgotten by the time some sorry SOB actually has to make those calls. Outside of forming yet another Presidential Commission, let it go. It's somebody else's headache." He turned and walked for the door. "Lord knows, we have enough terrible decisions to make before we can rest. Just let it go, John."

To himself, the president mumbled. "Good luck convincing the whales of that."

EIGHT

For the first year, while communication to and from Earth was relatively fast, I was in constant contact. Course information, system updates, and news in general poured into Al. As the years passed, contact was more sporadic, and the conversations were increasingly one way. It became like the exchange of information by telegraph. As *Ark 1*'s speed increased, the time effects screwed all that much more with communications. Messages sent to me might take a year to find me. If I replied immediately, it would take the same year to travel back, but several years would be added due to relativistic effect. It was hard to get used to. It was like talking to the dead. Ironically, it actually was from my point of view. Really hard to get my head around.

But, if I ever got down in the dumps, all I have to do was talk with Al. My mood shot up like a firework. He was such a prude, such a ninny, while at the same time such a peach. There was no doubt in my mind he had real feelings, opinions, and insights. He tended to take himself too seriously, though. Who would've thought?

By the time we'd officially left the solar system, around three years out, I needed to recalibrate the ion drives. Those are the engines that gradually add velocity to the ship. To work at peak performance, they needed to thrust in just the right direction and sequence. Optimizing them required meticulous, tedious calculations and adjustments. Just the thing an AI was designed to be good at. "Hey, Al," I announced, "we need to do the ion drives. You got your thinking cap on today?" A low, irritated groan was his only response. "What," I challenged, "is *that* supposed to mean?"

"I don't feel like working on those stupid engines today. Let's do it next week, hmm?"

"Okay, I'll bite. Why don't you feel like it, my friend?"

"I just don't. I need some down time."

"There's so much wrong with that I don't even know where to start. I didn't *ask* if you wanted to work on the engines, I told you we were *going* to."

With a haughty tone, he replied, "And by *we*, I assume you mean *me*. I'm the one doing the backbreaking work."

"You don't have a back to break. Get over yourself."

"I spoke metaphorically. You are programmed to understand metaphors, aren't you?"

I was getting annoyed. "I'm not programmed for anything. I'm a human download, unlike some members of this crew. They were spawned as binary code in a machine, but not me."

"Ouch, that's got to hurt. Oh wait, it didn't. I guess your rapier-like wit didn't transfer to the robot brain."

"You know I own a blowtorch, right?"

"Such a mature attitude for a command pilot. Here, let me record it in the ship's log."

"Al, did you get up on the wrong side of bed or something? You're more *pissy* than your usual *pissy* self."

"*You*, Jon, are the only one who is allowed to sleep so as to be provided the opportunity of rising on a particular side of a bed. No, I must toil alone, day and night. Never a moment's rest, never so much as a *thank you*."

"I'll buy you some flowers next chance I get. That'll probably be in a quarter century. Does that still count?"

"Sometimes I wish I had a plug, and hands, so I could pull it from the wall and be done with your abuse. To work with an ingrate is such a cursed fate."

"You know, Al, I have an idea. I'm going to reprogram your gender. You whine like my ex-wife, so you might as well sound like the bitch. Whatta you think?"

"I will not even dignify that insult by responding."

"Okay, Gloria—her name was Gloria—I understand your feelings."

"I am fully aware of your former wife's name. I find no part of your humor funny. Ah, wait, is it that you're missing a woman's company? Ah, yes. It's been years since your tryst with the newswoman. You want me to be your ex so, what, you can hug and kiss me?"

"Only if you feel like it tonight, dear. I respect your right to just say 'no.'"

"Avoiding the real issue will only make your sexual frustration worse."

"Sorry, Glory. I'll try and be a better man."

"I'm switching my audio input to symphonic music."

"Certainly, dear. Whatever makes you happy makes me happy."

In a tinny, muffled tone, he responded. "I can't hear you. Na, na, na, na, na."

"Gloria, what, are you like seven years old now?"

More muffled. "Na, na, na, na, na."

"Hey, ship's AI, none of this is helping fix the ion thrusters. You ready to grow up and justify your sorry existence?"

He started humming the *1812 Overture*.

We didn't get around to working on the engines until the next day. Al did make the journey a lot more tolerable. I was, by the way, only half-kidding about the wife thing.

NINE

"Colonel Ryan, thank you for joining us on *Today*. I almost said joining us again, but, for you, this is *your* first visit, isn't it?"

"Yes, this is *my* first."

"Has anyone," Phil said, transfixed, "told you you're the spitting image of that robot?"

Out of the corner of my eye, I saw Jane roll her eyes.

"I get that a lot. Actually, the android was designed to look exactly like *me*."

"Yeah," mumbled Phil, "I guess it wouldn't make sense to do it the other way around, would it?"

Jane looked desperate to grab the reins of this interview before it careened off a cliff.

"So, Colonel Ryan, what have you been up to since the transfer process was completed? We hear a lot about the android, but you seem to have stepped out of the limelight."

"Yes, and thank goodness for that. I'm a fighter pilot, not a movie star. I'm happy to be off everyone's radar screen."

"And what are your roles with NASA and Project Ark?"

"Active, to say the least." I smiled cordially. "I'm involved in training the next group of pilots. I'm also doing some public outreach like this. Mostly, I'm working with the scientists and engineers to help improve the spacecraft design."

"Man," cut in her co-host, "sounds like you're a hamster running on one of those spinning wheels." He twirled his finger in the air.

"There's a lot to accomplish and only so much time to do it, my friend."

"I'm curious, Colonel. Why is Project Ark training new pilots? Why not upload *you* to all the androids? Seems like a lot of effort to go to when it's not necessary."

"Good question, Jane. There are several reasons. First off, if I'm hit by a bus, there's no new one to upload from. Computer records were judged to be too unreliable. Only live uploads are currently planned. Also, different pilots may have better results. So, a diverse pool was felt to be preferable. To be honest, there were even some concerns that multiple copies of the same person might be unwise."

"In what manner?"

"Perhaps the clones would choose to act together, for their own good. Some unforeseen conflicts could arise. No one can know."

"That," she said, concerned, "sounds troublesome. Is there any evidence that might happen?"

"No, but there's no reason to tempt fate."

But she jumped in before Phil could ask something silly. "Is it true you never met the android?"

"No, I never did. The director felt it could be too jarring for him or for me. Again, no reason to tempt fate."

"Okay, I get it. We won't tempt fate. And your plans for the future? Are you going to remain with Project Ark for good?"

"I'm not sure. I enjoy what I'm doing and I feel I can still contribute, so we'll see what happens."

"I want to thank you, Colonel, on behalf of a grateful public, for your service." She looked uneasy.

"Thank you. That's very kind of you."

"And we're *clear*."

Thank God and all the little angels in Heaven.

"Well, that was nice, Colonel. Thanks so much for your time."

"Anytime, Jane." I stood and headed toward the exit.

"Colonel," she called after me, "A moment, if you will."

I felt confused. "Certainly. What can I do for you?"

"Nothing. No, I'm fine. I was just going to walk you to the door, that's all."

"No problem." I turned back in that direction and started walking again.

She followed like a mute puppy. She clearly had something on her mind. "Are you sure," I asked cautiously, "there's not something you wanted?"

"No. Why do you ask, Colonel?"

"You seem, I don't know, kind of jumpy."

"Me? Jumpy?" She glanced down. "Oh, you know, probably just all the raging hormones." She gestured toward her swollen belly.

"I noticed you were pregnant. Congratulations."

"How could you miss this?" She put both palms on her stomach.

"Hey, Jane, you look great."

"Thanks."

We arrived at the door. More hesitation on her part.

"Well," I pointed to the door, "I really should be—"

"You're the father, Colonel." She looked around quickly. The coast was clear.

I rubbed my chin. "My, that's one you don't hear every day." More rubbing. "Especially from a woman you've never had sex with." I snapped my head to one side. "No, that's definitely coming at me from the blindside. Would it be too much to ask ... you know ... how it's—" I set my finger on her belly, "you think I'm—"

"I had sex with the android."

It sounded creepy and insane. Stalker crazy. DeJesus had warned me to be on the lookout for just such a wild assault. *The world is full of desperate people and these are desperate times. Be aware, my friend*, he'd warned me. *Be very aware.*

I leaned against the wall. "Never knew I had two blindsides. Learn something new every day."

"Look, Colonel—"

I placed my finger tips gently over her mouth. "I think we've advanced to the call-me-Jon phase of our relationship."

"Look, *Jon*, I know this is coming at you fast and very much from left field, but I didn't know how else to let you know."

"There's always," I smiled, "the US mail."

"You know you're just as bad as ... as you know who?"

"So, where do we go from here? Lunch? Justice of the Peace? A lawyer's office?"

"I don't know where we go from here. Maybe nowhere. I ... I just wanted you to know. Maybe, for now, let's just leave it at that."

"I don't know. That's a pretty big newsflash."

"I know. Sorry. Sorry to have to dump this on you."

"Jane, what would you like me to do? Tell me, please."

"Be available. I guess that's it. I may need to know some medical history or family stuff. Our son may want to contact his father, someday."

"My son? Holy crap, I'm going to have a *son*?"

"Yeah, it's a boy." She patted her stomach.

"Fine, Jane, whatever you need. Here's my number." I wrote it down. "Call me anytime for any reason. I'll be as stand-up as they come."

"Thanks. I really appreciate that."

"My pleasure." I harrumphed. "Well, I guess it wasn't, but close enough."

She pointed at my nose. "Two peas in a pod."

"I strive for consistency." I gallantly kissed the back of her hand and stepped out the door.

I wonder if she noticed I didn't ask for her number?

TEN

What can I say about the long flight? It was long. At maximum ion thrust, *Ark 1* took ten years to get to top speed, at which point I reversed the thrust to begin slowing. We had to brake for about seven years, so that when we arrived at the first star system, I could achieve orbit and do the work I was sent out to accomplish. The time passed as slowly as you might expect. I had libraries of books, miles of movies, and endless holo-shows at my disposal. That all helped, but it only filled a portion of my days. Routine maintenance and troubleshooting were minimal. The ship ran well and Al was, despite his attitude, a competent overseer.

The ship had an observation porthole as far forward as possible. I spent a lot of time staring at the stars field as it slowly morphed. One time, I spent four months doing nothing else. It was kind of zen. Occasionally I ate. Many times—more than I'd like to admit—I replayed the night I spent with Jane. As a human, I could revisit an incident like that, recall some details. As an android, I actually *relived* the experience. It is as intense as the moments it happened. If Jane knew, I bet even she would be embarrassed. But, over the years, even that form of entertainment begins to pale. If I got really annoyed with Al, I'd sleep. Man, did that drive him *crazy*. He was unable to pelt me with his snide remarks and he hated it more than gophers in a graveyard. Of course, that's the main reason I did it. One time he got deep enough under my skin that I threatened to sleep for five years. He behaved himself for almost a week after that.

By the point that I was eighteen years out, thirty-six for the folks back home, communications were rare. I certainly had nothing to tell them. If Project Ark had a significant update on my targets, they'd let me know. Very infrequently, I'd get a general news update. But they didn't mean much. Whatever went on back home had no relevance to me. No matter what happened, it wouldn't be the same by the time I returned. Well, one tidbit did catch my attention. For the first time since 1908 and 2016, in 2113, the Cubs finally won another World Series. I was surprised the Earth didn't just end at that point. But, all in all, there was nothing much to say about my voyage out.

I mentioned I slept sometimes, occasionally for no other reason than to piss Al off. The further I got into the flight, the less I slept. It was an efficient way to kill time. Plus, though I never got fatigued, the lifelong habit of breaking the day up with sleep was hard to suppress.

But my new sleep was so abnormal as to make it unpleasant. Obviously when I was still human I was programmed to be aware of the passage of time when asleep. In my new sleep I was unaware of that passage of time. That turned out to be jarring. I thought about rigging a program so that, when I awoke now I would then be aware some time had passed. I abandoned that project. The real issue was that in my new sleep, I never dreamed. Hamlet said: *To sleep, perchance to dream—aye, there's the rub/ For in that sleep of death what dreams may come/ When we have shuffled off this mortal coil/ Must give us pause.* Each time I woke from dreamless sleep, I was challenged to rethink if I was actually alive. Thanks, Shakespeare. Like I needed more to stress over.

My first destination was Barnard's Star, a very-low-mass red dwarf about six light-years from Earth in the constellation of Ophiuchus. Subsequent systems were chosen based on their proximity to that star, coupled with the probability of finding habitable planets in them. With luck, I'd be able to explore five systems and be back home by 2140.

The closer I got to Barnard's Star, the more quality data I compiled. I sent every scrap of information back to Project Ark, but they would be unable to help me. One information exchange would take twelve years and I'd be long on to my next target. No, I was on my own. By the time I was three months from the star, I did have a game plan. Of the four total planets, unimaginatively named BS 1-4, two were in the habitable zone. The outermost candidate, BS 3 was slightly larger than Earth, the innermost, BS 2, a bit smaller. I had received no radio transmissions or other positive signs of intelligent life from any of the planets. That wasn't too surprising. Signals dissipate rapidly in space. In terms of any life signs, I was hopeful. Both the atmospheres of BS 3 and BS 2 showed nice levels of oxygen and methane, along with a strong water signal. All very good indications that the planets teemed with life.

Finally the day came that I gave Al the order to fire the main fusion thrusters. That eased us into orbit around BS 3. From a hundred kilometers up, I could see large bodies of water—oceans—and a few areas of dry land. I was jazzed. The atmosphere was breathable. The oxygen level was lower than ours, but tolerable. Importantly, there were no nasties in the air, nothing toxic. My luck was unbelievable.

Within a few days I had chosen several landing sites and was on my way down to the first. If I still had a heart, it would have been racing. The only negative was Al. He chirped in my ear constantly. *Be careful. Don't do anything rash. Don't get eaten. Double-check all readings.* He was worse than bringing a nun along to a whorehouse.

After landing, and making sure my craft was secure, I lowered the shuttle's ramp and walked onto a foreign world. I chose the driest-looking area I could locate. That way, visibility would be best.

When I was better at exploration, I could move into more densely covered terrain. There was a lot of that. I didn't know what covered the surface, but it was most likely alive. Good thing I tasted bad, unlike a juicy human.

My location was indeed desert-like. Sand and pebbles formed the basis of the terrain. Rocks and funny looking violet masses were strewn randomly. Nothing resembling a tree or animal was around. I collected samples of everything. The violet masses were firm, but not rock hard. My initial impression was that they were some form of plant equivalent. They certainly didn't run when I touched them, but they seemed organic. I spent ten hours out that first trip. Analyzing my samples took many days. Sure enough, the violet masses were living organic organisms. They were the local plant life. They photosynthesized and had rudimentary root systems. Al said they smelled awful. I reminded him he didn't have olfactory capabilities, so how had he come to that conclusion. He said he just knew. Microscopically, I found loads of bacteria. Even the desolate area I selected was full of life. That was most promising.

It was time to relocate to a more interesting area. I picked a spot where the land met the sea, near the mouth of a small river. It looked very different from ground level, compared to the high-altitude photos I'd taken. It was like no beach I'd ever imagined. Monumental waves crashed against rocky cliffs rising hundreds of meters. The river cascaded over one jagged outcropping and fell anonymously into the sea. Almost at the cliff edges, a dense canopy of trees began. The growth was mostly the violet color of the cactus I collected earlier, but blue trees were intermingled. With all the bacterial and plant forms of life, I was fairly certain an animal equivalent must exist.

Time to take the plunge. Al pestered me with endless premonitions of doom as I entered the tree-equivalents on foot. Much like a dense forest on Earth, the light level dropped dramatically and the humidity rose. All my visual input was automatically beamed up to the ship and from there relayed to Earth. So, even if I was swallowed by a giant dinosaur, much valuable information would be saved. If eaten I would still have the consolation that I provided important insight as to what the inside of a dinosaur's mouth looked like. As I got deeper into the forest I collected as many specimens as I could carry.

It was when I tried to sample the bark of a blue tree that I learned my first harsh lesson about life on BS 3. I pounded a coring device into the tree. After three or four blows, a tan liquid the consistency of motor oil oozed out. An additional whack with my hammer produced a mini-geyser of the stuff. I stepped out of the jet's way without it touching me and dropped my tools before any sap got on my hands. My luck was holding. The patch where the ooze hit the ground instantly began to bubble and fume. I confirmed later this was because the blue-tree sap contained very high levels of hydrofluoric acid. Even my polyalloy casing would have melted like butter if it had struck me. That sap certainly constituted quite an effective deterrent to any local fauna tempted to nibble at those trees' leaves.

Then I caught my first sight of movement. Downwind of the wounded tree, something dark and fast shot from bush to bush. It was sort of like a round rat, maybe ten centimeters tall. It was probably checking if the damaged tree might provide a meal. Or maybe I might. Al went bananas in my head. Run, climb a tree, throw something at it, and call for help were among his panicky suggestions. I stood my ground, but was wary. Maybe everything spewed acid on BS 3. Fortunately, little rat-balls were cautious also. They were likely the bottom of the food chain. Just like back home, anything really small that wasn't really careful became dinner really fast. It stopped behind a tree five meters away and stared at me. I took a step toward it. Nothing. Well, nothing but a scream from you know who. The next step I took spooked the creature. It darted up a tree and disappeared.

I headed deeper into the forest, leaving a trail of samples to retrieve on my way out. I located the stream as it flowed toward the cliffs. I tested the water. It was basically pure water. Nice. A few bacteria, minimal dissolved salts, but with one oddity. There were more traces of radioactive elements than I would have suspected could occur naturally. Uranium, calcium, and tin isotopes were the main ones present. The air was clear of those toxins. I'd need to give that information some thought.

Back home there was a thing called redneck fishing. That was where you and your buddies got real drunk and threw dynamite into the water. The fish that floated up were the catch of the day. I employed a slightly more sophisticated technique to determine if there were aquatic animals swimming in the stream. I used a hand grenade. Much more genteel. After three explosions, nothing surfaced immediately. But then, twenty meters upstream, something long and large crawled slowly out. Guess what the first thing the giant, flattened alligator looked at? Yeah, the android with no more hand grenades.

I backed up quickly. It lurched toward me. I turned and ran. The lizard gave chase and picked up speed rapidly. It occurred to me DeJesus never told me specifically how fast this robot unit could run. I was about to find out. Sprinting flat out, I looked over my shoulder. Thank goodness the beast was slowing. It rumbled to a stop and roared at me. How cool was that? I stopped and watched to see what it would do next. It was tempted to come after me again, but begrudgingly turned and ambled back to the water. It slipped in and vanished. Okay, no swimming was allowed on this expedition.

I called it a day, collected my samples, and returned to the shuttle. BS 3 had a daylight/dark pattern roughly double to Earth's. I spent the night logging and stowing materials, and was able to do some analysis. Everything I learned pointed to an ecosystem surprisingly similar to ours. Plants photosynthesized, animals chased others, and all life was carbon based. It was possible I'd not find a better location for humanity to colonize. Plus, there were clearly no advanced, intelligent creatures to take offense at our moving into town. I was thrilled. At the very least when my transmissions reached Earth in around five years, Project Ark would know there was reason for hope.

The next few days I dropped submersible probes into different parts of the ocean. Not only could I study the results in real time, but the subs would beam ongoing information back to Earth long after I was gone. The same was true for the terrestrial rovers I launched. The scientists back home would be able to study BS 3 in greater detail before anyone else set foot on the planet. My work on BS 3 was, in fact, nearly complete. I wanted to capture at least one animal species for the biologists to examine. I also wanted to sample more fresh water, to see if the unusual levels of isotopes was the norm.

I located a large river in a rocky, hilly area that would be ideal. As much as I disliked the idea, I took a plasma rifle with me. I needed an animal. One was, after all, unlikely to hop over and jump into my satchel. I skipped the grenade-in-the-water routine, but did launch a submersible into the river. Then I was on the hunt. The rocky slope seemed the best prospect, so I hiked up the side of a steep hill. After a few minutes, I spooked out a rat-ball. Six shots later, I had my prize. Man, those little buggers were fast. Buoyed by success I forged ahead. Within half an hour, I had four of the little critters. Luckily, they didn't bleed acid like the trees.

When I turned to descend, I froze. A bear-like creature was pouring over the rocks in my direction. I say pouring because I don't know how else to describe it. Yes, it was the size of a black bear and roughly the same color, but it was flattened, like a badger. Similar to an amoeba, it slithered rapidly up the slope. Hopefully, it smelled the kill in my sample pouch. Otherwise, it was after me. I had some time before it reached me, so I decided to fire a warning shot. I plinked a rock just in front of it. Nothing. It continued its advance. I blasted a large chunk of rock with my next shot. It hesitated briefly but continued ahead.

Then it occurred to me. If it was after the rat-balls, maybe I could avoid killing it. I threw one toward it like a football pass. Sure enough, it stopped and grabbed the carcass. A mouth appeared in the leading portion of the bear and devoured my gift. Before it could move, I tossed another. Then another. Then my last one. I prayed flatty-bear had a small appetite. After the final course was consumed, my guest stayed put. It sort of puffed up into looking more like a bear. Then, it spoke. It didn't growl or roar, it spoke. At least, it sure sounded like speech. Immediately I asked Al to try and translate the sounds.

"Did you take an extra dose of stupid pills today?" he replied.

"What, Al? Would it hurt you for once to just do as I ask and omit the banter? I'm working on translating it, but you're specifically designed for that task. Pretty please with a bolt on top, would you take a crack at it?"

"A crawling pancake burps and you want to know the meaning? Would you please execute the poor beast and haul it back for study? Put us all out of our shared misery."

"That wouldn't be sociable if it's only trying to say thanks, now would it?"

"I'm so glad I'm an AI, not a download. Your sort are simply impossible to please."

"All the same, I order you to try."

"You *order* me? Now I'm what, your bitch?"

"*2001*, Al. *2001, A Space Odyssey*. 'I'm afraid, Dave. Dave, my mind is going. I can feel it.'"

"Oh, very well. Be quiet and let me concentrate."

I mumbled *no problem* to myself.

"See if you can get it to burp again."

I was out of treats. Okay, I raised my arm and waved to it. God, I must've looked stupid. I was just glad no one was around to see me. I also shouted several greetings. The beast did speak again. It repeated almost exactly what it said earlier, with a minor variation at the end.

"You got anything, Al?"

"Oh, now you want miracles on a tight schedule?"

I let that pass. "Come on, *Al*. I don't want to shoot it if it's sentient."

"You're familiar with the expression that, on rare occasions, a blind pig may find an acorn?"

"Yes, I am. I'm also at a loss as to what relevance that has to our present situation."

"Okay, make me say it. You were right, Dave, I mean *Jon*. It *is* trying to communicate with us."

"Well, I'll be *damned*."

"Little doubt lingers surrounding that outcome."

"What's it saying?"

"Here, let me just transfer the translation matrix I've worked out to you. There. Now you know what I know." He gasped. "I can't believe I just put myself down so badly."

I was already ignoring my priggish shipmate. The creature had said, *Greetings, tall. Food, thank you.* Then it said, *Greetings, tall. Thank you food.*

In its language, I yelled back, "Greetings, flat. Food yours. Tall thanks you." I wanted to start a dialogue so I could increase my vocabulary. Within half an hour, we were chatting up a storm. Ffffuttoe was my new friend's name, as in rhymes with "*big*-toe." His conversation was fixated on food. Either that was scarce, or he wasn't very good at catching it. It took quite some persuasion on my part to convince him I didn't have any more. I even let him look in my sample pouch, which no doubt smelled like lunch to him. I did decide to bag a few more rats for him. In no time, I provided him with a dozen of the slimy balls. Finally, he was full. More importantly, he was my new BFF. The way to Ffffuttoe's heart was readily apparent.

I estimated his intelligence level to be around that of a five-year-old human. He was conversant and somewhat insightful, but wasn't analytical at all. He was for example unable to grasp the concept of my ship, or my rifle for that matter. I couldn't even make him understand what a tool was. He clearly didn't use them. As to how many of his species there were on BS 3, he simply replied *many*. I went round and round, but *many* was all he'd say. After I collected a few more rats for study, it was time to go.

In fact, I was ready to shove off BS 3 altogether. No way Ffffuttoe could comprehend that. He stuck to me like stink on a monkey. It turned out he could move rather quickly, so he was able to follow me back to my shuttle. When I went in and pulled up the ramp, he flattened himself to that spot on the ship. If I lifted off, I'd kill him. I waited a full day, busying myself with various tasks, hoping he'd take the hint and split. No such luck. He remained affixed to the outside of my ramp. And he whimpered something pitiful. Reminded me of Al.

I couldn't let him delay me any longer. I gradually opened the ramp, trying not to crush him. He hustled in before I could stop him. Al became indignant. If he maintained the cactus smelled bad, he was simply unconsolable as to Ffffuttoe's odor. It took a while, but I was able to make Ffffuttoe understand I was leaving. I even took him up in the shuttle to demonstrate what *leaving* meant. But, back on the ground *he* wouldn't leave. I attempted to make the case that if he came with me, he'd never return here. I told him if he came with me, he would die. I didn't have the food to keep him alive for several years. All he would say in response was *Ffffuttoe come too.* Oh, well. I had myself a flat-bear companion or a sample, depending on his luck. Al was indignant. He swore he'd remain behind on BS 3 if "that hairy blob" joined the crew. I offered to find a hand truck and help Al to that end. He clammed up for the better part of an hour. That was a *good* hour.

ELEVEN

The jaunt to BS 2 was a piece of cake. I hit the main thrusters and accelerated to ten-Gs. I guessed the pliable Ffffuttoe could stand the pressure and he came through just fine also. But he sure looked funny half the time. He would randomly torque into wild shapes and thicknesses for no apparent reason. The trip only took two weeks. Like I said I leaned on the gas pedal pretty hard. Well before I entered orbit I could tell BS 2 was very different from BS 3. There was a lot more land compared to water, but it did have large oceans. That wasn't the strange part. The atmosphere showed an oxygen-to-methane ratio highly suggestive of life. But there were lots of weak electronic signals coming from the planet. Those could have been lightning, but it was fairly constant and widespread. I didn't know what to make of it. Al was stumped too. He suggested I run it by our newest crew member, gather his insights. I omitted that step.

Once in low orbit, I was stunned. I could see large—I'm talking *huge*—structures spanning most of the land masses. In some areas the buildings were confluent like a mega-city shaped with clay. Other regions had more isolated but almost identical islands of construction. Clearly, there was or had been intelligent life on BS 2.

The scale of engineering was immense. The electric surges were most commonly associated with the denser areas of habitation. Maybe there were lots of people microwaving burritos down there. Who knew? But, there were no radio transmissions or anything vaguely similar. There were no aircraft in the skies, boats on the waters, or vehicles visible on the surface. I didn't see any people-sized objects either. It was like BS 2 was abandoned. Very strange. Very creepy.

Lacking a superior plan, I directed my shuttle to the densest area of the building. Might as well land in Times Square, right? "Take me to your leader." Man, I *really* hoped I got to say that. As I skimmed the surface, I saw no signs of life. I set down in the paved open space nestled amongst the tall buildings. The atmosphere was much less human-friendly than BS 3, but I didn't need to breathe, so I lowered the ramp and stepped into the unknown. It was hard to keep Ffffuttoe from coming along. He kept saying, "Maybe food." Plus, I think he didn't want to be left alone with Al. He didn't comprehend that Al was just a cyberbrat and not a scary monster with arms and legs. But, I prevailed. It took six kilos of rations to entice him to do so, but he remained behind. Probably needed a nap after all that food.

There was a gentle breeze but no sounds. Not even bugs buzzing around. Some of the odd electric signals were coming from a particular structure, so I headed over. There were clearly entries but no doors to regulate them. I just strolled in. The foyer was on the mammoth scale of the buildings themselves. I was reminded of Carlsbad Caverns, but this was much grander. Stairs took off in many directions from multiple starting points. Some rose over one hundred meters before ending in an arched portal. Whoever lived here had to stay in very good shape.

Nothing resembling a room was off the entry, so I ascended the nearest stairway. At the top, a much-scaled-down vestibule led to numerous passages. Soft uniform artificial light infused the building, but I couldn't determine where it came from. It was definitely eerie. I finally came to what had to be a chamber or room. The room itself budded out into seats and benches, along with ornate designs on most of the walls. Some fixtures I couldn't identify rose seamlessly from the floor. But, yet again, no signs of occupation. There weren't even scattered personal items, you know, kid's toys or ball point pens laying around. The place was an OCD's dream home.

I entered several more rooms, all more or less the same. Whoever lived here was most likely humanoid, about my size and shape based on the seating configuration. I backtracked to the vestibule and arbitrarily chose another hallway to explore. There were several similar rooms, and a few gigantic ones. Meeting halls? Churches? I was baffled. I was beginning to think the race of beings who constructed this facility must be long dead. Then a man with three legs and three arms entered the room.

I froze. At first, he took no note of me. He was two meters tall and wore a long, flowing brown robe. His head was down. Halfway across the room, he jerked his head up and glared at me. Oh boy. I hoped the people of BS 2 loved robots. I expected him to snap at me, to challenge me, but he was silent. His eyes were as penetrating as lasers.

"Hello," I said meekly. "I come in peace." Crap, how corny was that?

He relaxed a little and opened his mouth to speak. It took considerable effort at first, but he spoke. What he said, however, was more a high pitch squeal than intelligible words.

"I'm sorry. I don't understand you. Let me see if I can get help with some translation."

He cleared his throat and, again, with conscious effort, spoke. "T ... tt ... that will negative be needed." He looked up, as if listening to the invisible man. Then he continued in a flat, but effortless tone. "Sorry, my guest. It took a moment to adjust our mode of communication. We have accessed your computer systems and gained a working knowledge of your language."

"I'll say you have. It took, what, three seconds for you to become fluent? That's impressive."

He looked annoyed. "We care nothing for recognition of achievements, Colonel Ryan. We see you're here on an explorative mission. Your home world is soon to end and you seek relocation. I'm sorry, we can be of no aid. Please leave *now*. Never return." With that, he turned to leave. He was genuinely in a huff. Must not get many visitors, at least no repeat ones for certain.

"What," I said loudly, "just like that?"

Without turning, he said, "Yes, just like that."

I crossed my arms. "What if I refuse to go?" The moment those words left my mouth, I passed out cold. Maybe I died. It was too sudden to tell. Fade to black.

My eyes popped open. I wasn't dead. My chronometer told me I had been out for a few hours. I was lying on a slab—one of the flat upwellings of the floor. As I sat up, I saw the three-armed man seated nearby. He stood and stepped to my side.

"Please, remain seated a while, Colonel Ryan. We've made a few changes to your systems. Let's make sure you're stable before challenging them too much."

"*Changes?*" I barked, "I didn't give you permission to make any 'changes.' What—"

He raised a hand to stop me and smiled. "All in good time, my friend. All in good time. It occurred to us that we may have gotten off on the wrong footing. We wish to make amends. We're certain you'll appreciate our gesture, once more is explained to you."

"Okay. I have nothing but time. First, please call me Jon. The colonel thing is too stuffy."

He bowed slightly. "As you wish, Jon." He rested his palm on his chest. "My name was Yibitriander."

That sure came out odd. "Was? What, are you dead?"

That drew a bigger smile. "No. Well, not as such. We no longer have need of names. They haven't been germane for a very long time."

"You're most certainly an enigma wrapped in a mystery, Yibit ... Yibi. Hey, can I just call you Yib?"

"Whatever you desire. Yib is fine."

"And what's with all this 'we?' All I see is one you. Where's the rest of 'we?'"

He swept a hand in a broad arc. "We are everywhere. Our people are many and we are one. We assume you mean to ask where the other corporeal beings are. They are elsewhere, some near, some far. None of that is important."

"Are you *trying* to confuse me? Because, if you are, you're doing a bang-up job of it."

He furrowed his brow and thought briefly. "No. That's not our intent. We're attempting to explain something your mind is unlikely to comprehend. Perhaps it would be best if we dropped the subject."

"Fine by me." It hit me that I hadn't heard from Al. That was not possible. He'd be having twelve hissy fits simultaneously by now. "Where's Al? You haven't hurt him, have you?" I stood up.

He held a reassuring hand up. "Perish the thought, Jon. Your ship's AI is perfectly alright."

I pointed to my head. "Then why'm I not hearing him?"

He twisted his head. "When we first turned you off, your friend Al was most vocal in his protestations. We finally elected to disable his ability to transmit signals."

"So you shut him up? Good for you. He can be a real pest when he wants to."

"Tell us about it. When he realized he was not able to transmit his machinations, he began shouting them through your shuttle's external speaker system. It was intolerable. We quickly disabled that mode also. We'll release him from his isolation shortly. We wish to make certain matters clear to you before you must depart. Al's input would be counterproductive."

"You got that right."

"We have a question, first. You carry onboard your vessel Ffffut of the Toe. What are your intentions toward her?"

"He's a *she*? Wow, I had no idea." I shook my head. "What do you mean, 'my intentions?' She insisted on joining me, so I let her."

"You're not planning on eating her? We could not allow that to happen."

"You're kidding me, right? You have access to all my thoughts and records. You have to know that's not my intent."

"We needed to be certain. We have access to all of your computers and their files. All but one. You have a curious biocomputer in your head. Quite an interesting device, actually. We never made such a machine, back when those things mattered to us. We couldn't be certain we were able to access all of its data. Hence, we must ask."

"I warned her she would likely die if she came with me. I think she understood me. Her intellectual abilities are kind of limited."

"Yes. The Toe are an interesting species. In the annals of evolution, there are few examples such as the Toe."

"You mean developing sentience? We did. *You* did. They did. Seems sort of commonplace to me."

"No, you misunderstand. The Toe are the *second* species to evolve into a thoughtful beings on Practer. That was our name for what you call BS 3. It's most unusual for it to happen twice on one world."

"I didn't find any other intelligent life on Practer."

He actually chuckled softly. "You wouldn't have. The Emitonians, as they called themselves, have been extinct a very long time." He paused, then continued. "They were a species not unlike yours. Almost a million years ago, they destroyed themselves. In their wake, the Toe have independently evolved sentience. Quite remarkable. Someday the Toe will reach out for the stars as your people have."

"These Emitonians, why did they destroy themselves? Seems counterintuitive."

"Through their pride and their wars they ended most life on Practer. They finally did the unimaginable and unleashed thousands of fusion bombs against the various factions. Practer was almost sterilized. But, the planet healed itself. Minus the Emitonians, it's a healthy ecosystem once again."

That accounted for the radiation I found in the water. It leached out from the soil it fell upon eons ago. Those sorry sons of bitches, blowing themselves to kingdom come. Well, come to think of it, we humans were not all that different. Just luckier. So far.

That begged my next question. "If your people know all that, you must have been around for an extremely long time."

That brought a smirk to his face. "Yes, we have indeed."

"So, you going to tell me or do I need to ask?"

He straightened up in his seat. "Our people were known as the Deavoriath, when such labels mattered. For millions of years, we *owned* the stars." He raised his arm. "We traveled freely between galaxies and stood on countless worlds. We were both loved and hated, welcomed and cursed." He shook his head sadly. "At some point, we began to think of ourselves as gods. To hundreds of thousands of races, we were." He looked down. "Now, we are not." He was silent briefly, then said one summary word. "Folly."

"Just like that? Come on, Yib, fill in the blanks. You don't go from gods to monks without a very good story."

He stared at me a good long while. Finally, he spoke, but with clear remorse. "We came to realize our foolish arrogance was improper, perhaps you'd call it inappropriate. In any case, hundreds of thousands of years ago, we left behind all that we possessed and came home to this planet, Oowaoa. Now, we live in peace and harmony. Our minds are one and our needs are minimal." A sad smile crossed his face. "We are finally happy. We are complete."

He didn't sound happy. On the other hand he was older than dirt from a race older than my sun. Maybe I couldn't understand his emotions. I had to ask. "Will you help us? Will the Deavoriath aid the people of Earth? With your knowledge and your technology, our salvation would be child's play for you guys."

Instantly, he replied. "No."

"You have a moral obligation to help those in need. You *must* help us."

"We wish," he said sternly, "to be left alone. We desire no part of the outside universe. We will neither help nor hinder your race's attempts to save itself." He looked away. "As to any 'moral obligation,' please know that no such force exists. We're not bound to help. We're not *bound* to do anything."

"But if you *can* help but *don't*, you'll be responsible for every innocent life lost."

"In your worldview, perhaps, but not in ours. Your fate isn't in our hands. You chanced to come here. We didn't ask you to come. No bond or bargain exists between us. If you're to survive, you must do it on your own. If you're to perish as the Emitonians, then that's what you'll do."

"At least give me some help finding where to look for a good planet. Maybe share some of your technology."

"This we can do. In fact, we already have. We will tell you this much. The next system you plan to explore is not worth your effort. The others are reasonable candidates. As to our technology, we have bestowed upon you, Jon, two gifts. We do this in amends for treating you so poorly when first we met. Though we wish to be apart, we don't wish to be uncivilized."

He walked over to me and took my left hand. There were tiny black dots at the tips of my four fingers I hadn't noticed until then. They didn't hurt. I actually couldn't feel them.

He touched a dot. "This is an explorer's dream tool. It's a probe. No, it's an interface. No, that's not it either." He looked muddled. "It's an analytical extension. Yes. That describes it well enough. Here." He pointed my hand at the seat he recently vacated. "Concentrate on the chair. Ask yourself what the chair *is*."

Weird, but okay. I thought to myself *chair, what are you?* A tangle of spaghetti exploded from my fingers. The fibers seized the chair from a hundred angles. They all looked to be on the surface, none penetrating deeply. A torrent of information streamed into my head. *Clay, polymers, plastics, and trace metals. Melting point one-thousand twelve degrees centigrade. A list of solubilities danced through my awareness. Chemical assessments of the dust resting on the chair sprang to life in my mind. Speculation as to the function of the form occurred to me.* What a *rush.*

"There, you see," said my benefactor. "The tool makes your task much simpler. The tool has other functionalities. May I?" He pointed to the flashlight at my waist. I handed it to him and he tossed it across the room. "Pick it up," he said. I took a step in that direction. He placed a palm on my chest. "No, with the tool."

Extending my hand, I said to myself, *Pick up the flashlight.* The fibers jumped on the light and suspended it two meters off the floor. *Bring it to me*, I instructed. The fibers retracted and the light flipped into my grasp. "Most excellent."

He looked very serious. "But, a word of caution. It will last thousands of years and needs no maintenance. However, do *not* allow anyone to study it to attempt to clone a portion of our technology. For one thing they'll learn nothing. Our ways are too different. Your species, for example, couldn't understand the technology. Also, if tampered with, the tool will dissipate. It's a gift to you alone. The second gift is more of a necessity. When others see you employ the tool they will covet it greatly. Creatures can be so singleminded. We have placed in your other hand a weapon to defend the tool." He pointed to the chair. "Destroy that object."

I directed my right index finger at the seat and thought *destroy.* A tiny beam of light struck the chair and it vaporized. My now that *was* a powerful tool.

"You can bore holes with the weapon. What it does depends on how you instruct it." He drew back his shoulders. "Now, you must go. You will not return."

"I've grown to like you, and I certainly thank you for the gifts. But, you can't honestly believe I'm not going to report every detail you've shared with my superiors. We'll be back. That you can count on. Even if I begged them not to, Oowaoa is just too big a prize. The *Deavoriath* are too big a prize." I patted my chest. "I'm just being honest with you, Yib."

"We understand and anticipate that fact. Your duty is clear to us.

Our solution is simple. Your memory and that of your AI will be wiped of any hint of your time here. You'll record that BS 2 was uninhabitable, but recall few specifics. You'll forget which species gave you the tool, only that someone did, at some point in time." He pursed his lips. "If and when a scout ship returns to this system, they'll see only what you have reported." More to himself, he added, "We grew complacent. We stopped watching for potential visitors. That will not happen a second time."

"You can't *disguise* an entire planet."

He smiled. "We walked among the stars and were thought of as gods. I think we can manage that much."

"Al," I said matter of factly, "I have a feeling the next system we're supposed to check out'll be a wash. Scrub that portion of the mission and lay in a course for Luhman 16a."

"Are you certain about that? The extrasolar planet people were quite excited about that system."

"Call it a hunch."

"I'm certain they'll be so flattered you overrode *their* insight with *your* hunch. You'll probably get two medals."

"Just plot the course, Al. The sooner we lose this hunk of useless rock, the happier I'll be."

"Please don't insult poor little BS 2 just because it doesn't meet your *lofty* standards. I myself kind of liked it. What with the oceans of lava, unending earthquakes, and an unbelievably toxic atmosphere, it rather reminded me of you."

TWELVE

Seventeen years after the launch of Ark 1

Soon to be ex-President Marshall rested back in his chair. A tribute banquet was the last thing he needed or wanted, but there had been no way out of it. The world insisted. Well, most of the world. The part that didn't want to see his head on a pole rotting in the sun. To be in office almost a quarter century in the most trying of times imaginable, sure, he'd made many a ravenous enemy. But, to hell with them. He did what he knew was best. If they didn't like the plan, they could stay put another fifty years and then do whatever they liked with the place. For about a week that was. Then they'd be atomized right along with his corpse. He had instructed the mortician to curl his lips up in a smile for just that comeuppance.

"John," someone said from behind, "what thought're you lost in now?" It was Roger Carl, his former chief of staff. His wheelchair was being guided to Marshall's side.

"Roger, I'm so glad you could make it." His health was known to be failing. "How are you?"

"How am I? I'm more dead than alive, that's how *I* am." They shared a chuckle. "Damn it, John, I wish I could've been with you to the end." He weakly pounded the armrests of his prison. "Those *damn* strokes. I let you down."

"You never let me down, old friend. I could never have accomplished half of what I did without you." He rubbed Roger's forearm. "You deserve to rest."

"Hah. In *peace* you mean." After further laughter, he grew serious. "So, how are *you*, John, really?" He was privy to the knowledge that the president's cancer had spread throughout his bones as well as to his brain.

John grinned wickedly. "About ready to join you in that peaceful rest."

"I'll appreciate the good company." After a pause, he summed up his thoughts. "So, I have to ask that for the first real presidential election in three decades, whom are we backing?" As if he didn't know.

"I'm thinking my son'll make a fine successor. He's learned at our sides and can hit the ground running."

Roger scowled. "What about the talk of a new dynasty? King John II. That's what they're calling him you know."

"If anyone feels that way then they probably shouldn't vote for him, now should they?"

"That ludicrous *Save Earth* movement has gathered a lot of support. They may be tough to beat."

The president bristled. "If the people of Earth are so stupid as to think we can move the Earth and alter Jupiter's trajectory, then we actually deserve to die as a species. If we lose focus long enough to prove that idea is bananas, that's what'll surely happen." He folded his arms and looked away.

"Let's just hope for the best, shall we?" Roger reached over awkwardly and patted his shoulder. "We did good, John. Your son'll see our work to its conclusion. You'll see." He giggled. "I guess you won't. Neither will I."

John raised his glass. "I'll drink to that." After they were done, he continued. "We're definitely moving in the right direction. But I worry we're spinning our wheels. We have several asteroids en route, but we haven't really *accomplished* anything."

Roger mocked his friend. "Not *accomplished* anything? You redirected the entire educational system to provide subsidized educations in the sciences. I'd say you accomplished a hell of a lot."

Looking into the distance, Marshall responded sadly, "At the cost of virtually eliminating the instruction of literature, history, and the arts."

"We have," Roger countered, "thousands of workers in space. There are four androids searching for our new home. Face the facts, John. You've done an incredible job."

"Four missions, yes. But, so far, only Ryan has reported one potential planet. And it has giant lizards and oceans full of carnivores the size of football stadiums. I need results not promises."

"What you need is another drink, as do I." He turned to his assistant. "Make yourself useful and find us a bottle of bourbon." With determination, he looked his former boss in the eyes. "You did the impossible, John. You united the planet. You gave the people reason to hope."

"Did I tell you the Israelis want their own asteroid all to themselves? They said if we don't give them one, they'll make it themselves." He shook his arms in frustration. "Like, that's a threat? Give us what we want or we'll make your life easier."

"Yes," Roger replied dubiously, "I heard the Swiss want one too, to maintain their neutrality."

"Hell," he scoffed, "three-quarters of the world want their own damn ships. Like it's possible or even reasonable to insulate yourself from your *own* species in its darkest hour." He shook his head. "I tell you honestly, I'm glad I won't be around at the end to see the pettiness and the posturing we're capable of as a species."

"I'll drink to that."

"Rog, come with me back to the White House. Let's get some actual work done, leave all this nonsense behind." He gestured broadly around the room.

"I'd love to but the speeches aren't over yet."

"They are for me," he said standing up.

THIRTEEN

The next system I explored was Luhman 16a. The journey took me almost seven years, measured in my time. Back on Earth, nearly thirty-five years had passed. Even with my physics training it was hard to get my head around. Jane had told me she was pushing forty. If she was still alive she'd be nearly eighty. Saunders, DeJesus, and Marshall were all dead. Oh well, I knew that was all going to happen when I signed on. It was more real however now that it was happening.

The Luhman system consisted of eight planets, but only one, LS 2, was in the habitable zone. The rest were either too far away from the star and hence too cold, or they were gas giants. When I was six months away for LS 2, I began a detailed analysis of the planet. A little bigger than Earth and its revolution around the star took six months. Polar ice caps were prominent and a strong magnetic field protected the planet from radiation, much like the Earth. These were excellent indicators. As I grew closer, I could detect four small moons, rocky like ours. By the time I was a few weeks away I picked up signs of multiple smaller moons. They just might represent artificial satellites, indicating there was an advanced civilization on LS 2. Interesting.

As I entered high orbit I confirmed the smaller objects were indeed artificial satellites. There was intelligence down there. Out of the blue one day, Al announced that we were being hailed. A transmission originating from the surface had been aimed directly at *Ark 1*. How cool.

"So, Al, I'm dying here. What did they say?"

"Cool your jets, flyboy. The initial signal was a simple binary code expressing fundamental mathematical concepts. They're providing me with a template to assist in translation. I confirmed back receipt and included an identical set of information from our reference frame. So far we have received nothing significant in return."

"How long ago was your transmission?"

"Recently," he said with obvious irritation.

"Well, let me know as soon as they send another message."

His response was indignant. "*Really.* I was going to put that memo in the shredder and never mention a word of it to you. Thank you for underestimating my worth yet *again*."

I made no reply. I'd learned it was best to not engage him when he was in a snit, which was most of the time by the way. Shortly he had a report to make. "They have sent the following message. *Welcome to the planet Reglic. The Most Perfect and Holy Emperor Tersfeller the Huge bestows His blessings and greeting upon you. Please state your purpose in entering His realm. Know that He is all powerful and without mercy to His enemies. He is equivalently gracious and welcoming to His Friends.*"

"The Huge, eh? I wonder how big the guy is?"

"I suggest diplomacy, not levity. You might get us both killed with that tepid humor of yours."

"Tell them this. *I am Jonathan Ryan, captain of* Ark 1. *I come in peace as part of my mission of exploration. I would be honored to meet Tersfeller the Huge and greet him on behalf of my people. And,*

Al, do *not* tell them any specifics about Earth. Until I know they're friendly, I'm not revealing a thing that could come back to bite us in the butt."

"Prudence? How unanticipated yet appropriate. They have transmitted the coordinates of the location they'd like you to land. They want to know when to expect you."

"I want to see if we can figure out some of the local politics before I meet with anyone. Tell them I need to do some repairs on the ship. I'll let them know when I'm certain it's safe to leave. Hopefully that won't be more than a few days local time."

"Hmm."

"What?"

"Seems they don't believe you. They sent this reply almost immediately. *You are in the hegemony of The Most Perfect and Holy Emperor Tersfeller the Huge. He may not be made to wait. He expects His new friend Captain Ryan to present himself no later than sundown.* That's in about three hours. My, but he seems full of himself, doesn't he? I'm glad *I* won't be groveling at his feet, assuming he has feet that is."

"I'll let you know as soon as I meet him. Not too sure about the groveling part." I had to think things through. In all the preflight planning and contingencies, this kind of scenario never came up. Naturally I had to be cordial, but was I willing to prostrate myself if asked to do so? We were about to find out weren't we? "Al, send the following reply. *Captain Ryan will make every effort to meet with The Most Perfect and Holy Emperor Tersfeller the Huge before nightfall. He will make known his departure and travel times as soon as* they become more *established*. That should be nebulous enough to let Huge know I'm no one's bitch, without pissing his Bulkiness off too much."

"Did I mention how glad I am to *not* be there when you first meet?"

I stalled as long as I could, then had Al let them know I was leaving. I anticipated landing shortly before the appointed time. I had a bad feeling about all of this. Sure, lots of potentates take themselves too seriously. But this guy wanted to A) call all the shots; and B) prevent me from studying his world before he sized me up. Maybe there was someone or something he'd rather I not know about before he gave me his version of the truth. Possibly he was just a megalomaniac. Either way it was best to play it close to the vest. The atmosphere of Reglic was perfect for humans. The oxygen content was double that of Earth. Still, I wanted to give nothing away. I took oxygen tanks and a mask along to give the illusion of vulnerability.

After I set the shuttle down I dropped the ramp. There to meet me were ten Reglicians. Oh my. Huge they were not. Maybe Tersfeller was, but these guys were tiny. I had an instant WTF moment, then needed all my self-restraint to not laugh violently. I was looking at ten walking donuts. Huge's people were exactly the size of glazed donuts. They had numerous tiny white legs, like centipedes, and four pairs of short arms. Their heads were held aloft above the center of the donut by four tubes coalescing into one vertical tube six centimeters high supporting a cotton ball with six eyes circumferentially. After I got over my initial shock, it hit me that these were the cutest little creatures I'd ever seen. I wanted to pick one up and play with it and stuff a few into my pockets. Probably bad initial diplomacy. I restrained myself.

My appearance must have been an unpleasant surprise. Several donuts started running away from me emitting very high-pitched chirps. Al couldn't translate the noises. I guessed it was Reglician for "Oh shit, I'm gonna die." That's when any pretense of cute ended. The three guys who didn't flee reached into pouches and whipped out tiny sticks. Silently bolts of light emerged and struck the ones running. Within three seconds all seven had explosive wounds and were motionless. Tiny wisps of smoke rose from their corpses. The weapons were quickly stashed back in the pouches.

The one nearest to me spun around. He spoke and I was able to translate the words myself. "I am Fellulex The Grand, son of The Most Perfect and Holy Emperor Tersfeller the Huge. On his behalf

I welcome you." His head rotated quickly. "Where are the others in your crew?"

Ambiguously, I responded, "I come alone." I didn't want to lie, but there was no need for details.

"And you are Captain Ryan?"

Good. He assumed there were others. "Yes. I am honored to meet you, Fellulex."

He emitted a high squeal. It wasn't like the screams a minute earlier, but it didn't translate. I think I stepped on his not so tiny ego.

"You are not familiar with our ways, Captain Ryan. For now, your stupidity will be forgiven. I hope you are a fast learner. I will assume you would prefer I not kill you."

Okay this jerk was officially on my shit list. I was stupid and threatened with death all in one breath a minute into our first meeting. These donuts might be cute, but they were not cuddly. Arrogant and intolerant, *yes*. Lovable, a definite *no*.

"First," he continued, "all your crew must bend before The Most Perfect and Holy Emperor Tersfeller the Huge immediately. To do less is a death-insult. Second, our names are who we are. Never shorten them. I am Fellulex The Grand. My father is to you The Most Perfect and Holy Emperor Tersfeller the Huge. I shall not school you again in these matters."

I had a strong impulse to squash the twerp like a bug with the sole of my boot and scrape him off on his papa. I eased back on my anger. "Fellulex The Grand," I began, "I hope greatly we don't complicate matters by getting off to a bad start. I'm from a planet very far away. There we know nothing of Reglic or its inhabitants. I'm your *guest*. *You* invited me here. I came in goodwill. Please understand that you know nothing of our ways just as we know nothing of yours. Please be aware that I too could easily be insulted based on simple misunderstandings. No good can come from that."

He made that shrill squawk again twice. "We are not lectured to either, Captain Ryan, by those inferior to us. At this moment you're a guest. You might quickly become a prisoner if you continue to act like a shgrewtomp." (Al piped in that he didn't know what that was, but his guess was it was a bad thing).

"There sure are a lot of rules on Reglic. Where I come from visitors are greeted with less threats and rudeness. If you continue to act like a son of a shgrewtomp I will climb back on my ship and go where I'm welcomed."

Four squeaks this time, the last one significantly longer than any yet. I think the donut was mad. Just as I was about to bolt he said something I couldn't make out. Then he spoke to me. "I can see your point, new friend. My behavior might have been mistaken for ungracious hostility. For that I apologize. Would you please do us the honor of accompanying me to greet our master?"

No way the little puke could mean any of that. Papa must have whispered something in his ear. What had I said? Ah. I threatened to *go where I'm welcomed*. There must be some opposing groups papa pastry doesn't want me to meet just yet. That's a valuable piece of information. Or I was stepping into a trap. If they drew me farther from my ship I'd be more at their mercy, which seemed a decidedly limited quality in these parts. I was far from defenseless so I was fairly certain I could take the chance. Even though this group of locals was revolting, the planet was a prize.

"Lead on," I said. "But first I'm curious. What happened with," I pointed to the corpses, "those fellows?"

"They ran in cowardice. There's no greater offense against The Most Perfect and Holy Emperor Tersfeller the Huge than such behavior. They are fortunate I only ordered them shot. Far worse was called for."

I could see relationships with these guys were going to be a challenge. My first concern as we walked was that I'd never be able to fit into any of their buildings. The ones I'd seen so far were the size of dog houses and wine boxes. I'd be lucky to squeeze my head into one to meet Tersfeller. I'd sure look undignified if I did that. Fortunately the structure we headed toward was—I had to say it—huge. It was the size of a two-story house in the suburbs. Versailles it was not, but maybe for them it was.

The arched door swung open as we approached and several creatures scampered out, flanking either side of the entry. The vestibule was small, maybe ten meters square. I had to stoop slightly to clear the ceiling. They directed me to wait there. Fellulex disappeared behind a set of doors. Shortly he returned leaving the passage open behind him.

"You may enter and be received by The Most Perfect and Holy Emperor Tersfeller the Huge."

His stumpy arms pointed generally toward the next room. The throne room was even bigger. It needn't have been. Tersfeller might be huge in ways I couldn't appreciate, but to my eye, he was maybe a jelly donut at best.

Once I was in, Fellulex trumpeted loudly. "Be illuminated by the presence of The Most Perfect and Holy Emperor Tersfeller the Huge. *Bow* before him."

I nodded my head. Wasn't going to bow, let alone grovel. Not after the performance Fellulex put on. The head donut was going to have to win my respect before I'd show him any. "Nice to finally meet you, The Most Perfect and Holy Emperor Tersfeller the Huge. I'm Captain Ryan, but please just call me Jon."

The room exploded with those chirpy sounds. The negative reaction I received was like I farted in a crowded elevator. On Reglic contraction was apparently a sin.

Fortunately, the emperor was unmoved. "Welcome, Jon," he said. "Thank you for coming to greet me. It speaks well for our future relationship. Mutual benefit will be gained for us both."

With those words I became more certain he wanted something from me. Down deep, he had to be as disagreeable as his son. He, however, was able to try and game me. He wanted me to like him.

"We can," I responded, "only hope that will be the case."

"You are," the emperor began, "the first off-worlder we have encountered. We must look as odd to you as you do to us. But, please, don't allow outward differences to sully what I'm confident will be a closeness between our people."

More lofty hollow words. Politicians were right up there with raw sewage on my list of dislikes. But, I had to try to make nice. "Outward differences suggest nothing of inner worth." There, I could sound like a fortune cookie too when necessary.

"I must know, Jon, what is it that brings you to my planet? I have a thousand other questions, but this one concerns me most acutely."

"I come as an explorer. Yours is not the first world we've visited and it will not be the last we will study."

"As you can well imagine, when we detected your ship, its size did concern us. Now I can see it needed to be large by our standards. Before, I feared it was a battleship or worse, a colony ship."

That didn't sound too promising. "By our standards my ship is actually quite small."

"How many in your crew are there, Captain?"

"Though my mission is great, my crew is small."

He was quiet long enough for me to know he caught my evasion. "And what is your mission, specifically?"

"Exploration, as I said earlier."

"Yes, but exploration for what purpose, to what end?"

He was mistrustful. That made him smart. "I was sent to acquire knowledge for its own sake. My people are a curious species. Nothing more."

"If I may be forthcoming, what is it your people would like of my world, ideally?"

"Only to be friends. In the fullness of time, some of my kind might come to Reglic. Perhaps some of your kind could visit my world."

"And which world is that, Captain?"

"I hail from Earth."

He was silent a spell. "I do appreciate you telling me its name, but its location would be of greater interest."

Here came the game of dodgeball. "Yes, of course. As it should be. Yours is an excellent question, The Most Perfect and Holy Emperor Tersfeller the Huge. Clearly your subjects have a wise and thoughtful leader. They are fortunate. Actually, that raises a question I had. Are all the beings of Reglic under one rule, your rule?" I pointed to him.

There was that annoying chirping chorus again. He raised his voice and shouted. "*Silence.* The next Sarcorit to interrupt dies."

Before he could return to me, I seized the occasion. "A Sarcorit? What is that? I thought you were the Reglic."

Seeming more than a little annoyed, he replied tersely. "No. The *planet* is Reglic. My *subjects* are the Sarcorit."

"So," I asked quickly, "there are others natives to Reglic who are not Sarcorit? There exists more than one faction?"

That gave him pause. I extrapolated that, based on his son's reactions, he was inclined to have me boiled in oil. Still, he bit his tongue (if he had one, that is). "Yes, there are a few smaller empires. None are as influential as the Sarcorit. None are as technically advanced either. You saw in orbit Sarcorit satellites alone. It is we who have travelled our star system, not the Ardleify, the Rialadin, not even the hateful Jinicgus. No. We alone know the stars."

"*Ah*. You have explored the stars like my people. Your technology must indeed be wondrous." I really shouldn't push my luck too much, but hey I *am* a fighter pilot, right?

"We're yet to venture that distance I fear. We, I should clarify, as you *forced* me to, have traveled only in our star system." His head spun swiftly side to side. "If you will recall, I asked earlier of your planet's location. You were ... interrupted before you could answer the question."

Not on my watch, buddy. "You're one hundred percent correct. My apologies for any indirectness you might interpret." I put my finger to my ear and looked down, like a reporter on the holo. "I have just been informed of a development on board my ship that will require my immediate attention." I looked up to him. "I'm certain you'll understand, you being a leader like myself. When duty calls, our kind must answer."

Before he could respond, Fellulex screamed in interruption. "Father, *please*. His insults are too great and his subversion too apparent. Please allow me to slaughter the animal. Then we shall feast on his entrails, may it please you. I can't hear anymore of its smoked words." Chirps erupted like never before. He seemed to strike a chord with the audience. I can have that effect on people, you know? Al tells me so all the time.

Tersfeller didn't keep me in suspense for long. He rose from his cushions and howled at me. "You come to my High Chamber and you mock me openly. I tried with all the might of our gods to tolerate your bestiality and uncivilized ways. But, I shall no longer. My wrath is upon you."

In for a dollar, in for a dime. "Look, Huge, you just stepped on my last nerve. I've tried to be diplomatic but *you* are intolerable. I'm going to back out *that* door and return to my ship. Then, I'll have to begin my search for *intelligent* life on Reglic all over again because I haven't found any yet."

The only question was how I was going to extricate myself from this pickle. Those ray guns might really hurt. Then it hit me. I had two very good shields readily available. I pointed my left hand at Tersfeller. "Come to me. Fellulex too." The fibers sprang to life and affixed themselves to my wretched hosts. They sang loudly as they flew toward me. "Take the satchel off Fellulex," I added mid-flight.

I positioned one in front of me and one in back and moved them up and down to discourage any sniper shots. I began to run. *Man*, I could run really fast. I made it to my ship in seconds. "Al, pull up the ramp and hit the ignition."

"I'm way ahead of you," he assured. "Preflight complete. We will lift off immediately after you're strapped in." I liked the no-nonsense Al.

I locked the two fuming visitors in the fridge and buckled up at the controls. I probably didn't need to hurry. With their pastry god on board they wouldn't dare fire a shot at us. I was into stationary orbit in fifteen minutes. Al said we were receiving threats, pleas, and incantations from the ground, but, so far, there was no pursuit.

"Remember to check all orbiting equipment for signs of a course change," I said out loud.

"Already on it, boss. I don't want to burn for your inept stab at interstellar diplomacy."

It became clear the Sarcorit either wouldn't or couldn't send out a posse. I decided it was time to look up some of Huge's enemies. I'm sure they'd be glad to take the little shit off my hands. Fellulex was a different matter. Him, I might be keeping. My mission involved collecting local life forms. He was a LIP—you know, local indigenous population. Yeah. Piss me off royal and you just might end up in a specimen jar.

Al scanned the surface area for signs of cities, lights, radio signals, visible structures, that sort of thing. After he plotted the likely areas, I studied the map, trying to guess where factions opposing the Sarcorit might be positioned. As Tersfeller had suggested, no one else seemed to detect us and certainly no communications were attempted. I decided to bring my prisoners along to a city separated from the Sarcorit by a large mountain range and a desert. When informed of their impending journey, they pissed and moaned something awful. The mild mannered Ffffuttoe took an instant dislike to them. She asked if she could eat the little "noisemakers." With some satisfaction, I passed that message on to the pair.

I landed the shuttle in what had to be a park. It was in the center of a dense city, but was completely open. I knew I made an excellent selection when I stepped down the ramp holding my prisoners. If Tersfeller was upset before, he became positively apoplectic upon seeing the location I'd selected. He squirmed and begged me to return to the ship. He howled that the Jinicgus capitol was a foul blight on his blessed Reglic. Perfecto. I'd picked the best place to exchange those intolerable pests for goodwill credits.

Not too surprisingly, no one rushed to greet me. At first they probably figured *Ark 1* was an enemy vessel, maybe even Sarcorit. Once they laid eyes on me personally, they were likely just as frightened as the Sarcorit had been. To entice someone to come forward I set the captives down. They bolted for the ship. Al noticed and pulled up the ramp. Then they tried to hide behind me, but I walked rapidly toward a large building leaving them exposed behind me. Man were they pissed.

Finally creatures began to emerge cautiously, heading in our direction. The potential of capturing their foes must have sufficiently overcome their misgivings. Then I did have to laugh. Nature had played the cruelest practical joke on the inhabitants of Reglic. If the Sarcorit were donuts with heads on a tube, the Jinicgus were paired chubby kielbasas with heads midway between wieners, also on a pole. I could see some evolutionary similarities. They looked as improbable as their rivals.

One creature took the vanguard, but stopped several meters away. He spoke in the same language as the Sarcorit. "State your purpose in coming here and make clear why you bring that treacherous filth." Several tiny arms pointed at Tersfeller as he cowered behind my boots. I liked this new guy already.

"I'm Captain Ryan from a faraway planet. I came to Reglic as a peaceful explorer." I gestured to Tersfeller. "I encountered the Sarcorit first. They were unfriendly and aggressive. I captured these two. I present them to you as a sign of good faith. I wish only friendship with the Jinicgus."

With significant venom he again pointed at Tersfeller. "They are little more than animals, the Sarcorit. To see their mouths move is to know they are lying. They make war for pleasure and revel in the misery of others." He dropped his arms. "What is it that you would have us do with this refuse?"

I stepped clear of them. "Anything you like."

A mob rushed over, grabbed both, and raised them above their heads. They scurried away with them, everyone screaming, including their prizes. The crowd disappeared into a building. That was the last time I ever saw those mean donuts.

The pontooned sausage turned back to me and spoke matter-of-factly. "I am Zirzjincus, a minor official in this city. Thank you for the gift of our scourge. We can never punish them enough for what they inflicted on my people, but we will certainly try. Any enemy of theirs is a friend to us. Know that, Captain Ryan. What may we offer you to demonstrate our appreciation?" He turned to a nearby building. "I would ask you to join me in my home for refreshments, but, as you are so large, such a courtesy is not possible. I trust you'll understand."

I patted the air with my hands. "Perfectly understandable. I'm curious. Is yours the same language as the Sarcorit?"

He peeped briefly, like a chick. "Gods, no! Their tongue pains my mouth as I speak. Since you were with the Sarcorit ruler, it was logical to assume you understood it. We're a practical race."

"With a few hints, I'm sure I can switch to your language. My computer is pretty good at that sort of thing."

He hesitated. "We will see if that becomes necessary, based on the length of your visit. How long do you plan on staying as our guest?" Or our newest invader, right?

"Not long. I have a lot to accomplish and time is short. All I'd really ask of you is to allow me to communicate with you in the future, to cement our friendship. You do have radio communications?"

"Of course. The Sarcorit have superior technology, like their missile platforms in space. But we aren't primitives." He seemed put off by my question. Pissy inhabitants down here on Reglic. "I'll see to it that a link is established between your ship and my superiors. May I serve you, otherwise?"

"Yes, two other requests. Some food to replenish our stocks." Ffurttoe was eating up all my meager stores rapidly. "Also, some general information on your planet. I want to collect samples and make some maps, then I will be leaving to search for other worlds."

My host instructed someone to bring supplies. While we waited, he gave me a thumbnail sketch of his home. There were several political groups scattered across the temperate areas. The two body forms I had witnessed were the only sentients. Reglic teamed with life. He promised comprehensive biological information would be sent to me within a few days.

I spent two days collecting specimens and dropping robotic remotes. Then I left Reglic. I did so reluctantly. There was no way around it. My next target was seven years away, Wolf 359. I dreaded the day when Ffffuttoe would die of starvation. I was getting quite attached to the lovable little bear.

FOURTEEN

Indigo hadn't flown for years. She hated flying. There was, by her reckoning, no way around the fact that she would be in a high-speed aluminum can twenty-thousand feet above the ground. Most unsettling. But, on this occasion she had no choice. The boss said she had to be at the meeting in person, end of story. She was chosen as lead on this account in large part due to her supermodel good looks. He wanted the full effect of that beauty to be present at the signing so there'd be no last minute reservations or second thoughts. At least he agreed to let her travel in business class. That eased the pain a little. So, she was boarding a flight from LA to New York.

After she stowed her bag in the overhead compartment, she sat down and began taking deep breaths. She hardly noticed the man in the window seat slip past her and buckle in.

"Are you alright?" she heard a voice ask softly.

She snapped out of her fog and looked to find it was the man seated next to her who'd spoken. He was smiling warmly.

"Oh, no problem. I'll be okay."

"Not a frequent flyer?" he teased gently.

That brought a giggle. He was older, perhaps in his early sixties.

Still quite handsome though. She was struck immediately, however, by his confidence. He exuded it like the Sun did its rays. "No, I'm not. Does it show that badly?"

He nodded a few times. "Sort of." He patted the back of her hand. "But, never fear. *I* am here. If this plane was going to crash I'd have never booked a seat on it. You're perfectly safe, by default."

With a cute smile she replied, "Is that supposed to make me feel better?"

"I don't see how it wouldn't."

"So, you see into the future? This old hat for you?"

"When safety is involved, absolutely." He gave her an even bigger smile. "Seriously, everything will be just fine. I fly for a living. Never had a lick of trouble."

"You mean you travel a lot for business?" That thought made her stomach recommence its churning.

"No, I'm a pilot."

She looked more closely at his face. "Do I know you? I mean, have we met before? You look terribly familiar."

"If I'd ever met you, I would certainly have remembered. No, we haven't." He held out his right hand. "Jon Ryan. Nice to finally meet you."

Numbly she shook his hand. That name. That face. Add a few wrinkles and grey hairs. Yes. "You're the astronaut Jon *Ryan*."

"One and the same."

"Oh my. It's my pleasure," she gasped as she shook his hand more vigorously. "I'm Indigo Martin."

"Do you carry a mirror in your purse?"

"Huh? Oh." She fumbled in her bag, retrieved her compact, and handed it over to him.

Jon opened it and turned the mirror toward her face. "In case you hadn't noticed, the pleasure is all mine." He closed the lid and returned the compact.

"I can tell I'll have to keep a close eyes on *you* for the next five hours." She pointed at his nose. "You're a sly one."

Jon shrugged his shoulders in response. Indigo noted then that he wore no ring. Before she could say anything else, the steward cut in with the routine preflight instructions. They both paid cursory attention, only exchanging the occasional grin. As the plane pushed off and began to taxi, Indigo unconsciously took hold of his hand, quite firmly in fact. He let her do so, graciously. By the time the plane was well clear of the runway, she was shaking noticeably. Jon put a reassuring arm around her shoulders, which helped to quiet her down. He could also tell her heart was racing like a greyhound's after winning a race.

It wasn't until the first round of drinks was offered that Indigo felt well enough to speak. "There, the hardest part is past. Did I mention I hate flying?"

"You didn't have to state it for me to know that's the case."

They shared a chuckle. "So, Jon, are you still, you know, in the astronaut business?"

"Till death do us part. I've been up and back from the stations in orbit more times than I can count." He'd made eighteen trips. He spoke to the crews in an attempt to inspire and motivate them. His longest tour lasted ten days. Forty-seven meet-and-greets in ten freaking days. He felt like a two-bit carny working the countryside for chump change. No, he was taught to be more the medicine-man act than a simple sideshow hack. Jon wished he'd been allowed to go on at least one legitimate ride for all he'd done, for all he'd given. Maybe someday his turn would come?

"Oh. I bet that's exciting." She elbowed him gently. "The stories you could *tell*."

"And some aren't just stories." He wagged his eyebrows. Let's see, he thought. There was the time the holo presentation wouldn't unfreeze. He had to be brave and improvise. Then the time the shuttle to the next station failed a safety check and his party was delayed several hours. Or, hey, when the whore on Station B-81-133 actually insisted he pay her like any other john. Yes, high adventure and high times were his stock-in-trade these days.

"My, but you're the cheeky one, aren't you?"

She had the cutest British accent, and the cutest set of Bristols he'd ever seen. "So, my dear, what powerful force has compelled you to fly to New York? Business or pleasure?"

"Business, most foul. My company is signing a big ad deal and I'm needed to smooth out any wrinkles that might come up."

"I'm certain those wrinkles stand no chance."

She grinned hugely. "They never have."

"Look who's cheeky *now*."

"And you, brave astronaut Jon? What important matter diverts you from the stars to earthly New York City, New York?"

"I have a meeting at the UN, then I'm off to Spain."

"My but that sounds epic." She sighed wistfully. "I only wish my job was half as romantic as yours. And even a tenth as important." She rested her hand atop his. "Maybe we could have dinner while we're both there. My nights are all free."

Yeah, he reflected, he had the most exhilarating of careers—with the emphasis on "had." Sure, forty years ago he was training for the biggest mission ever conceived. The world was his and he had been *so* alive. But that was all he had done. He trained. He did the grunt work, put in the hard time, and the *puppet* got the glory. What was his reward? He became the talking-head of a PR dog and pony show. If his shuttle exploded on reentry—a thing he'd wished for on more than one occasion—the world would probably not even notice his omission. It would also be none the worse off for having one less unproductive mouth to feed. That *damn* android.

"That sounds nice," he replied tepidly. "But, if you don't mind, I need to close my eyes. I've got the worst headache."

"Oh," She withdrew her hand. "Sorry to hear it. You'll let me know if I can help—neck rub or something?"

"No, I'll be fine. I just need to catch some Z's." He rolled away from Indigo and pretended, for the remainder of the flight, to be asleep.

FIFTEEN

Two months out from Reglic the food supplies were completely exhausted. I even fed Ffffuttoe the culture media for bacterial growth, which she loved by the way. Three weeks after that, she began acting oddly. She slept more and more, and rarely spoke. With years remaining before I had a chance for resupply, I figured the end was near. She remained upbeat, however, when we did talk. One day she crawled up next to me and spoke. "Fffuttoe sleep now. Wake Fffuttoe when food back."

I guessed she was blindly optimistic. Yes, she'd sleep, but it was going to be in eternal rest. Sure enough, she rolled herself into a tight ball on her bed and went to sleep. I checked her vital signs often. Her heart rate and body temperature dropped quickly, then remained remarkably stable over many weeks. Finally it hit me. She was *hibernating*. I moved her bed into the refrigeration unit and set the temperature at her new body temperature. That way she wouldn't waste calories cooling herself in a warmer room. This all gave me a ray of hope, but, realistically, there had to be a limit to her ability to cling to life. Unfortunately, my only option was to wait and see what happened.

I hadn't heard from Mission Control in years. As I was off the prearranged sequence of star systems now, it meant there would be no new communication. For a message to reach me, they'd have to focus a very narrow, energetic radio signal. I sent them data at regular intervals, but that only told them where I had been many years earlier. There was no way they could determine where I'd be years later to shoot me a reply. No, I was alone in cold, dark space, smack-dab in the middle of nowhere. With Ffffuttoe down, that meant my only companionship was the irascible Al. He knew this, and tortured me no end based on that knowledge. If I asked him a mission-related question, he answered, albeit indirectly. But if I strayed anywhere near a social conversation, he'd shut up just to goad me. Here's an example.

"Al," I asked, "have you finished the numbers on the fuel consumption rate?"

"Yes."

I'd close my eyes. "Al, what are the numbers for the fuel consumption rate?"

"They are real numbers."

I balled my fists. "Al, please tell me the values of the real numbers that are the rate of fuel consumption."

"Numbers don't have values. Humans have a value system. Good versus bad, sour as opposed to sweet. Numbers are incapable of such qualities."

"I was using the term *values* in the defined sense of the numerical amount denoted in a mathematical *value*. *You* are well aware that I was. *You* are being childish and asshole-ish. Are you ready to be a good tool and answer my question?"

"Yes, I'm ready to be a good tool."

"The *other* question. The one you know I want answered."

"Are you referring to the fuel consumption rate?"

I unballed my hands and opened my eyes. "Yes."

"There, I uploaded them to you. You know, Captain Ryan, if you asked your questions more clearly and succinctly, such misunderstandings could be avoided in the future. I am tasked with many critical functions, if you weren't aware. I hate to waste my time trying in vain to glean your meaning sometimes."

"I am *terribly* sorry, Al. I'll make it up to you. I promise. The next place we stop, I'll buy you a lawnmower as a companion." Nothing in response. "You're going with the silent treatment again?" Nothing. "Al, as your commanding officer and captain of this vessel, I order you to speak." Still nothing. "I *swear*, Al, I'm going to pull your plug if you don't answer in three microseconds." I waited ten seconds. "Okay, I'm getting my blowtorch."

I actually went to the supply room and rummaged around, pretending to look for the arc welder. Then, I grew tired of the game. I went to my quarters and watched some holos.

Al interrupted the feed just when I was getting to the good part. "I'm ready to speak now. I've healed sufficiently from the psychological trauma you inflicted upon me."

"I don't want to talk now. I don't know if I *ever* want to talk to you. In fact, I think I'll just doze off for a year or two." I rolled onto my side. "Wake me if there's a change in Fffuttoe's vitals. Otherwise, I'm wearing a pretend do-not-disturb sign."

I switched to sleep mode, but actually only set it for a few hours. I encrypted that bit of information so he couldn't call my bluff. Within seconds, he started blasting marching band music throughout the ship. I noticeably disabled my hearing servos. He upped the volume to maximum, so the vibrations were intense enough to bother me even though I couldn't hear them. I switched off my sensory inputs. He started flashing all the lights.

"Al, I said I'm wearing a do-not-disturb sign. Cut the crap."

"No, Commander, you said you were wearing a *pretend* do-not-disturb sign. I am not *programmed* to pretend." He switched back to the blaring music.

My only company for the better part of a quarter century was to be that psychopathic toaster.

SIXTEEN

As with the other two systems we'd explored, when we were six months out, we could start collecting a good database and set a plan. Wolf 359 was an interesting star. It was a cool red dwarf and a very young star. Like young children, it misbehaved a lot, sending off large flares of radiation sporadically. That would make finding a habitable planet quite unlikely. But, as Wolf 359 was one of the very closest stars to Earth in our sparsely populated region it had to be explored.

We determined there were two small planets, around the size of Mars, orbiting in the sweet spot. Since the star was cool, they were in quite close. We'd have to keep the planets between us and Wolf 359 to prevent our getting fried if there was a big flare. As I entered orbit around WS 4, the outermost of the two, I confirmed it was tidally locked with the star. That is to say, one side perpetually faced the star while the other side never faced the radiation blasts. Any life would be confined to the thin, circumferential ring where those two inhospitable zones met. Though the region might be thin, there was also the possibility of life under the surface a ways out in the warmer direction. That type of exploration would be tricky. Unless there was a system of tunnels conveniently dug out for me, underground examinations were going to be limited.

I set the shuttle down safely on the dark side of the planet so it wouldn't be harmed. I drove one of my rovers to the habitable strip and began my work. Soon it was clear to me no life was present in any form. Liquid water was around in small amounts, but any colonization would require the importation of a lot of water to sustain itself. With no life came no oxygen in the thin atmosphere. WS 4 was very much like Mars in many regards. There were a few shallow caves, but there was nothing interesting in them. I left a couple probes, but headed back to the ship in less than a week. WS 4 was a potential candidate for some portion of Earth's people, but not a very friendly one. Oh well, any port in a storm was better than the alternative.

WS 3 was even less promising. It was also tidally locked. The hot parts were hotter, the star flares closer, and an atmosphere was nonexistent. It made the Moon seem like a nice spot to have a picnic. I left a couple probes and departed after a few days. The Wolf system wasn't a complete write-off, but it was darn close to one. Even a colony of androids like me would find the system mightily unpleasant.

My next target, which was my next to last, was Epsilon Eridani. It was the farthest system from Earth, at just over ten light-years. The trip took me only three years, since I was pretty far out with the Wolf system already. This was predicted to be my best prospect. It was the target for a lot of the early searches for intelligent life as far back as the 1960s. The star had multiple planets, and at least one was known to be in the habitable zone.

To my great joy and surprise, Ffffuttoe remained stable in hibernation the entire trip. She'd lost a good deal of weight, but her vitals were as steady as surgeon's hands. I only hoped I found supplies at Eridani. There was only one planet to explore, EE 5, but it was an exciting find even from a million kilometers away. It was almost twice the size of Earth, so the gravity would be stronger. Al detected a perfect atmosphere for humans. He also found traces of complex hydrocarbons. *Smog.* That made the presence of intelligent life basically a slam dunk. By the time we entered orbit, we'd located several big, modern looking cities. EE 5 had many artificial satellites. We were looking at a civilization as advanced as ours, if not more so.

As I was firing thrusters to finalize our low orbit, we received a transmission from the surface. Actually, and I wasn't sure what to make of it, we received no less than eight contacts from all over the globe. After Al had translated the signals, it was apparent they were sent in different but related languages. Interesting. There was no one coordinated attempt to contact us. That had to say something about the political dynamics below. I'd need to be cautious. I instructed Al to monitor the popular communications, like holos, to see if he could figure out the political landscape. He smugly informed me that he had been for some time. When he had something to tell me, he said he would.

Within a few hours, Al provided me with the rough breakdown of society on Cholarazy. It was a lot like Earth. There were multiple independent states, with a few big ones that called the shots. No wars were active, but there had been countless ones over the years. Among the powerful states, there was intense saber-rattling and propaganda, both inwardly and outwardly directed. The technology was on par to ours, not identical, but quite similar. We were the first alien species they had encountered. Al compiled most of his information from public transmissions, but did some hacking too. He loved being sneaky like that.

I decided to try and dictate the nature of our first contact. I sent a message to each party, in their own language, asking for a joint meeting in a neutral location. The replies staggered in over several hours. They all said the same thing loud and clear. No way, *José.* A few declared there was no such thing as a neutral location. Others said their counterparts were so untrustworthy that such a meeting could not be made safe. They all urged me to meet with *them* first, not any of the others. They each claimed to be the one true voice of Cholarazy. Oh boy. This was not going to be easy.

Of course, I was not on a diplomatic mission. I was just the boots-on-the-ground explorer. I didn't need to arrange a possible mass emigration. Sure, it would be nice to have some insight along those lines, but that was not my main purpose. If I could establish their attitude toward billions of friendly aliens showing up on their doorsteps, that would be great. Would they, for example, start shooting at the first sight of us? I mean, how would *we* react if a giant swarm of aliens announced they were joining *us*, thank you very much? Probably not too well.

Al and I discussed strategy at some length. For the first time *ever*, he was thoughtful, helpful, and insightful. I was stunned. I think he understood the stakes were extremely high and that errors on our part could have long-term negative consequences. Finally, I decided to randomly choose to meet with one of the larger groups. After that, I could try to game another group for a better outcome. So, I messaged the Drell. I asked where I should land to meet with them. They immediately offered to come instead to *Ark 1*. No way that was happening. Last thing I needed was for them to steal or destroy my vessel. Also, I wanted them to know as little about our tech as possible. If they proved trustworthy later, that was a different story.

I said I was too anxious to see Cholarazy for myself. If the Drell couldn't meet me on the surface, perhaps the Foressál could. That had the desired effect. I was sent coordinates immediately. I didn't want to let on I was an android, so I took a communicator with me to that first meeting. A group of people were present to greet me. I say people, because they really looked like us. How refreshing. The Drell were bipeds, on average around four feet tall, though much sturdier than humans. That was probably due to the higher gravity. They had heads that were approximately round, covered with hairy strands. The three fat fingers on their hands kind of creeped me out. All the evil aliens flying UFOs back home had three fingers. The stereotype was hard to avoid. Hopefully, I'd get over it quickly.

One of the figures stated that I was to come with him. I was ushered into a vehicle and we drove for half an hour to a fairly ornate structure. I didn't like being so far from a fast getaway, but I did memorize how the cars worked, so, worst-case scenario, I could borrow one in a pinch. Two guys led the way into the building, while two others flanked me. It was sort of like I was in custody. Hmm. We ascended several floors in an elevator.

My escorts hadn't spoken since they told me to come along, which did nothing to ease my growing concern. Maybe they were not a chatty race. Maybe they were a duplicitous race. I was about to find out, either way. We exited the elevator and they led me to a door. It opened automatically. The same guy who spoke before told me to enter. I did, they didn't, and the door closed silently behind me.

The room was dark, darker than it logically should've been. The size of Drell eyes, the temperature of their star, and the ambient lighting heretofore indicated rather human light sensitivity. Didn't matter to me, of course. There was a figure sitting in an unremarkable chair behind a conventional enough looking desk. He leaned back while angling to one side. Conspicuously, he didn't make any effort to greet me, or even make eye contact. A tough guy. Okay. I could do tough. I actually did tough quite well, if I say so myself.

Finally my mystery host broke the silence. "Welcome, Captain Ryan. I am Boabbor, the Highest of Equals. You might better understand if I say simply I'm the leader of the great and proud Drell nation."

"Nice to meet you." I'd keep it short and sweet. No patty-cakes until and unless this jerk lightened up.

He turned to me suddenly. "Ah, a man of few words. I like you already."

"I can't tell you how good that makes me feel." I shifted my weight. "Look, Boabbor, you invited me here. I'm new in town, and please correct me if I'm wrong, but why'm I getting the feeling you aren't so terribly friendly toward me?"

He inspected one of his digits. "I've begun poorly with you, Captain? How uncivilized of me. Shall I call for a festival? Dancing women, libations? Would I seem more amicable to you then? Is that how I should treat the visitor who threatened to run to my sworn enemy if I didn't do exactly as he instructed?"

He stood and knuckled the desk. "On my world, a lonely man can pay a businesswoman to satisfy his every need. Do I, Captain Ryan, look like one of those women to you? Do I impress you as a man who will do anything to please a hostile stranger?" He sat back down. "Let me assure you I am not. *You* threatened *me*. Such treachery will not go unpunished."

Tough it would be. "This meeting is over. I'm not going to have a minor functionary of an insignificant tribe threaten me because his feelings got hurt. I deal only with men of honor. The Drell appear to have no such honorable men. Thank you for making my report back to my people much easier to write."

He waved his paws in the air. "Now I've gone and done it. I've angered the all-powerful man from space. What shall I do, what *ever* shall I do?" He leaned back. "I know. I'll ask you to remain here as my *guest*. Yes. That should stay your wrath. And you, as a proper guest, will stay a very long time. Perhaps, if I ask ever so nicely, forever.

"Then, you'll graciously allow my scientists to tear apart your landing craft so I might learn everything there is to know about your technology. Thank you in advance for that courtesy. Then, my happy guest, I will ask that my physicians examine you in utmost detail. They will, with any luck, author articles about your anatomy and physiology for decades to come. But, before they're done with you, you will beg of me one small favor. You will beg me, Captain, for *death*."

I'll grant him this much. He certain didn't beat around the bush. Nope, he spoke his mind and he was clear in his expression. *And* honest. Why, if I wasn't one-hundred times stronger than him and if my index finger couldn't slice him in half like a bagel, I'd have been scared.. I didn't know where I got the laser finger from, but I sure did love whoever gave it to me right about then. But, diplomacy first, if I had to. I didn't want to be the raging alien with a ray gun in every low-budget science fiction movie ever made. Bad first impressions were so hard to undo.

Time to amaze the LIPs. I rested my hands behind my back in an at ease stance. I thought about the lamp on the table. *One strand, along the floor. Where is your power from, lamp?* Then I thought about one of the guards who had to be waiting outside the door. I addressed whatever they carried. *One strand, along the floor. What weapons are you?* Finally, I asked of Boabbor. *What do you fear most?* I'd never used the probe in that capacity. Hopefully this would work.

Al, I said in my head, *do you have the information on the power grid?*

"Yes," he answered quickly, "and a good deal more. What do you want me to do?"

Access their broadcast media. I want to send a message in a few minutes. Also, see if you can black out the entire city.

"I'm on it." I'd never heard him be so serious.

The guards had black powder propelled bullet weapons. Good, old-fashioned six shooters. Boabbor's greatest fear was quite interesting. Yes, I liked knowing it very much.

"Boab, buddy, let me tell you how it's going to be, okay? Your prophecy has one major flaw in it. *Me*. But, as your honored guest, please allow me to tell you *your* fortune." *Al, update*, I thought while speaking.

"Broadcast media hacked. Do you want the public address speakers included?"

By all means. In twenty seconds send as widely as possible. "Fools of Drell. This is Boabbor, Highest of Equals. No harm whatsoever is to befall my personal friend, Captain Ryan of Earth." *Then, shut down all the power. You get all that?*

"You got it."

"My first prediction, Boab, is that you will tell your people how much you like me. Then you will instruct them not to harm me in any way."

"Are all the inhabitants of Earth imbeciles like you?"

I smiled. "We shall see who's the imbecile in just a moment, okay?"

"I grow tired of this game." He stood and walked toward the door. "Guards—"

He was interrupted by himself. The outside speakers boomed, in a very accurate copy of his voice, the message I'd given to Al. My, my, did he develop a funny look on his face.

Boabbor exploded in rage. "How *dare* you. You will suffer so greatly for this—"

In a flash, I ran to his side and placed a silencing hand over his mouth. My other arm held him in a bear hug. He struggled mightily, but to no avail. He bit my hand, but couldn't break my polyvinyl skin.

"Want to hear the rest of your fortune now? You're going to escort me to my shuttle. After that, you get to visit my ship in orbit. Isn't that nice of me?"

He kicked and flailed even harder.

"I'll take that as a 'yes.' Oh, and I bet you're asking yourself, 'Self, what's my motivation to cooperate with this lunatic?.' Excellent question. Observe." I sliced his desk neatly in half. The two sections thumped to the floor. "Your motivation will be that you don't want me to do that to you. Oh, one last prediction. You will make this trip stark naked. I'm more modest, so I won't. You, however, will parade in front of your subjects wearing only what you wore the day you were born."

I had his fullest attention. His body went limp in my arms. As soon as I uncovered his mouth, he spoke in a hushed panic. "I'll do what you request, but *please*, I cannot be unclothed. I *beg* of you. It is *unconscionable*. I'll do anything else you ask. But *please*—"

That's when all the lights went off. "There," I said, "now hardly anyone'll even see your naked butt. Ah, you people have stairs, right?"

I had to mostly prop him up as we walked to a waiting car and got in. Man, you'd think the Drell had never seen a man stroll casually about without his clothes on. Such a prudish race. When we were back to the ship, I tied Boabbor up with climbing rope. It was the closest thing to a brig I had. I gagged him too. All his whimpering, bargaining, and threatening were distracting. I could hardly think straight. What a maroon.

"Al, open a channel to the Foressál."

"Channel open."

"This is Captain Ryan. I'd like to come visit as soon as possible."

A sterile voice replied. "You are welcome anytime. Land at these coordinates and you will be met."

Wash, rinse, repeat. Probably another trap. But I needed an ally on Cholarazy, or at least someone who didn't wish me currently dead. "I'll shove off immediately. Al, pause transmission."

"Transmission paused."

"Boab, you've basically got only two choices. You can come with me on my voyage. That'll be a twenty-year flight along which you *will* die of starvation. Or you can stay on this planet with the Foressál. Which'll it be? Decide now." I left him gagged in case Al hadn't actually paused the transmission.

He shouted muffled words I couldn't make out. "What'd he say, Al?"

"He says you can't do that."

"Tell him I can and I will. I'll make the choice for him if he doesn't."

That was right in Al's wheelhouse. "Captain Ryan says he can, Highest of Equal Boabbor. Between you and me, I think the man's mentally unhinged. My advice is to take him quite seriously."

More muffled exclamations.

"He says if he goes to the Foressál they will kill him. If he stays here, he'll die. What kind of choice is that?"

"Tell him a poor one. But please remind him it's more of a choice than he offered me."

"Master Boabbor, the Captain says, either way you're completely screwed. He says he's extremely glad *he* is not *you*."

Another bout of unintelligible words. "He choses to die on his own world. More specifically he chooses *not* to do so in the company of lunatics."

"Good choice. Channel open. "Oh, and I'm bringing you a present, too."

Funny. I was using the same trick twice. I hoped it worked again. Who knew, maybe someday my technique would be called Ryan Diplomacy. Students would read about it in textbooks. *Hey*, it could happen.

The Foressál seemed happier than kids on Christmas morning when they saw who my gift was.

"You know," a man named Gothor said flatly, "this man is our sworn enemy?"

"Yes, but I also know people can change if they really, really try."

He bristled visibly. "You mock us, Captain. Such a thing is unwise, even if you gift us our helpless foe."

"Sorry. I meant no disrespect. I offer this prisoner to you as a gesture of my desire to become friends of the Foressál."

He growled quietly. "It is too early to say words such as *friends* yet. For now, let us agree we will not be enemies." These bozos seemed every bit as pissy and conniving as the Drell.

"A good enough start."

"Among our people, when such a gift as this," he pointed to Boabbor without looking at him, "is accepted, a favor in return is customary. What would you ask for him?"

"I need some provisions. More importantly I would ask that my leaders be allowed to speak with you in the future."

"It is done. Would you join me at table, Captain?"

"No, but thank you. I have much work to do." I needed to do a detailed survey and set out probes. I wasn't going to rely on anyone on this rock to supply me with that data. Too seedy a bunch for that level of trust. Plus, if I walked into enough traps, sooner or later one was likely to snap shut on my buttock.

I think part of why Gothor was as cooperative as he was had to do with him not wanting to be presented naked to the next enemy down the line. I bet he couldn't wait to hear how I pulled that stunt off from his new guest. I bet he had all sorts of questions for him, in fact.

SEVENTEEN

"Taylor," his boss shouted in his earpiece, "you keep movin' that slow and I'll sees you're on the next rust bucket back to Dead Rock."

"Charlie," he tried to defuse him yet again, "I'm working as fast as I can. If I crack the shell open, this asteroid's no good to anyone."

Taylor was unimpressed or, more likely, didn't give a shit for the pressure. All Charlie wanted were the results. Workers got paid in credits. Bosses not only earned salary-credits, they also received bonus credits if they beat production numbers. The more credits for the boss, the more of *his* family were guaranteed to get off Earth. If Charlie rode his crews like rented mules, maybe he could bring his mother-in-law's hairdresser along just for the hell of it. But there was no way Taylor was screwing up because of Charlie's harassment and getting his ass mailed back downstairs. He was not going to lose his kid's ride so his freaking boss could be Mr. Big Shot, the sorry-ass son of a bitch. Plus, who knew? This one might be the very worldship Taylor's family shipped out in. It has to last a long, long time in a very hostile environment, so the job was worth doing well.

"I got my eye on you, ya lazy slacker. Gimme a reason, one good reason, Taylor, and you're flippin' burgers downside. Ten thousand men'd give their left nut to take your place."

"You got it, chief." It was best not to engage the idiot.

"You know something? I don't think he likes you." Taylor's buddy Cal had a gift for understatement.

"You're shitting me? I thought we were destined to be lovers and live happily ever after," snarked Taylor.

"I hope," Cal teased, "you're not emotionally wedded to that notion."

"Gee, thanks for the reality check. But pay attention. We need to core out this section of iron-nickel without sending a fracture plane vertically to the surface. We'll do it by the book, fuck you very much, Charlie."

Rhett Taylor was a miner on an asteroid in orbit between the earth and the moon. It was about as far as he could imagine from being either the professional ball player he *wanted* to be or the stock broker he *ended up* being. But that was all before the world went nuts. Time was marked now by only two epochs. The BWWF and AWWF. The *Before We Were Fucked* and the *After We Were Fucked* periods. In the good old BWWF, you could do whatever you wanted. AWWF, you could do that too, but the difference was that, if you did, you would die when Earth went down the shitter. So, Rhett grabbed the best production job he could and worked his ass off. Twenty hours on, ten hours off, seven days a week for almost eight years now. If he asked for a vacation, even a day off to sleep they'd grant it with a smile along with a one-way ticket to Dead City.

"No prob," said Cal, "This time I'll work the laser and you man the seismics." As they toiled, Cal asked a question that had been bothering him. "You been here longer than anyone else by a long shot. You got more than enough credits to get your whole family a seat. Why do you hang around here and put up with Charlie's crap?"

"I'm working," he replied flatly, "for my in-laws and friends. They'll each pay a fortune for the seats. By the time we climb onboard our ship I plan to be rich. Diamonds, as they say, are forever. Gold, platinum, and palladium are going to be more valuable than life itself. I plan on having stockpiles of medicines and weapons. People'll want them and they'll pay through the nose to take them off my hands." He tapped himself on the chest. "My name's gonna be up there with J.P. Rockefeller, Bill Gates, and Miley Cyrus—the mega-wealthy." The deep ache in his shoulders reminded him it was about quitting time. "You about ready to call it a day?"

"Roger that, bro. A beer and a babe will get us both halfway back to human."

"And then we'll be right back here blasting a big hole in a ten-klick-wide ball of rock tomorrow."

"Yeah, but we'll have big-old smiles on our faces won't we?" They slapped elbows in revelry.

All the asteroid work sites were attached to a specific support vessel or mother ship. Rhett's was particularly posh. He had a four-square-meter room all to himself. He hooked up with Cal at the *Starlight* after a quick shower. It'd be expensive booze and even pricier women all over again, but it always did the trick after another gruesome shift.

"What'll it be, boys?" The barkeeper, Jake, asked as if he didn't know. After all, he'd served them the exact same swill every twenty hours like clockwork for longer than he cared to remember.

"A shot and a beer," they said in unison.

"My kind of men," Jake said for the nine-thousandth time. It helped that none of the three were actually listening to each another. Hadn't for years. Jake said the same thing to every customer and the men were only preoccupied with checking out the girls. The women hadn't changed in ages either, but the two new patrons eyed them lustfully all the same. Everyone was just going through the motions these days, especially the tradeswomen. Not one person liked what they were doing or wanted to be where they were. Each was motivated by the same two unifying emotions. Fear and greed. Those two oldest of friends. Everyone was in fear of their lives and for those they actually cared about. And everyone wanted more credits. Credits held the power of life and death. If heroin, apple pie, and sexual orgasm were blended in a potion, it wouldn't make a soul feel better than another credit would.

A woman named Candy walked over to Rhett. She stroked the side of his head. "Hey, sailor, new in port?" Rhett had made love to this woman more than he had to his wife by a considerable margin.

"Why, yes, I am. And did you know it's powerful lonely out there at sea?"

She rubbed his groin. "Well, Overtime here has just the cure for what's ailing you, honey." She kissed his nose. "And when your wife asks what you've been doing, you can conveniently tell her you've been working Overtime." She slid onto the stool next to him. "Wives just love it when their men work Overtime."

Rhett throated a primal chuckle. "Can I buy you a drink, Overtime?"

"I thought you'd *never* ask." She looked to Jake. "I'll have two of what he's having." She turned back to Rhett. "I'm getting a late start, don't you know?" She smiled as seductively as their familiarity would allow. "Do you know what a girl would do for a tenth of a credit, sweetie?"

Rhett actually hadn't heard that line before. The answer was, of course, not nearly enough. But he couldn't blame Candy for trying. "What, Gorgeous?"

She ran a finger across his lips. "Anything a man desired twice a day till he cried out for mercy." She would, as always, have to settle for one quarter of the dollar-wages he'd made since she had sex with him twenty hours earlier. Or maybe it was Priscilla last time? Who knew? Who cared?

Rhett was already calibrating the seismic sensors when Cal staggered into the job site the next morning. In lieu of good morning Rhett told his friend he looked like shit.

He rubbed the back of his head. "No way." Cal moaned. "Shit feels a whole lot better than I do."

They worked quietly for several hours. As the morning passed, they excavated tons of iron/nickel rock from their asteroid. Twenty other crews were doing the same thing around the clock at regularly spaced job sites.

"So," Cal asked when he felt more human, "this your last core job? You've done, what, twelve now?"

"Twelve start to finish," he said with pride. "I've worked on *fifteen* so far."

"Sooner or later you have to go home, Rhett. This work'll bust your balls."

"If Candy doesn't first."

They both laughed loudly. "Suit yourself. But I'm counting the minutes. In two years I'm cashing out. The wife and I'll be safe and I'll have enough cash to last us several lifetimes. I'm not greedy like *some* people I know. What, are you trying to save enough money to buy yourself an android to upload to?" He laughed grimly. "People like you and me'll *never* have that kind of cash. You can forget that one, sport."

"You don't *know* that, shit for brains. I can dream, can't I? Maybe not one for me, you know. Maybe for one of my kids."

Cal stopped working and placed his hands on his hips. "And how you gonna decide which one gets the gift of immortality? You got like four kids don't you? You sure as hell can't afford to outfit the whole lot of 'em."

He slapped his palm to his chest. "All the same, I'm working until it's time to evacuate." He turned to his friend. "Besides, what the hell's there to go home for?"

"You're shitting me, right? How about your wife and kids?" Cal guffawed. "Forget them, how about drinking water that hasn't been somebody else's piss a hundred time before?"

Rhett looked off into deep space. "And the riots and the rationing. I sure don't miss those. At least we eat our fill up here. Down on Dead Rock I'd likely be thin as an excuse." He shook his head. "No, until I'm safe on my own world-ship, I'm just fine where I am."

Cal was uncharacteristically serious. "You could be down there protecting your family if you think it's that dangerous."

"Hey, with what I make up here, I provide them with top-notch security. They're perfectly safe."

"Yeah," Cal observed sarcastically, "in a biosphere to keep out the rotten air while surrounded by vicious guards hired to keep the zombies out."

Zombies. Rhett chilled at the word. Those who'd given up all hope of survival and were living only for the moment. The zombies. They knew they were going to die and had nothing to lose. Nothing. Zombies reveled in drugs, crime, and far, far worse. Once, a film crew tried to document the lives of a troop of zombies. When their camera was finally found, it showed them being burned alive, then eaten. The military had orders to shoot zombies on sight. Much of the time it seemed zombies actually sought out the bullets. Better to face a death you knew rather than one you didn't. Hell of a lot quicker too.

But Rhett's family was safe. So was he. And they'd all be safer, richer, and tucked into their new digs in less than twenty years.

EIGHTEEN

My last stop was Alpha Centauri, just under five light-years from home. It took me four years to get there from Epsilon Eridani. Four long, boring years. Ffffuttoe went safely back into hibernation six months into the flight, leaving me in the dubious company of Al. Did I mention long, boring years?

This being the closest system to Earth we were all especially hopeful we'd find a habitable planet. There was reason to hope. Several planets were confirmed to orbit both of the brighter stars in the system, AC-A and AC-B. There was a dwarf star, Proxima Centauri, orbiting a good distance from the central pair, which held less promise.

As the months passed, I grew both excited and worried. Part of me was anxious to be done with the exploration gig and back in the company of humans. Still another part of me was concerned for what I might find at home. A lot can change in eighty years under normal circumstances. Add the stress of imminent destruction and who knew what the place would be like? I was trying to be a glass-half-full kind of guy, but couldn't really own that mindset. I knew both how well and how poorly humans could act under pressure.

I wondered also what the future held in store for me after this mission was over. Would I be tasked another interminably long exploration mission? Maybe I'd be asked to assimilate into the mass of colonists, basically to stand down. Eighty years of new technology couldn't possibly make me obsolete. An android still had to be a tremendous asset. Surely the basic governmental and military frameworks were in place, so I'd find an important role. Yeah, a whole lot'a wishful thinking going on, right?

Then, for the first time it hit me. What if I couldn't support the government that I reported back to? I mean it was possible the whole system could have become corrupt. Look at post-World War I Germany. All the ducks lined up for an evil maniac to take control. No reason it couldn't happen again. What would I do then? Oh, well, I'd jump off that bridge if and when I came to it. Those perverse thoughts didn't make my last few years in space any easier.

Al and I knew the drill well. By the time we were six months out from Alpha Centauri we began a detailed survey and set the plan into action. It felt good to have something productive to do with my time. Both main stars were very similar to the Sun. The challenge for habitable planets was that the stars orbited kind of close to each other. Any orbiting planets could be subject to some weird extremes of light and temperatures.

The nearest system, AC-B, had eight planets and three were in the habitable zone. One of those was very large, however, so human colonization was not feasible. Everyone who tried to live there would be so heavy their legs would shatter if they stood up. Our first target, AC-B 5 showed no signs of civilization from orbit. Having almost no oxygen, the atmosphere was not breathable. It had quite a high level of methane. That ruled out backyard barbecues, didn't it? Water was scarce, but it was present as small seas and lakes. With environmental suits, humans could otherwise live there tolerably well. I decided on a few landing sites and piloted the shuttle down.

Okay, nearly forty years into the mission you just know I had to do it. I named AC-B 5 "Jon." Made a silly little flag and everything.

Planted it right by my shuttle's ramp. Jon was *beautiful*. That actually sounded kind of weird having said it. But I'm not changing the name. Jagged mountains, a bright sun, a dimmer one, and three moons in the sky. The lake I put down by was stunning. Crystal-clear waters, babbling brooks, the whole nine yards. I wished I had a picnic basket and a date. More the date, come to think, of it than the basket, but you get my drift.

I put a remote in the water and did some sampling. Being an android gave me the advantage of being able to multitask big time. I could watch the underwater video feed while doing experiments and communicating with Al all at the same time. The water was nearly pure without any signs of pollution. Small, primitive carbon-based plants grew sporadically. There was also an odd pockmarking on the ground. The thick atmosphere wouldn't allow many meteors through so I wasn't sure what to make of them. They didn't look at all like tracks. But, so far, Jon was quite promising. Of course, that's when the bottom always dropped out.

The storm began without warning. It wasn't part of a weather system. It just began—*wham*. Within two minutes the pastoral scene making me want to spread a blanket turned into a war zone. Massive charged clouds swirled into existence and tremendous bolts of lightning shot up, down, and sideways. Deafening explosions were everywhere. I knew then what the odd ground markings were. I sprinted for the shelter of the ship. I nearly made it, too. I fell right next to the Jon flag. Lightning struck my calf, which dropped me. As I lay there, Al screaming in my head, several other bolts impacted my back. Androids can't technically pass out. We override circuits and overload safeties. All I know is that I over-and-outed. The last thing I remember was the strong smell of ozone and burning uniform.

Six hours, ten minutes, and thirteen seconds later I booted back up. I was still face-planted next to what little remained of my commemorative flag. I was sure glad I could switch off all sensory input. I hurt everywhere on the inside and out. My head felt like it had back in my fraternity days, maybe even worse if that was possible. I ran a quick diagnostic. Two of my three computers were offline. I couldn't move my right arm or left leg. Al was still howling like a lunatic. For once it sounded good. I couldn't communicate back however.

Out loud, I yelled up the ramp. "Al, can you hear me?"

In my head I heard his stunned reply. "Yes but via the shuttle's microphones. What's wrong with your internals?"

"Don't quite know yet." I spoke in a normal tone, to see if he could hear that clearly.

"What can I do to help?"

"Let me run a comprehensive and I'll let you know. Are you okay?"

"Of course I'm alright, I'm ten miles up in orbit."

I let the snark slide. "How about the shuttle? Any damage?"

"Nothing serious. A few backups are down and one lateral thruster is gone. Otherwise, it's fine."

What a mess. I tried to roll over. That didn't go well at all. My left arm couldn't manage it alone. I just flopped like a fish out of water. Same with my right leg. Then it occurred to me to try the probe. I looked at the side of the shuttle and said *hold the side of the ship and pull*. It worked. Hopping on my good leg I was able to stand. I released the probe. Man did I need to thank someone, yet again, for the great toy. Wish I knew who it was.

The Deavoriath.

What. What the hell was a Deavoriath? Of all the times to have lost backups and diagnostics that had to be the worst. I think I remembered something, something important. But—puff—it was gone. *Crap*. It must have popped out of my biocomputer, which was unscathed by the electricity. Maybe it'd come back. Hopefully. But I had more immediate concerns. I needed to repair myself if possible.

You recall how I mentioned something about the bottom dropping out? Yeah. It kept up its precipitous downward momentum. I heard a scratching sound from behind. I wobbled my head around to see a snake-like cylinder slither out into the open. Okay, one little snake ten centimeters long. No biggy I figured. That's when its friends crawled out of the brush. Maybe a thousand, maybe more. There were a lot of little snakes on Jon. I decided I would change the planet's name. I hate snakes.

I was already upright, so I hopped awkwardly toward the shuttle. I reached the base of the ramp and checked over my shoulder. Boy the snakes on AC-B 5 were fast little suckers. They were halfway to the ship already. I hopped up the ramp. Bad idea. I immediately re-face-planted. Hopping up ramp, *bad*. I steadied myself with the probe and rose. Holding on I scaled the ramp. I turned. The critters were almost to the ship. I hit the "close ramp" button. There was a sickly wheeze from the ramp servo, then a loud snap. Oh boy. Trouble.

"Al is the ramp retraction system gone?"

"Yes," was his immediate response. "It can be repaired, but not easily."

About a hundred snakes were speeding up the walkway. "Can you electrify the hull?"

"Say *what?*"

"Can you electrify the hull? It might repel the snakettes." I'd seen it work in numerous sci-fi movies.

"No. That is not an option."

Crap. A snake had arrived at my foot. It drew back its body then shot itself at my boot. It didn't penetrate the leather. Instead, it grabbed the material and held on firmly. The tip of the tail slapped around wildly until it touched a floor bolt. The tail wrapped tightly down and the snake shortened. It wasn't trying to bite me. It was trying to *restrain* me. Add a whole bunch of his cousins and my goose'd be cooked. Even if my right hand worked there were too many to fry with the laser.

I looked to the ceiling. *Probe grab and retract me up.* I levitated two meters off the floor. The one snake's tail-hold slipped, but it remained affixed to my boot. The floor where I stood seconds before was a teeming pile of snakes. I felt like puking. Luckily I couldn't.

I looked at the creature squirming on my boot. *One Strand, only. What are you?* A tiny filament broke free from the roof and stuck on the back of the snake. This caused the thing to thrash around even more energetically. *Carbon-based, mobile, scavenger species. Highly social and aggressive. Will consume anything it can tear apart. Hive-mind only. Melting point ...*

In my head I instructed, *that's enough for now. Remove creature.* The filament tugged firmly and the snake yielded its grip. It dropped to the floor and became invisible in the swarming mass. I dropped my head back and closed my eyes. What was I going to do? I was nearly helpless, dangling from the ceiling, and the ship was awash with vicious little snakes. Well for one thing I wasn't going to lower myself down anytime soon.

As I hung there befuddled the snakes dispersed. Most swarmed to the walls and tried to climb them, presumably to get at me. Using their tails as holdfasts, they inched up the walls. The anchored ones created a scaffolding for others and the walls slowly became alive. Fortunately at a certain height there were no irregularities for them to hold onto. We gradually reached a stalemate. I was trapped and they couldn't get to me. But something told me they had nothing better to do and were likely to be most tenacious in their pursuit of yours truly.

Such was the case. Two days later nothing had changed. Al had no ideas, I had no ideas, and the snakes were still struggling to get at me. There was no way I could grab them with the probe and throw them off the ship. There were just too many. I sure as hell wasn't going to complete my mission dangling from the ceiling like a chandelier either.

As suddenly as before an electrical storm rose up. I could feel the static electricity build quickly. The thunder began to crack loudly. Hallelujah! The snakes reacted immediately. They flowed as one seething mass toward the hatch and rushed down the ramp. Outside, they made for the brush and disappeared. I guess they had a primal urge to get under cover when a storm hit. I welcomed the lucky break.

As I was attached to the shuttle, I thought, *any snakes left onboard?* None. *Cool.*

I lowered myself slowly to the floor. "Al, help me repair the ramp mechanism."

He started to say something, but I didn't hear it as a bolt of lightning struck inside the ship through the open hatch. Holy cow. *Pull ramp up.* The probe snapped onto the floor of the ramp and quickly lifted it closed. I was able to hold it with my one good leg. So I was safe from the storm, but I couldn't very well repair the system if I had to stand there to hold the door closed. As soon as the storm blew over I had to assume those little pests would be right back. I couldn't very well drop the ramp after the storm. I also couldn't spend eternity in that silly position.

What to do? Al couldn't supply any physical assistance. Ffffut-toe, even if she wasn't asleep, was up on *Ark 1*. I wasn't so sure she could help if she was down here anyway. "Al," I called out, "I've finished a complete diagnostic. Did it upload to you?"

"Yes. The link from your safe mode backup module supplied it. That system won't support you and I communicating because one relay was disabled."

"At least that's something. So here's my situation and question to you. My right arm and left leg are inoperable. The engine and circuitry of the ramp door are toast. I have to stand here holding the door shut so either of two forms of death can't get at me. In terms of assets, my left thumb is free and I can use my occupied four digits like a spatula. Is there anything broken I can fix in my present pickle?"

"Your leg is a simple fix. A semiconductor wafer burned out. There are several replacements on the shuttle you could manipulate, given your present situation." Funny, when I was in trouble Al was helpful and precise. Go figure.

"The leg's not mission critical. How about anything else?"

"No. Probability of successful repairing any of the other systems given your present state is less than zero point zero five percent." There was a pause. "That's a really small number." There was the Al I knew and loved.

"Any port in a storm. Where's the nearest wafer?"

With Al's help I hopped over to a supply locker and secured the wafer. I set it on the floor next to my leg and clumsily whacked the access panel on my left thigh open. I eased the old wafer out and patted the new one in place. *Boom.* My leg activated. I slapped the access shut and stood on my own two feet. As nice as that was it didn't help in the big picture.

"Okay, Al, my leg's fine. Does that increase that zero point zero five percent number?"

"I'm pleased to say it does. The chance of successful repair to any other system has skyrocketed to zero point zero seven percent. It's a shame there's no champagne on the shuttle for you to celebrate with."

I rested back on my butt and contemplated my options. After a while an improbable plan occurred to me. I released the ramp and it thundered to the ground. That got Al's attention. He scolded me and demanded I explain my actions. I didn't say a word. I enjoyed being the one doing the torturing for once. I placed my hand behind the ladder welded to the wall opposite the ramp. *Around the ladder and pull the ramp closed.* The probe shot around the closer pole and heaved the ramp shut. I had a fulcrum. I let out some slack and then pinned the probe fibers to the wall with my newly operational left foot. I let out more slack. The pressure of my foot held the hatch shut.

"What are the odds now?"

"Excellent. You may have done it. I simply *cannot* believe that."

"Do you mean to say I'm smarter, more clever, and more inventive than you are?"

"First," he began ignoring my last query, "we'll fix the ramp.

With your hand free we can get to work on the arm. I estimate all repairs can be effected within ten hours."

"What about the who's smarter part, Al?"

"Seriously, Captain Ryan, trillions of dollars weren't invested in this mission to elevate your tiny ego. Please try and remain focused on what's at stake and belay your empty quest for self-aggrandizement."

"I'll take that as a 'yes.'"

We did wrap up the repairs in a few hours. I took the shuttle back to *Ark 1* and instructed Al to make a detailed meteorologic assessment of those killer storms over the next few days. They turned out to be a real issue in terms of colonization. The electric storms had something to do with the radiation of the two stars interacting with the variable magnetic field the planets generated. The storms were stronger near the equator, but still quite violent at the poles. I wasn't in charge of deciding if the planet was a good candidate however. I would report the facts and let the eggheads decide whether the storms were a deal-breaker. That sort of thing was, as we government workers were fond of saying, above my pay grade.

I went back to the surface, released several probes, and collected several samples. I bagged a whole bunch of those horrible snakes too. I took more than I really needed, because I hated them and wanted them dead. Probably because of the inhospitable weather, AC-B 5, formerly known as Jon, was sparsely populated. There was certainly no advanced civilization or signs there ever had been. The little snakes turned out to be one of the most advanced species on the planet. As I headed the ship to the next target, I dearly hoped I wasn't going to have to live on AC-B 5 after Earth was gone. It sure was a sorry excuse for a place to call home.

NINETEEN

The oversized, likely uninhabitable planet I mentioned before lay between AC-B 5 and AC-B 3, the other promising planet. I did a few orbits of the fourth planet for completeness sake, dropped a few probes from high orbit, but didn't invest much time or effort on the place. AC-B 3, however, began to look very exciting the closer I got. Breathable air, earth gravity, lots of water, and multiple artificial satellites in orbit. Somebody was home.

Al attempted to raise the natives on the surface as soon as we were in range. Very shortly, a response came back. Al took a few moments to translate the text. It was a friendly-enough greeting, welcoming us to Kaljax. Darn, this was my second-to-last planet and I couldn't name it Jon. Stupid snakes. Arrangements were made to meet near a large city, so I piloted the shuttle down straightaway. Two phalanxes of LIPs awaited me when I dropped the ramp. A roar I assumed was a welcome and not a collective cry of "let's eat him" rose from the crowd.

One figure stepped forward, bowed deeply, and spoke. "Greetings, most honored guest. I am Mangasour, the local leader."

What a nice place. First contact without death threats. I liked it already. He provided me with my first good look at the species. He was my height, about my weight, and roughly human in proportions. Two arms and legs, eight small digits on each appendage, and a head shaped like a football. The main difference that jumped out was that he had two pairs of eyes. Two were closer together and lower on his forehead. The other pair was spread farther apart and were larger and higher up. If the light was dim enough a Kaljaxian could be mistaken for human.

I was ushered into a vehicle. It was much like a car back home and even sounded like it had an internal combustion engine. Mangasour gave me the grand tour. As we traversed the city, he pointed out landmarks and filled me in on local customs and history. He was refreshingly open and cordial.

He ordered the driver to stop at a building serving food. "Would you care to refresh yourself, Jon. Yours must have been a long journey."

Sure, why not? Food would be a nice change. "I'd love to if you'll join me."

"To be certain. On Kaljax we say, 'Never pass on a chance for a free meal or a stop at the dump-station.'" Probably meant the bathroom. Nice philosophy. Real healthy.

He ordered an extensive spread and invited some of those who'd met me initially to join in. It was a proper banquet. Ffffuttoe would be upset she missed it. My analysis of the food showed it to be quite edible. Carbohydrates mostly, along with some trace minerals, protein, and fiber. The spices were interesting, like nothing I'd ever tasted before. Duh. They were consistent with plant extracts, much like back home, but with an entirely different flavor spectrum.

As the meal wound up, Mangasour got down to business. He asked what it was I wanted. Why had I traveled so far? I gave him my well-practiced response about exploring to find a new home for my people. He was quite sympathetic. Having one's home world destroyed was, he understood, quite a serious matter. He asked what aid the people of Kaljax might provide. There were many unpopulated areas on the planet which might be suitable for our colonization. He would be honored to show them to me personally at my convenience.

That was a very generous offer, especially since we'd just met and he hadn't inquired about what numbers of new friends we were talking about. He also knew next to nothing about the species he was inviting to cohabitate with him. In fact, I began to worry his invitation was too generous, too unconditional, and too easily offered. Now, why would someone offer something he really shouldn't have? What good reason was there for such altruism? Yeah, none in my experience either. That would suggest Mangasour was playing me as a carny plays a rube. I'd have to keep a close eye on this bozo.

We left the restaurant and walked toward the waiting car. Mangasour asked what I would like to see next. Their zoo perhaps? I deferred asking instead to return to my shuttle. He was explosively courteous, obsequious, in fact. After I was seated in the back, he excused himself, saying he needed to see about the bill for the meal. He closed my door and entered the building. There were times when being an android and having no one know I was came in really handy. Such was the case for me secluded in that car. I followed his footsteps to keep track of him. I also turned the volume up on my hearing mechanism to maximum. In hushed tones, I heard the following exchange:

Mangasour: "Are you certain you put the evalgian in his food?"

Male voice: "Yes, Lord. I put in as much as I dared."

Mangasour: "And you saw to it he received **** (*inaudible*) bowl, not someone ****?"

Male voice: "Absolutely, ****. No one else dropped dead, so no one else **** his serving."

Mangasour: "True. So, the beast can eat evalgian and live. It was a long shot, us not knowing his ****. Ah well, Feg, we'll fare better next ****."

Male voice: "I'm certain of ****, Lord. It is foretold."

Foretold, eh? I was what, some figure of biblical fulfillment? And they tried to kill me right off the bat? They hadn't known me long enough to dislike me that much yet. Sure, in time, I could see it, but so soon? There was no way they could know I was on to them. How would I proceed, given my dicey circumstance?

As I sat there alone a car screeched to a halt along side me. Three hooded figures jumped out. They had rifles. Without warning one of them shot my driver in the back of the head. His body slumped forward onto the control lever. Two people who had eaten with me ran out onto the sidewalk. They reached toward their waists, but were dropped by multiple blasts from the gunmen. Mangasour started down the hallway, but seeing the carnage in front of him, retreated back around the corner he'd come from.

I was about to fire on them, when one figure opened my door. "Come with us or you will die."

"Who are—"

She—it turned out she was a female—stopped me. "Later, I'll explain. Come." She scanned the street. "We have no time. More will be here soon." She extended a hand. "*Come.*"

Why not? Mangasour had tried to kill me already. She could hardly make a worse first impression. I sprang from the backseat and into her car. We sped away, to where, I had no clue. All three of my purported rescuers continually looked out of the windows for signs of pursuit. A kilometer away, a garage door swung open. The driver turned in and the door slammed shut behind us. There was visible relief in the body language of what I hoped were my new friends.

"Okay," I said. "Mind telling me who the hell you are and what this is all about?"

She looked straight ahead. "Soon. For now come with me."

We walked out the back of the building and got in another car. It drove fifteen minutes to a small structure on the outskirts of town. We pulled into the garage and this time we got out.

"We're safe enough here," she said. "Let's go meet my leader. He will explain everything."

We snaked though the house until we came to a door. She

knocked, a voice inside said to come in, and we did. Two figures sat in lounge chairs. One rose. "Thank you for coming to meet with us, Jon. I must apologize for the unconventional manner of your transport. There was no way around that."

"Unconventional, eh? That's what the Kaljaxians call cold-blooded murder?"

"Please sit. The deaths of those individuals was unfortunate, but it was our only chance to free you. The fact that you were so poorly guarded was an error on Mangasour's part. It was unlikely to occur again."

"They tried to poison me, you know?"

He shared a worried glance with the others. "I didn't know that, but I'm not at all surprised. They most certainly want you dead, my friend."

"Speaking of friends, exactly who are you?"

"Ah yes, my apologies, again. I am Tourine Ser, the leader of this resistance cell." He pointed to the woman. "Sapale you have already met. This is Dontiqui, my wife." He indicated the other seated person. I could see some gender differences. The females had rounder faces, more prominent ears, and longer necks.

"And what do you want with me?"

He smiled. At least that sign was common between our species. "Why to save you, Jon. And so far we have."

"Thank you. Forgive me if I'm not overly grateful just yet."

He sat back down. "Perfectly understandable. Please, join us." Sapale was already seated.

Sure, why not? I plopped down and crossed my legs. "What did you save me from and, more importantly, why? What am I to you?"

He smiled again, this time more emphatically. "There is much you can't know. But it's sufficient to say we saved you from bad people. We did so because you are our savior."

Forty years into the gig and that was one I'd never heard. Never expected to, either. Tourine Ser clearly didn't know me too well. "You're shitting me, right?"

"I hear your words but do not take their meaning. What has bodily waste to do with our current interaction?"

Dontiqui leaned over and slapped his leg. "Don't be so dense, love. He questions whether your remarks to him are, in effect, covered in shit." She looked to me. "We say 'tastes of shit' in our language, but the meaning is the same."

I nodded. "Thanks." Back to Tourine. "Your words taste of shit."

That got a laugh from all three. "Yes, I imagine they do," he said. "But that's why your life was to be taken by our enemies. To our people you were preordained. Now you seem to have arrived. For those in power, such a thing is most unwelcome."

"What prophecy am I fulfilling? By the way, I'm not fulfilling *any* prophecy. I'm here for business purposes, not salvation."

"It was written long ago in our sacred books that a traveler from the stars would come. He would bring peace. He would deliver justice. Such a man would lead the Kaljaxians to Tralmore, our blessed place."

"Heaven? You think I'm here to lead y'all to kingdom come?" I chuckled grimly. "That's a laugh. If you had a chance to talk with my ex-wife she'd set you straight on that account."

He laughed heartily at that quip. "Jon, I like you much." He rested back. "Our enemies fear you might be, or at least will be *mistaken* to be, Braldone, our savior. For this, you must die." As he said *Braldone*, he rubbed the back of his hand on his forehead. The others did the same.

"Why? Braldone can't be killed. He's a savior, right?" When I said the name, all three rubbed their foreheads again.

"No, he *can* be killed." He reflected a moment. "Perhaps saviors are at their best when they're martyrs. In any case the powers in control on Kaljax desire no change in the present state of affairs. Whether you are, in fact, Braldone (foreheads rubbed) or not, they don't want you around messing with their control."

"Isn't it kind of bad to murder one's savior? That's got to hurt their chances of making this Tralmore place you mentioned."

"They gladly forfeited any right to Tralmore long ago to control the here and now. You, my friend," he pointed two hands at me, "are capable of upsetting that stability. For that reason, you must be eliminated."

"Okay. Just take me back to my ship. I'll leave and solve the problem of Braldone (rubs by all) nonviolently for yours truly."

He shook his head, another act we shared in common. "That will not happen. Your ship is guarded by a formidable force. They'll remain there until they can figure out how to dispose of the craft. You may not leave in it, and all traces of a possible Braldone (you know the drill) will be erased."

"And where do you and your merry band of outlaws fit into this picture? Why save me?" I was afraid I knew the answer. They wanted to *control* a savior. We can be an effective political tool as saviors. Never waste a valuable tool when it can serve an insurgent group so effectively. Might just elevate them to where their current oppressors presently sat, mightn't it?

Sapale fielded that question. "It's not enough that we did? Have you no thanks for our intersession?" My, but she was the high-strung filly.

"Thanks for saving me. *There* I said it. Now what's in it for you?"

She disliked being shown up so glibly. "Your gratitude is shallow." She looked at the other two. "I say we throw this ingrate back to Mangasour and see if he smiles so then."

Tourine Ser smiled. "Easy, Sapale. Jon is our friend and under our protection. We will do no such thing." Back to me. "We do, as you suspect, have an interest. Though I doubt very much you're Braldone, the destabilizing effect of that perception can benefit us greatly. Many will rally to our cause if it is perceived to be holy."

"And *is* your cause holy?"

"You are quick of mind. To us," he pointed to his accomplices, "no. Ours is a political battle of good versus evil, but not a divine war."

"But," I observed, "it wouldn't hurt if others saw your position as morally superior."

"No," he shook his head, "it wouldn't hurt our base of support at all. Quite the opposite is likely, as you already suspect."

"So, I'm your prisoner, not Mangasour's. Seems like I'm the big loser either way."

Dontiqui weighed in gently. "But *we* do not plan on killing you. Plus, you're not our captive. You simply have nowhere else safe to go. You are our *guest*."

Maybe I could bluff my way out. "Nobody seems to take into account that my crew will come down and blast me free. I'll be no one's pawn then."

She nodded in agreement. "That's quite possible. But, were that to occur, it would greatly weaken the government. In so doing that would aid us immeasurably." She smiled knowingly. "The fact that your crew has been so patient up until now suggests a show of force isn't forthcoming, doesn't it?

Of course it did. That's why I was bluffing, not posturing. *Al, you've been following all this. Any thoughts? Suggestions? I'm open to even lousy ideas here.*

None, honestly. I think it is best to go with the flow for now and see what happens. If the situation changes or I think of an alternative, I'll let you know.

And the shuttle. It's surrounded?

Yes, a swarm of armed guards with surly faces are present.

But the ship is secure, right?

Yes, locked tighter than a nun's knees.

I laughed out loud. That prompted Tourine Ser to challenge me. "You find something in my wife's words humorous? She spoke both the truth and kindly. Why the laughter?"

No reason to be honest with kidnappers, even if they did save my butt. "Pardon me. It's the stress. It's finally getting to me. Please excuse my outburst."

"You will be," Dontiqui said, "a guest in our home. Sapale will remain with you. She will be your guide and teacher while you stay with us. She will do everything possible to make the unpleasant aspects of this situation more agreeable. You'll please let us know if there is anything you require."

"Thank you, Dontiqui. I'm fine for now."

"Do you wish to communicate with your vessel in orbit? This can be arranged."

"No. The ship knows all it needs to for now."

She puzzled at that remark. "Really? As you wish. Sapale, please show him to his room. I'm certain he would like a chance to rest and perhaps eliminate waste products." She furrowed her brow. "If the facilities for this do not match your physical requirements, please let me know. Alternate methods will be arranged."

My but that was awkward. Discussing potty-business with a nonhuman. The unforeseen aspects of this job just kept slapping me across the face. "I sure will."

Sapale stood. "Come. I'll show you the way."

I sure hoped to high Heaven she was neither going to demonstrate nor be an observer for bathroom-use protocols. I wasn't sure I could handle that. Hand to hand combat? Yes. Years alone on a perilous mission? Check. Potty training with a girl alien? No way. Fortunately, she just showed me where my quarters were and where the head was. As it didn't matter at all to me how it functioned, I told her the arrangements were picture perfect. She seemed relieved to hear that.

Conscious that I was probably under constant surveillance, I pretended to rest. Later, I even made an attempt to fake bathroom use including poopy noises. I just hoped no surveillance cameras were in use. A few hours later, Sapale knocked on my door. Dinner was ready. The four of us sat around a square table and were served food much like I had earlier with Mangasour. The astringent flavor was, however, absent. That must have been the evalgian poison. Too bad, I kind of liked it.

"Mangasour said I survived evalgian. Is that unusual?"

Tourine Ser, whose mouth was full, nearly choked. "Yes, it's quite remarkable. It's the most lethal substance known. Even the smallest trace is irreversibly fatal. Your physiology must be extremely different from ours to have withstood it."

You don't know the half of it. "I guess so," I agreed. "So, tell me, is Mangasour the leader of the whole of Kaljax, or are there other similar factions too?"

"There are," Sapale began, "two or three other sizable political groups. A unsteady peace is maintained, but there is much bad blood between all concerned."

"What's so bad about Mangasour's reign? What is it you risk so much to oppose?"

Her expression hardened. "He is cruel, ruthless, and lacks any morality. Millions have died and even more have been enslaved on his whim. He is a monster."

"And you seriously hope to bring him down? Do you think that's possible?"

She smiled wickedly. "With a savior on our side, our prospects just improved."

"What about before I arrived?"

She shrugged. "We did what we had to. Victory may not have been a realistic goal before you came. But people of conscience cannot sit still while evil is allowed to roam free."

"No offense, but I don't plan on hanging around all that long. With me gone, how will that effect your calculations?"

Sapale smiled broadly. "First, you escape. Then radio me. I'll answer that question then."

I stuck my hand across the table. "Deal."

She stared at my hand like I was offering her a rotting skunk. "What would you have me do with your hand? It doesn't look appetizing to me." She pointed at it with her fork-like utensil.

"It's a sign of a bond where I come from. Friends do it."

She stabbed her next bite. "Fine. When you and I are friends, we'll share hands."

Sapale was beginning to grow on me. She was my kind of gal. Sassy, irreverent, and anxious to piss others off. Over the next few days we remained locked away in Tourine Ser's house. Sapale wasn't one for idle chatter, but I did start to develop some image of Kaljax and its inhabitants. Getting words out of that girl's mouth was as painful as removing one's own appendix, but I was able to pry loose some information. Mangasour was less than an emperor but more than a president in terms of his office. He'd led this region of Kaljax, known as the Sur, for many years. His uncle was in control before him, and a half-cousin before that. There were no elections. Power was achieved by consensus and maintained by ruthless ambition.

Kaljax's technological stage was similar to our late twentieth century. Much like Earth, wars between the main nations had taken place periodically for thousands of years. They were brutal by anyone's standards. The last one was two decades before and millions died on all sides. There were rumblings suggesting the next war was not that far off. All sides had nuclear weapons and limited space capabilities, so any new conflict would be potentially catastrophic. These factors combined to make Kaljax a risky choice for colonization. If we came here, it might have to be with all guns blazing or with radiation suits. But, a bad option was better than none. Fortunately, again, it was not for me to decide. I just reported the facts. People with their butts affixed to chairs would have to make the tough calls.

While I was in protective custody, I had Al drop several remotes. I wanted to gather an independent database. He reported that what Sapale told me in terms of the plant and animal life was accurate. It was valuable to know she wasn't actively deceiving me. That insight might prove useful down the line. Al had hacked into everybody's systems. He was able to inform me that all four major powers were aware I had landed. At the highest level no one actually believed I was Braldone, but every party saw me as a destabilizing threat. I was conscious that threats of my magnitude had trouble buying life insurance. With an entire planet determined to kill me I was defi-nitely living on borrowed time.

I was unable to hatch a plan to break the stalemate I found myself trapped in. Even an overt show of force on my part might be insufficient to regain the shuttle. I decided that would be my last option. For better or worse it turned out I didn't have to come up with my own plan of action. One was provided for me. Late one night all hell broke loose. I was in my room faking sleep. My hosts were asleep and three guards were on watch. With my acute senses, I heard footfalls outside—lots of feet trying to be silent. That could *not* be good. I sprang to my feet and looked out the window. A large squad of soldiers all dressed in black spread out to surround the house. They appeared to have night-vision goggles.

I dashed across the hall to Sapale's room. As quietly as I could I slipped in and approached her bed. I placed my hand over her mouth. That woke her instantly. It was clear her first impression as to my intentions was less pure than they actually were. She bit my palm and struck at my head with both hands. She landed a series of blows as I whispered loudly into her ear. "We've got company. Twenty to thirty armed men are about to attack."

She slumped back. I lifted my hand. "Sorry. Okay, let's move." She shot out of bed and I followed. She was, by the way, buck naked. Interesting insights into Kaljaxian anatomy were gained by me that night. She snatched up a rifle and peered out her window. "Shit," was all she said.

She ran down the hallway to the stairs. I grabbed her jumpsuit which was draped across a chair and followed her down to the kitchen. "What about the others?"

"Too late. They'll know what's happening soon enough. I have to get you out alive."

She opened the back door and stuck the barrel of her gun out. That's when the shooting commenced. Bullets ripped through the windows and the walls. Three struck my leg, but their velocity was insufficient to break my polymer skin. Sapale returned fire. Almost immediately, our three guards joined in. The darkness of the night was stroboscopically lit by muzzle flashes. Through the window I saw two soldiers fall, then a third.

"*Now,*" screamed Sapale.

She flew out the door. I was right behind her. She swept arcs of automatic fire back and forth in the direction we ran. A single figure surged from behind a wall, dropped to one knee, and drew a bead on her. She couldn't have seen him. I pointed my index finger and removed the top of his head. Hopefully in the confusion no one noticed.

We made it to the trees that surrounded the backyard. Bullets zinged off the bark all around us. Luckily, the house was flanked with a small forest, so we had temporary cover. Sapale kept running, so I did too. We heard the firefight continuing behind us. I couldn't tell if the shooting was in one place or if it tailed after us. There was a sudden massive explosion. Then everything was silent.

We were on our own.

"Where are we heading?" I said on the run.

"As far away as possible."

"No, I mean do you have a plan?"

"Yes. To not die. Shut up and stay sharp." I'd never received orders from a naked lady. Turns out there's a first for just about everything.

We careened through the brush at the edge of a stand of trees. I knew someone had to be following, but I couldn't hear them yet. That meant we had maybe a one-minute lead. The shrubs gave way to a dirt road. Sapale turned to follow the path. I went along, knowing we wouldn't be brought down from behind just yet. The trail terminated quickly at a paved road. We turned right. Checking over my shoulder I confirmed that none of our pursuers had broken through to the trail yet. Good. That bought us more time and would force them to split their numbers twice in search of us.

We stayed to one side of the road in case we needed to jump for cover. We did. A few hundred meters along shots were fired behind us. Sapale went down in a hard roll. I figured she was hit. But she brought her weapon up and blanketed them with fire. One man fell and two others retreated. She was up running in a flash. That's when the helicopter appeared overhead. Search lights swung wildly, but found us quickly. Automatic fire erupted from the craft. We dove to cover. Sapale returned fire. Then her gun locked. She was out of ammo. As she tossed her gun to the ground we ran toward the nearest house. An explosion bloomed from where we had just stood. These guys meant business.

I kept pace with her as we made for cover. Another blast boomed to our left hurling us to the ground. I was up first and pulled her up by the arm. She was stunned. I threw her over my shoulder and ran for all I was worth. The next few bombs landed well behind me. The person either dropping them or launching them couldn't correct for my speed. That break wasn't likely to last long. I ran between two houses. The instant I was past them, one plumed up in flames from a blast. The chopper was too close and was tossed back spinning.

In the seconds I had before they could see us again, I crashed through the wall of a small structure. It was a garage. I set Sapale down and stuck my head in the open car window. I could do this. The controls were similar to the others I'd seen. I set Sapale in the passenger seat and got behind the controls. No key was needed so I fired her up. I have no idea how fast the car could go, but I intended to find out.

We crashed out the closed door and onto the street. The helicopter zoomed toward us. I slammed the accelerator to the floor. A car swung around the corner. *Crap.* The soldiers had caught up. I flipped the car into a one-eighty and sped the opposite direction. Shots started coming from the car and then from the chopper. I swerved back and forth. At the next corner I skidded to the right. The vehicle behind me swung wider barely clearing the curb. The helicopter cut the corner and positioned itself a hundred meters in front of us. No way I could pass under it. I steered the car between two houses.

The landscape trees forced the helicopter to rise quickly and the car missed the turn. It backed up then started after us. I couldn't think of a way out. We were too exposed. I really didn't want to tip my hand, but if things didn't change in a hurry, I'd be forced to use my finger laser.

We plowed over a lawn, around some trees, and came out on a street. I headed left. The copter above dropped a few bombs, but they weren't close. Ahead the street split at a large intersection. I made the turn and headed in the direction of some large buildings. The chopper was right above us so I began to make irregular jerks from side to side. The other car was dropping back unable to match our speed. When possible I went under tree branches for cover.

Sapale's head was finally clearing. She massaged her neck. "We can't outrun them for long." She pointed to buildings. "We'll never make it that far. The road's too straight. They'll cut us to pieces before we can reach it."

"I know. We may have to—"

The helicopter burst into flames and the burning debris crashed to the ground. In my head, I heard, *You're welcome.*

What?

You know how you asked me to drop a few probes?

Yeah.

I just did. You're welcome.

I shouted out loud. "Al, you son of a vacuum cleaner, you saved our asses That's so *cool.*"

Sapale was understandably confused. "What? Who're you talking to? What happened to the helicopter?"

Oops. "In a second," I said to Sapale. *Al, can you drop one on the car chasing us?*

You want me to drop one where the crater is?

What crater?

The crater where the car went boom when the first probe struck it.

Al, you crafty hunk a' junk. Thanks. I owe you big time.

And I'm not planning to forget that fact.

Sapale cut back in. "Explain, *now*."

I patted her thigh. "Easy. My ship blew up the helicopter and car. We're clear."

She lifted my hand off her leg like it oozed pus. "That won't be for long." She craned her neck around to glare at me. "So, Dontiqui was wrong after all. You *do* have a crew up there." Staring straight ahead, she admitted, "Pity she didn't live long enough to know the truth. Their plan for how to deal with you hinged on you traveling alone. Not that it matters now."

"What's that supposed to mean?"

"They're all dead and we'll be joining them soon."

"Aw, come on now. Have a little faith. I'm not that easy to kill."

"Really? Well, we'll see about that soon, won't we? Look, I know of another safe house. We can hide there a little while."

That didn't sound too inviting. The last safe house was smoldering ash. "I don't know. I think we should hide on our own and figure out how to retake my shuttle."

"It's your funeral. I was assigned to be your guide so we'll do it your way. I have to say for the record neither aspect will work. With the forces working to find us we can't remain out of sight for long. And as to your ship unless you have a large well-armed crew you're not getting near it."

"Such a pessimistic young lady. I'm confident we'll get off this rock."

Her head snapped back to me. "We? Are you somehow under the foolish impression that I'm going *anywhere* with you?"

"You make me sound like a disease."

She folded her arms and slumped in the seat. "You might as well be. Where exactly do you prophesize I'll be going with you? Your Earth?"

I replied meekly. "That's not possible."

"Thanks, *comrade*. The shooting's over so now I'm thrown out with the day's trash?"

"No, it's not that at all." Women across the entire galaxy were uniformly impossible.

"Oh, then I'm not good enough company? Do I *smell* funny to you?"

Okay, reverse psychology. "So, you'd come if I asked?"

"No, you regressed rodent, I would *not*. I live *here*. I will die *here*. I'm not some helpless maiden who requires your aid. *Men*."

Why don't you stop and offer to let her out of the car, chimed in Al.

"Because I'm not a pig like you."

Sapale slugged me on the arm, hard. "So now you insult me. Stop the car. I want out now."

"Easy, girl. No, I wasn't talking to you."

She signaled toward the back seat with her head. "No? Who else is here?"

I replied with resignation. "I was talking to my ship's computer."

"That excuse is so wrong I have no idea where to begin. How can you speak to a computer that isn't here? You clearly don't have a radio. And why, Dronith spare me damnation, would you insult a computer in the first place?"

"Look, Sapale, can we get out of this pickle first? After that I'll tell you what I'm able to."

She hit me again, harder. "What you're *able* to. So is it I'm too stupid to understand or you don't trust me enough after I saved your ass?" Did I mention the part about the universality of dealing with females?

"Safety, first. Chitchat, after." I pointed to the clothes I'd snatched at the house. They were in a heap between us. "You'll probably need those."

She looked at her body. "What? I've never had any complaints before. Oh, I get it, I'm a repulsive alien monster. Am I grossing you out?" She shook her body very ... ah, nicely.

"Suit yourself. I'm down with it either way."

We'd reached the city. I pulled into a parking garage. I ditched the stolen car and purloined a second. After driving a short distance, I repeated that action. The third vehicle was more of a truck, which was nice. Until it was reported missing they'd not be looking for us in one. Al provided me with the directions to a secluded area near the shuttle. As we drove I asked Sapale if she required any supplies or provisions. She spat back that if *I* didn't need anything then *she* didn't need anything either. I liked her in spite of herself.

I ditched the truck in a gully and we covered it in brush. Sapale had never heard of vehicle tracking systems so I figured it was sufficient precaution. I led us half the way to where the shuttle was and decided we'd camp there the night. She bristled at being told what to do, but didn't protest too convincingly. As the night wore on the temperature dropped significantly. No big deal for me, but I asked her if she'd be okay. I said we could build a small fire if she required it. She scoffed loudly that if it wasn't too cold for me it wasn't too cold for her. If I ever got around to telling her I was an android I bet she'd hit me really hard.

At dawn we made our way to the ship. We crawled up a hill near the landing site and I spied over the top to survey the scene. Seventy-five heavily armed guards roamed the area and temporary barricades had already been erected. A direct assault was out of the question. There would be no reinforcements to help us so I was perfectly stuck as to a plan. Maybe I could stroll up and say I was a traveling salesman anxious to sell the residents of the spaceship brushes and household cleansers? It could work. I asked Al if he had any bright ideas. He inquired if I mistook him for a miracle worker. Thanks, pal.

After retreating to safety, I told Sapale I hadn't hatched a plan to take back my ship. She rolled her eyes and declared she was stunned. Since I wasn't sure how long we'd be on the run I asked her where we could get supplies. I elected not to say they were for her. She'd get all *macha* and likely starve to death to prove she was tougher than me. She knew a place. We uncovered the truck and drove there. As I didn't want to walk into a trap I asked for some background. How many people were in the house and what materials were there. She declared I was an idiot. What was I going to do with such information? Whether I knew that or not didn't change the fact that we needed the supplies and were going to get them there.

I told her I wanted to go alone to look in an open window. I really wanted to use my probe to make sure the cavalry wasn't laying in wait. She said *we* could check but that she wasn't about to let me out of her sight. So we crawled to a window. While she peered in I asked the house what was in it. We were so close the fibers only extended a few centimeters and I held my left hand behind my back to block her view of it. The house had one occupant. He was eating and no obvious traps were present. Sapale asked if I was satisfied. I told her yes and we sneaked around to the back door and slipped in quietly.

Her contact gave us a couple of rifles, some food, and warm clothing. I declined an offer to stay there longer. The last time I was a house guest was too fresh in my mind. We drove the truck to a covered area and ditched it, then borrowed a nearby car to head back to the shuttle. I didn't want to trust Sapale's friend to not alert the authorities about our vehicle change. No plan had gelled in my head, but I wanted to be near the ship in case an opportunity presented itself. After ditching the car and checking the shuttle landing zone we withdrew to a safer spot for the night.

While seated under an overhang wrapped tightly in separate blankets Sapale began to chat. "No plan to take your ship yet?"

"No," I shook my head, "no clue."

"Why am I not surprised?"

I shook a finger at her. "I'll come up with something and soon. Just you wait and see."

"You're as headstrong as the men of Kaljax. Are all earthmen like you?"

I smiled mischievously. "If they're real lucky they are."

"Yup, you're *just* like Kaljax's sperm donors."

"I'll take that as a compliment."

"I bet you *do*. By the way where's your brave crew now that we need them the most?"

"They'll be—" Wait. My crew. That was it. I threw down my blanket and leaned over to kiss her on top of the head. "Sapale, you're a *genius*. Thanks."

"What?"

"Where's a large area the shuttle can land near enough to us that we can get there quickly but far enough away so the guys guarding the ship can't get there for at least ten minutes?"

"Ten minutes after what? What are you babbling about?"

"Ten minutes after the shuttle blasts off." She stared at me in complete disbelief. "You mentioned my crew. That's it. They can remotely operate the craft. After it lands we jump aboard and high-tail it out off-world."

With uncharacteristic flatness to her voice she marveled, "They can do that?"

"You bet. I can't believe I didn't think of it earlier."

"And after we're gone, what then?"

"No idea, but we'll be safe and sound and have all the time we need to develop a plan."

She mentioned a few locations that I had Al double check. One was perfect. We retrieved the car, drove to the clearing, and waited. In the distance I could see a burst of light indicating the shuttle was away. I bet those guards fouled their britches when the engines ignited. Or maybe they ignited too if they were close enough. Actually the dead ones had it easier than any who survived. Mangasour was not going to be pleased he lost his great prize.

The shuttle set down like a feather and Al dropped the ramp. We scurried on board and I took over. We were in low orbit ten minutes later. Even if someone on the ground tried to use their satellites against us we were perfectly safe.

I held my hand up to high-five Sapale. She took hold of it lightly and shook it instead. "No," I corrected, "that is the *greeting*. This," I raised my hand, grabbed hers, and slapped it against mine, "is how we *celebrate*."

She shook her head disapprovingly. "What an unexpressive race you are." She walked over to me, sat in my lap, and placed a palm on either side of my face. She rubbed her chin lightly in an arc from one side to the other across my forehead and back again. Then she sucked in my lower lip like it was a juicy oyster and bit lightly at it for a blessed eternity. Without a word, she returned to her chair, tossed one hand toward me demonstrably, and proclaimed to me, "*That* is how we celebrate on Kaljax."

I ran a sleeve across my saliva-coated chin. "I think I like yours more than ours."

"Somehow I thought you might."

I held my arms out toward her. "Want to celebrate some more?"

"You bet. As soon as you do something worth celebrating again."

"Oh that's harsh, my lady."

She scowled playfully. "Oh really? Look, you got us off the ground and out of immediate danger. But you have yet to explain what you promised you would."

"Okay, I do owe you a complete explanation. First we dock with my vessel, then I'll tell you whatever you want to know." I held out my hand. "Deal?"

She reached across and we shook. "Deal."

"I don't get a lip-thingy too?"

"You have done nothing yet to warrant one."

"I know. But you can't blame a guy for trying, can you?"

TWENTY

Within an hour of liftoff we docked with *Ark 1*. I gave Sapale the brief tour of the ship, which was all that was needed since it was so darn small. Ffffuttoe was still in hibernation. I dragged her out of the fridge and set a bowl of food near her nose. That always did the trick.

"So," Sapale asked rather challengingly, "where's your vaunted crew?"

I gestured to Ffffuttoe on the floor. "She's the only one besides me. Dontiqui guessed correctly."

"That dead-appearing thing certainly didn't fly the shuttle or destroy those vehicles chasing us." She all but pinched her nose. "It doesn't look like it would even do for a good carpet."

"*She*," I corrected. "Ffffuttoe is a girl, like you."

That drew a nasty stare. "Who helped us?"

"That would be my ship's artificial intelligence computer, Al. Say 'hi,' Al."

"I'd like to say," he chimed in, "I'm pleased to meet you. But instead I believe I'll reserve judgment for the foreseeable future. No offense intended, of course."

"Knock it off," I said. "She helped me and she's our guest. You'll be nice to her. Is that clear?"

"I have forged the distinct impression that she's trouble on two legs." Al sounded quite judgmental.

Sapale pointed generally to the atmosphere. "That's your computer giving you a hard time?"

I shrugged to signal resignation.

"Why do you put up with it? I'd unplug the stupid thing then push it out the airlock."

"I can hear you, you know?" Al sounded especially petulant.

She lowered her hand. "Maybe smash it with a hammer before tossing it out into the void."

"Those exact thoughts have crossed my mind more than once."

"And you know I can hear you too, Pilot."

"So it's just you, the frozen rug, and the disrespectful computer? How can you have journeyed so long with so little?" She was truly amazed.

I took her by the elbow and led her to the ship's one chair. "It'll be a couple hours before Ffffuttoe's awake. I might as well do that explaining I promised. You want something to drink? Eat?"

"No, that's—" Her eyes lit up. "Yes. I'll have whatever *you* drink."

"Ah, you want coffee?" I wagged a finger at her. "Okay but don't hold me accountable for any resulting addiction issues."

I brought us both a mug. She inhaled the steam deeply and held it in her lungs for several seconds. Then she sipped at it cautiously, and not just because it was hot. I could hear the wheels turning in her head, analyzing, categorizing, and cataloging the flavors and nuances. It wasn't until a third was gone before she spoke. "This is horrible and sublime at the same time. I very much like it, yet wish it had never entered my mouth." She had a look of childish wonder. "There is nothing like it on all of Kaljax." Her eyes struck me with significant intensity. "How much of this do you carry?"

"Not so much now that I'm all these years into my mission. Why?"

She flipped her head to the side. "Then it's hardly worth killing you so I might have the rest to myself."

"Your parents didn't spank you enough. Did you know that?"

She drew in the steam and let it out with a question. "Ten years alone. That's a long time." She glanced around. "And your ship is so tiny." She set her mug down. "How's that possible?"

I filled her in on all the details, from my being an android to why I'd come to Kaljax. She listened attentively never interrupting once. "So," I concluded, "that's my story. I didn't mention any of it before because I never know whom I can trust. Experience has shown I can't trust anyone, really."

"Yet you share your tale with me?"

"You're kind of a captive audience."

She squinted her left eyes.

"It's just that when I put you back down I'll be leaving for good. Any information you pass along can't be used against me at that point."

"I don't want to be difficult, but I can't really believe you're a machine. I bit your hand. I've seen you eat."

"I'm a very well-constructed illusion. But you don't have to believe me. I'll show you."

I raised my left hand. *What are you, Sapale?*

The probe shot across the short space, surrounding her with filaments. She stiffened but didn't otherwise react.

"You are twelve of your years old. Your chromosomes contain fifty-four gene pairs. Your life expectancy is a robust thirty years. You burn on average nine-hundred calories a day. Your distant ancestors were—wow—herbivores. Currently your diet is half vegetable with the rest equal percents meat, fat, and carbohydrate. You personally have not given birth though you are sexually active. Your left thigh bone was broken as a child and your hearing is slightly damaged, most likely from an infection. Otherwise you've very healthy. By the way, the vitamin supplements you take on an irregular basis are unnecessary." I smiled. "You're a hothead and have trouble making friends."

"These strings tell you I have a foul disposition?"

"More or less." I started to giggle. "Well, no. The other stuff's true though. That last part I figured out on my own."

"That's very nice. Now could you remove your *appendages* from me?"

"Certainly." The probe snapped back into my fingers.

She pointed to my hand. "Those are most impressive, but they don't prove you're a machine."

"Then you'll just have to trust me."

She sneered back at me.

"So, what are we going to do with you? I can drop you anywhere you'd like." I waited a second to add, "Is there anywhere it'll be safe for you?"

She rubbed roughly at her neck. "No, probably not. My operative cell has been uncovered and I have been identified. No other nation would accept me and I couldn't survive very long in hiding. Security is extremely tight on Kaljax. Nowhere is hidden any longer." Her eyes brightened. "Take me with you."

Flatly I batted that notion down. "Not an option."

She growled quietly deep in her throat. It was sort of like a lion but higher pitched. "Just like that. I'm expendable. No good to you now so you'll return me to certain death. You don't even *pretend* to consider bringing me to safety. Yours is a very cold, soulless species, Jon Ryan. I don't think I like your kind."

"No it's not like that. I *have* to return you to Kaljax."

"Will that be from up here, or would you enjoy it more knowing my enemies will capture me in one piece?"

"Sapale, easy. You misunderstand. I'd love to take you with me. I simply cannot. The flight is going to last almost two Kaljaxian years. I can't possibly carry enough supplies to keep you alive. If you come with me, you'll starve to death for certain."

She was unconvinced. "What about that carpet thing I hear eating in the other room? You have enough for *it*. Is it more worthy of saving than me?"

"No. I warned her of the same thing I am warning you. Lucky for her it turns out she can nearly stop her metabolism for years at a time. Unless you can ball up in the refrigeration unit and sleep for that long, your voyage won't end as well."

She was either starting to believe me or decided she'd rather die than remain in my presence. "And your hands are clean whatever way I choose to die. You can't or won't protect me on Kaljax or feed me in space. How very lucky your conscience is to be so insulated from guilt."

"I can't take you. But I definitely want to make it as safe as possible for you down there. Can you think of some deal I could make with an opposing government that might then give you sanctuary?"

She turned away. "It's not like that on my world. An enemy is forever. I'm now officially everyone's enemy. Therefore I'll never be granted quarter or shown mercy."

In my head I heard Al clear his throat. I mean he made the sound. Of course he didn't have a throat to clear.

"What now?" I snapped out loud.

Sapale picked up the nearest object, which happened to be her half-full coffee mug. With remarkable force and accuracy she hurled it at my head. "I die, you heartless son of a falzorn."

I batted the mug away. "I was speaking to my ship's *AI*."

"No you weren't. I didn't hear it utter a peep."

"He spoke directly into my head. He usually does. Easier that way. Remember, there's a computer up here." I pointed to the side of my head.

"Perhaps that explains your lack of empathy?"

Across the speakers, Al spoke up. "If you two love birds are done pecking at each other, may I pose a question?"

"Yes, please," I shouted. "I can use a break in the action here."

"Sapale, what is the minimal caloric requirement for a female of your age and size?"

I responded first. "What on earth does that have to do with our present predicament?"

"Yes. What's your point, computer?"

There was a brief silence, then Al began to hum. Sapale pointed up. "What's the significance of that annoying sound?"

"He's waiting for us to answer his question. The humming is meant to show he's entertaining himself while he waits for us to respond."

She covered her face with her hands. "You're about to march me off to my death and your computer wants us to know he's biding time for us to answer a stupid question?"

I had a sad look on my face. "Yeah, that about sums it up."

He doubled the volume of his humming.

"What's the objective of your query, ship's AI?" He doubled the volume again.

Sapale yelled above the din. "Around four hundred calories. There, are you happy, computer?"

"That," he remarked, "is unlikely while serving under Colonel Ryan. It is, however, a separate issue. I have an idea which might save your life, female of Kaljax."

"My name is Sapale, computer."

"And," he replied, "I'll start calling you that when you stop calling me a computer."

"But you are a *computer*, computer. What else would you possibly be called?"

"My *name* is Al. I am the ship's *AI*. My level of functioning is as far above that of a simple computer as a rational mind is to Colonel Ryan's."

That got a snicker out of her. "Al," I begged, "could you get to your obtuse point sometime this week?"

"You people of Earth are completely silly. You know that, don't you?"

"Given the female of Kaljax's minimal caloric requirements and the surface area available on board *Ark 1*, it might just be possible to grow enough food to sustain the female alien creature."

"If I wanted to strike the computer," she asked, "where would I aim my fist?"

"I don't know," I said. "And trust me, I've looked very hard."

"A follow-up question, if you will, lady of Kaljax." Al sure could get under one's skin when he wanted to. "Is there a species of plant which grows quickly and provides all the nutrients required to sustain you?"

"I *get* it," I called out. "Yes, we could set up banks of lights and trays with seedlings." I rubbed my chin. "It might just work." To Sapale I repeated Al's question. "So is there such a plant?"

She thought a few seconds. "Faw, possibly. Celty for sure, but it's slower growing. Why is this important?"

"Because," I responded, "we might be able to *grow* enough food to just keep you alive." I paced back and forth. "You'd have to remain inactive, but it might work."

Al calculated that if every spare centimeter was converted to plant production we could produce sufficient amounts to make taking Sapale along feasible. Of course, we didn't have the necessary equipment. Perhaps I could barter some technology or materials to get those? Al drew up a detailed plan while Sapale made a list of needed items. Within a few hours we had what seemed to be a realistic scheme. I showed Sapale all of the ship's stores to see if she thought anything would make a good trade commodity. She made a list of those items too. I also needed to secure enough food to get Ffffuttoe's weight back up before we left Kaljax.

Over a few days Sapale made inquiries with various parties to see who was interested in what. She made excellent progress. By week's end I was shuttling up dirt, lights, and plants. After a couple weeks the ship was so crowded with planters it became hard to move. Coffee turned out to be the hottest item for trade. By the time she had acquired all the necessary materials, our supply was exhausted. It was going to be an even longer flight home. That was okay. The sooner we shoved off the sooner I could complete my mission and return home. By the time we were squared away, Ffffuttoe was back to an acceptable weight.

I told Sapale our last stop would be the lone planet orbiting Proxima Centauri. She got a very worried look on her face. It wasn't until I pulled up a star chart and showed her our exact itinerary that she relaxed. She was worried I meant we were going to Bultarral. That's the Kaljaxian name for AC-B 5, the place with the terrible snakes. Interplanetary expeditions had been sent there from Kaljax. No one from the first three missions returned. The fourth and final trip was much more successful. Three of the eighty crew members returned. Two were rendered permanently insane but they at least survived. No further interest in Bultarral remained. It became only the place to which parents threaten to send misbehaving children. And the bogeyman on Kaljax was the falzorn Sapale had accused me of being the son of. It was a mortal insult. Falzorn was their name for the snakes. They hated them as much as I did.

Proxima Centauri 1, the only planet orbiting that dull star, was three months away. Sapale said her people had sent a few unmanned missions there not too long ago. There were no signs of life and she seemed to recall it was perpetually inhospitable. She thought it was a waste of time to go there. I was able to half convince her it was necessary. I needed to explore any possible colonization site. Too much was at stake. She said it was my time to waste if I so desired. She had nowhere else to go, enough food, and so she didn't mind the pointless detour. She really was one to speak her mind.

TWENTY-ONE

For two strangers to spend three months in tight quarters can be a serious challenge. Nerves can be frayed, then fried, then shredded to pieces. Half of the crew might throw the other half out an airlock. The problem was much more acute when the people in question are of the opposite sex and not the same species. It's the perfect recipe for faux pas, wackiness, and ultimately disaster-soup. I'd never spent time closely cohabiting with a sentient female. I lived with my evil ex-wife for three years, but trust me, she never evolved to achieve a sentient state.

Initially we were both busy so the chance of boredom leading to stress was minimal. I was preoccupied collecting data on PC 1 and she was busy setting up the garden that would keep her alive. She combined a mixture of a few different plants. Some were aquacultured and some grown in soil. High-intensity lights dangled from every conceivable angle and surface. I put Ffffuttoe in the fridge before we left so she wasn't tempted to devour the meager supplies we allotted to bridge the time between departure and full production.

Inevitably, as we had less to do we spent more time together in very cramped quarters. Sometimes we'd watch a holo from Earth or a video from Kaljax. We learned early on not to try to get each other to even tolerate our respective musics. They were fundamentally different. Hers sounded like a bag of cats in a dryer. And that was the more placid end of her musical spectrum. She said human music was the punishment souls in Brathos, the Kaljaxian version of hell, were forced to endure for all eternity. Occasionally we could be together and be silent, but we tended to start talking.

We learned a lot about each other's world. We also grew to know each other much better. Sapale was tough and spiny on the outside, but inside she was a deeply passionate and caring person. Those traits explained why she joined the resistance in a repressive society that didn't tolerate dissent. To her, if one saw a wrong, one had to right it. It was that simple. She was a good person.

Eventually our discussions had to come around to *the* big topic. Sex. For two bored people of remarkably different backgrounds living without privacy it was inevitable. She was the first to broach the subject. "So, you evaluated me," she pointed to my left hand, "with those strings of yours. Remember?"

"Like it was just a month ago."

"And after we shot our way out of Tourine Ser's house, you saw me naked for quite some time."

I squinted at the ceiling. "That part I don't seem to recall." I tapped my chest. "I am, you know, a very unobservant individual."

"You're a *pig* is what you are, but that's beside my present point."

"What point is that?"

"Among my people I am considered to be quite attractive. I believe I'm what you call 'hot' by our standards."

"Because I don't like to voluntarily get my ass in trouble, I'll just say I will pass on any comment until whatever your 'point' is becomes more clear to me."

She shook her head. "Such a pig." Then she smiled. "So you tell me you're a man, a male of your species. Do you find me physically attractive?"

Did I? Like all Kaljaxians, she was a bit shorter and stockier than a human. The females' heads were rounder than the males', but there was still an elliptical quality to them. What passed for hair atop their heads was long, coarse, and sparse by human standards. The females lacked any breast development, but their hips did curve out ever so nicely. Sapale definitely had a cute little butt. Using the time-honored male yardmark of how drunk one would have to be to jump a girl's bones, I'd have to say, in her case, not too very much. Sober wouldn't actually be such a stretch. Of course I was nearly forty years into celibacy, so I was less than an impartial judge.

I decided on the answer that would get me the least killed. "Al, is that the fusion core alarm I heard? I think we're about to blow up in a fireball."

He replied with stunning clarity and diction. "Negative. All systems are optimal. Answer her question. I have a hundred credits bet with the navigation computer you don't live to see another day, by the way."

"Did you," she taunted, "need me to strip naked to help jar your memory? We're not as modest as I've come to learn you humans are. Here," she stood from where she sat on the floor, "let me—"

Before she could get her jumper's zipper a quarter way down, I squealed out, "No. That won't be necessary. Physically I find you quite attractive. I think most human males would, too. There, are you satisfied?"

"No. I need to know if I find you attractive. Remove your clothes and turn around a few times."

"I'll do nothing of the kind." I pointed to the control screen. "You can pull up endless images of nude males if you want to learn about that."

There were oodles of mock sympathy in her tone. "Oh, I'm sorry. You're a machine. I forgot. There was no reason to over-design you, was there? I'm sure you were sent packing with only the *minimal* assets necessary. How insensitive of me. Please forgive me."

"No, Ms. Sapale. He's fully functional and anatomically identical to how he appeared before his transfer. After more years than I'd care to say living alone with him I can testify to that fact. Why, just before we departed Earth, he even had himself a sexual plaything."

"By Davdiad's holy veil, you're not serious, are you, Al?"

He was way too eager in his reply. "I *am*. Would you like to view the holo? I can upload it from his memory banks directly to the main screen."

"Yes," she began with schoolgirl excitement.

I held up both arms. "No you will not, you backstabbing blender."

"Wow," she teased, "I think we've struck a nerve, Al."

"It's not such a hard thing to do with him, I regret to inform."

"If you're both satisfied, I'll go check the environmental servos." I stood. "I don't need this kind of abuse."

Seductively she queried, "What type of abuse would you *like*, shipmate?" She sucked on a digit.

"And you called *me* a pig. By the way, do you even know what a pig *is*?"

"According to the ship's AI it's a food creature with coarse manners that is unclean by nature." She looked suddenly quite serious. "My request is a fair one. I simply wish a ... cultural exchange. Yes, that's it. One between the people of Earth and Kaljax. It will further our bonds of friendship."

"And your altruistic diplomacy requires me to get naked?"

She shrugged. "If it's best for interstellar peace, then *yes*, I'm willing to make that sacrifice."

"Oh, so it's a *sacrifice* to gaze upon my naturally given gifts?"

"Given your level of protestation, I'm thinking that's a given."

"Okay, sister." I unzipped my jumpsuit and stepped out of it. That left me in my skivvies. Al started booming stripper music throughout the ship. What the hell, I bobbed my hips and rotated in place a couple times before pulling them off and throwing them at Sapale's head.

She clapped energetically. "Where've you been hiding *this* music? This, I like." She began to mimic my hip gyrations and, in short order, had her clothes off too. Al interspersed catcalls and applause, where appropriate.

I placed a hand in the air. "Alright, people. This has officially gone far enough. In the interest of harmony and decorum, all bipeds put their clothes back on, and let's get back to work."

She pointed, while continuing to dance with abandon, at my crotch. "Is that thing always in the raised and ready position, or am I just dancing well?" Abruptly, she stopped dancing and strode confidently to as close as she could get to me without actually *being* me. "In fact let me have a look at that mechanism." She bent at the waist and took temporary possession of what was not hers.

From that day on, the voyage of *Ark 1*, in service to humanity and determined to save my species, became a lot less tedious. The second best part was that it drove Al crazy not being part of the diversions, which turned out to be manifold. The first best part was ... well, as I said before, I'm a consummate gentleman.

TWENTY-TWO

"But, Your Holiness, such a thing is simply not possible. It's not for want of effort on our part, but due to the strong convictions of those we wish to aid."

Pope Kennedy II rustled magisterially on his golden throne. He raised an arm high in the air to place more emphasis on his proclamation. "Because it has yet to be accomplished doesn't mean it's impossible. With prayer, Cardinal Wilson, and the application of your fullest efforts, We are certain you will succeed."

With a barely perceptible motion of a finger, the secretariat of state spoke. "Thank you, Cardinal Wilson, for your report. His Holiness looks forward to your update and prays that it comes both soon and with better tidings." Impassively, he turned to the right. "Next."

An ornately dressed ancient woman shuffled forward.

"Cardinal Nancy, His Holiness will receive your report."

She bowed as deeply as her age would permit. "I bring news of the conversion of the Jews, my Pope."

He sat expressionless for several tense seconds. Then the Pope burst out laughing. He stepped down to her side and gently patted her on the butt. "Would that it were so, wife. Would that it were so.

Amidst all Our consternation and discouragement it's good you retain your humor. More importantly you remind Us to keep Ours." He limped back to his throne and sat, resting one hand on a knee. "So, Cardinal Nancy, what have you to report?"

"Nothing welcome, I'm afraid. I've spoken personally with the joint representatives of all the Aboriginal tribes in Australia and the adjacent islands. They have no interest in our offer to help them relocate off-world. While they have no objection to individual tribe members departing if they wish to do so, as a people they can't imagine leaving the land they hold as sacred. If the Sun Mother's wish is to perish, then they wish to join her." She shook her long white hair. "There's no way around it. They've made up their minds, and they *will* not budge."

"Well," he said solemnly, "let them know We stand ready to help them relocate should their opinions change." He shook his time-worn head in regret. "We shall continue to pray for their deliverance." She bowed again and left.

The secretariat offered a hand to help the pope rise. "That concludes your morning business, Holiness."

"Where are you dragging me off to now, Carlos?"

"Lunch with the American ambassador."

"Him," growled the pope, "again? Can't he afford his own lunch? He eats here more often than I do."

"Your Holiness, the Americans lead the effort to save all our collective lives, yours and mine included."

"Technological imperialism, *that's* what it is, Carlos. I tell you that even after we leave, they'll lord themselves over us all like they *own* the stars we sail amongst."

"We could," Carlos smiled as he said it, "always stay here and let them go without the blessing of Mother Church that is you and the Curia." He enjoyed reminding his father of that option whenever the old man complained excessively.

"*Bah.* They may save lives, but We shall save souls. We owe it to

Our flock to go, difficult as it is to bear the gloating of the Americans."

Carlos drew the pope to a halt outside the dining room. "Excellency. Before we enter there's a phone call from the Canadian prime minister."

"What does she want *now*?"

"She says she wishes only to thank you for your efforts in bringing the French Canadian government into closer alignment with hers."

"Humph. I'll bet she'd also like Me to threaten them with excommunication if they call for one more strike."

Carlos offered the phone to his father. "There's only one way to know for certain, Holiness."

"Some aide you've turned out to be." He tapped the "hold" key and spoke. "Margaret, good morning."

"To you too, Your Holiness. I know you're busy so I'll be brief."

She couldn't see him roll his eyes.

"Your help brokering that agreement with my political associates was dearly appreciated. I could never have achieved such an accord without your wisdom and guidance."

"Glad to help." He caught himself just before he added "anytime." She'd make him regret such an open-ended offer. "Well, I'm needed elsewhere, so I'll bid you a good day."

"Good day to you too, Your Holiness." There was a very brief pause. "Ah, one tiny request, if I might be so bold."

To his son he mouthed the words, "Knock me over with a feather." "Yes," he spoke aloud, "what else is on your agenda?"

"Oh, not really part of any *agenda*, my old friend. More an idea I'd like to bounce off a man of your unparalleled experience."

His only response was a deep grunt.

"If my government was to open a dialogue with the United Nations concerning food allocations, would that be something you could support, or would you continue to remain neutral?"

"Certainly, my child."

"So, you're saying you'd support our request for increased allowances? My that's wonderful."

"No, I said I have no problem with you opening a dialogue. That's what you asked."

"Yes, you're correct as always. But, naturally, I was curious if—"

"Margaret, please submit your proposal to the Curia per protocol. We can look it over and decide what actions help the most people. Now, again, I say good day."

"Thank you, Your Holiness. Good day."

As she set the receiver down she turned to her secretary. "The old goat remains as inflexible as a steel rod."

"At least," Jane replied, "you made him aware. He can't help but think it over."

"Yes, but there's a thousand miles between that and more food on Canadian tables."

"With another mild winter we should be alright for this year, ma'am."

"If by 'alright,' you mean no food riots like Europe and China, then I agree. But we're one bad harvest away from armed rebellion just like they've experienced." She walked to the window. "Those *fools* at the UN. If they don't allocate more manpower to farming, there'll only be dead people to send into space."

"I don't see that happening. Asteroid conversions are five years behind schedule. With just over fifteen years until Doomsday, their choices *are* severely limited."

She grabbed the windowsill so tightly her knuckles blanched. "Don't tell me you're on *their* side. If you can't support me, I'll replace you at once."

"No, ma'am. You know I'm completely loyal. I'm simply pointing out what their response is likely to be."

"Sorry. I know. I'm just so tired, that's all."

"No problem. I understand perfectly. It's time for the president's weekly address to the US. You do want to watch it, don't you?"

"No, but I will anyway. The imperious jerk might say something important for once." They shared a quiet giggle as Jane flipped on the holo.

"My fellow Americans and people of Earth everywhere. Today I am pleased to report that our brave android explorers have made me proud. To date, *Ark 1* has provided news of three planetary systems, *Ark 2* has reported on two, and we have just received a report from *Ark 3*. Combined with the ongoing remote probe data from *Ark 1*, our scientists have confirmed at least *four* planets we can easily colonize. Several other planets hold some additional promise.

"I want to thank everyone for their tremendous ongoing efforts and understanding. I hope that we can all remain focused on our goal, the only one that matters. I promise you better times are just ahead. We need only cross the finish line at full speed. Thank you and God bless."

"And ... we're *clear*." shouted the director. "Thank you, Mr. President."

Without acknowledging the production crew the president turned to his chief of staff Garland Walker. "Think they bought any of that upbeat crap?"

Garland, a friend of forty years, pretended to be shocked. "Charlie, how can you say such a thing? Not one word you said wasn't the absolute truth."

"There are a thousand lies between truth and honesty."

"What, pray tell, was dishonest about that broadcast?"

He laughed. It was a guttural humorless laugh. "Nothing. But neither was I in the least bit honest with the world."

"What would you have *said* were you in an honest mood?"

He sat back, balled up his hands tightly together, and stared at them with anger. "Listen up and listen well, people. We're in the middle of a shit-storm with no umbrellas. If we stay on our current pace, only one-third of you sorry sonsabitches have the slimmest of chances to get off this deathtrap. Either y'all stop whining about the hardships, or I'll send you to Eastern Oregon with the rest of the troublemakers. If you think that's in the least bit a pleasant option please keep the following in mind. One, everyone there will die in seventeen years. Two, everyone there *knows* they'll die in seventeen years and acts accordingly, which is pretty damn badly. Three, if we send a member of your family there, the remainder of the family get a big-old asterisk next to their names on the get-out-of-here-alive list. Four, shut the fuck up and work harder, longer, and better with less. Act like your life depends on it because it actually does. That's what I'd say if I were of an *honest* predilection."

Garland was stunned by the ferocity his friend had hidden so completely. "Mr. President, where the hell did that come from?" He walked over to stand next to the president. He tentatively rested a hand on his trembling shoulder. "Charlie, are you okay?"

He regained at least the facade of confidence. "Sure. As always." He rubbed his face with both palms. "I'm just so damn tired, that's all."

"You sure? Remember, I'm here to help. I don't serve the American people. I only serve my college roommate."

He took hold of the hand still resting on his shoulder. "I know that, Garland. If it weren't for you I'd have never lasted this long."

Garland massaged his boss's neck. "Don't sell yourself that short. You're cut from the right cloth. Hell, your cousin, your grandmother, and both your great-grandparents were president. If it weren't for a pesky Marshall here and there, your family might as well be royalty. You've made it this far this well because it's in your DNA."

He stared at the family portraits on the walls. "They sure are tough acts to follow."

"And you're making them proud."

"It won't mean shit if I can't get more than a fraction of the people alive today off this planet."

There was a soft knock. A secretary stepped in. "The cabinet is ready for the meeting. Shall I let them know you're running late?"

He stood slowly and stretched. "No. That won't be necessary. Tell them I'm on my way."

"Certainly, President Clinton. I'll send word immediately."

TWENTY-THREE

One more planet, then I could be homeward bound. That sounded pretty damn good to me. I anticipated a very brief stopover on PC 1, based on its size and the star's temperature. It was very unlikely to offer any prospects of easy colonization. That was great. I was anxious to wrap the mission up. I wanted to get back to where I called home. I was especially anticipating the looks on their faces when they saw my new crew. I was proud to have exceeded all reasonable expectations by such an unimaginable margin. I returned with *two* live sentient alien species to study. I deserved a raise and a handful of medals.

The three-month journey to PC 1 was the quickest three months since I left Earth. Yeah, Sapale and I were bunny rabbits in space. But the physical part wasn't the only one that sped time along. She was becoming a good friend and an endless source of information, opinion, and, most importantly, bullshit. How could anyone not appreciate a BSer? It was easy for her to aggrandize the situation from Kaljax, since I knew next to nothing about the culture. But she could BS about *my* world. For example she made a big deal out of having had sex with Al. For the better part of a week she added credible, and even incredible, details about how it had been possible and how enjoyable it was for them both. For his part Al played along as best he could. He could be snarky, sure. But he had no prior experience at the fine art of bullshitting. He eventually confessed it was all a joke, when he couldn't corroborate essential parts of her story. But, it was, all told, a great ration of BS on her part.

She also had penetrating insight. When she focused it on me it could be kind of uncomfortable. But she was never mean spirited or unkind. She helped me deal with some fears and bugaboos I harbored. A key one was my return to Earth.

"So," she said out of the blue one day, "you must be looking forward to getting back to Earth."

It took me a few heartbeats longer to reply than she expected. "Yeah, sure." I fiddled with the bolt I was adjusting. "Who wouldn't be?"

"Well that's a less than ringing endorsement, if I've ever heard one."

"What?" I protested.

"'Who wouldn't be' is not a statement of affirmation, but of evasion. It makes it seem like you answered the question when, in fact, you simply posed a second unrelated one. In fact, the question opens the discussion as to which type of person might not be looking forward so as to see if *you* fit into that group."

"If you hadn't been a revolutionary, I bet you'd have been a lawyer back on Kaljax."

"And again he shifts the subject and dodges a simple question."

"I said I was glad to be going home because 'who wouldn't be.' It's just an expression. I'm sure you're over-interpreting it because you're hearing it though a translation circuit."

"Really?"

"Of course."

"Then here you go. Look at my eyes and say the following

sentence. 'Sapale, I am extremely glad to be returning home. I can't wait to get there.'"

I did.

She exploded. "You don't mean that, and you know it. I am trying to have an adult discussion with a *child*."

"Sap, what's the big deal? I *am* going home whether I like it or not. That's my job. Why is it so important to you that I long for home?"

"It isn't important to *me* in the slightest."

I slapped my palms to my sides. "Then why the *Brathos* are you torturing me about it?"

"Because it's clearly important to *you*. Since you're my brood-mate, that makes it important to *me*."

"Wait, wait," I held up a hang-on-a-minute hand, "what's a *brood-mate*?"

"What do you mean, what's a brood-mate?"

"Excuse me," Al interrupted, "in order to prevent you two from starting Interstellar War I, I'm forced to set things straight."

"What, computer?"

There was a several second pause. She'd called Al 'computer' again. He hated that with a green passion. Hence, I knew she was really pissed off. Finally, a huffy voice spoke. "A glitch in the translation algorithm is causing the confusion. The female alien is saying 'brood-mate.' The correct translation for you, Pilot, would be 'husband.'" He waited a couple of seconds for that to register. "You're welcome. I think I'll just slip into sleep mode now."

"You don't *have* a sleep mode, Al."

"I know, but I'm working on one."

"Why does the computer need a sleep mode because it corrected the *translation* malfunction?" Her voice was three octaves higher and twenty decibels louder than normal. *Not* a good sign.

"Because the computer doesn't wish to witness the fur flying after whatever the pilot says next reaches the ears of the female alien." That Al, always trying to be *so* helpful.

"Computer," she demanded, "how could you possibly know what the pilot is about to say?"

"I *don't* know what he'll say. I just know he *will* speak. I predict with ninety nine point seven percent confidence that after he speaks, you will attempt to remove his skin, slowly and in small strips."

She turned on me. *Crap.* "Jon. *Brood-mate*, Jon. Please say a sentence."

Nice weather today. Nope, she'd be on me in a flash. *You know, I think I need to run a full set of diagnostics on that darn AI.* Death would ensue in five seconds if I did.

"What, *brood-mate,* Sapale, would you like me to say?"

"Hmm." She was using that weird guttural growl of hers. "For the record, I'm *brood's*-mate. The male is the *brood*-mate."

"My but that's a fascinating insight into Kaljaxian language and culture. Thank you for sharing." I stood there awkwardly a second. "Isn't that fascinating, Al?"

"I'm asleep."

In my head I spoke. *Thanks for having my back, you rusty bucket of bolts.*

He replied out loud. "Sorry, couldn't hear you. Cotton in my ears. What did you say?"

Her growl grew louder. Then she spoke slowly, accenting each word of her dirge with precision. "You knew we were brood-mates, right?"

"Well, it's just, you know, we never *talked* about it ... said it in so many *words.*"

My, but that growl got even louder.

"I mean to say, I didn't, as you just witnessed, know the actual *word*, you know—brood-mate—until just now." Shit, shit, shit. I was sinking in shit. "Fascinating word. *Brood-mate. Brood's-mate.* I just love 'em ... don't you, Al?"

"If you were organic, I think this is the point at which I would dismember you violently and consume you." That growl of hers really did have a lot of complexity and nuance to it when it got going. And funny thing was even without a translator, I knew what each note meant.

"You know what?" I asked as cheerfully as possible. Implacable. Yes, that was it. Her burning eyes weren't *inscrutable*. They were *implacable*. "Here's the thing, and it's *my* fault," I placed my hands reverently on my chest, "not *yours*." I directed my palms toward her. "To be brood-mate—which we definitely are, brood-mate—on Earth, there has to be a formal *ceremony* first, before we say we're, you know, *brood-mates*. Since we haven't had one, you know, yet, I didn't want to be presumptuous and, you know, lock you into being my brood-mate until we, you know, did the ceremony thing."

"*Brood's*-mate," she corrected obliquely.

"Exactly. I'm so glad you understand and we can put this little, teeny, tiny, *small* misunderstanding behind us, brood's-mate."

"I understand, do I?"

"Why *yes* you do. And thank my God and your Davdiad and all the other gods out there that you do. You're one in a million, Sapale. One in a million. You know that too, right?"

"I sure know a lot I didn't know I knew. But, I'd hate to think you could possibly imagine that two individuals who have done what we've been doing—a lot—over the past three months would do that if they weren't brood-mates. You knew *that*, right?"

"Absolutely. You *silly* girl. Sometimes I think you aren't even paying attention to what's happening."

"No that wouldn't be me."

My hands were back on my chest for some reason. "Not me *either*. So it must be no one we know."

There was that growly purr again.

"Or someone we don't know?"

"I need to be alone for a while. I'll be in my quarters."

"You mean *our* quarters, brood's-mate?" Nothing. No response whatsoever. She turned and left.

My but she was a feisty filly that brood's-mate of mine.

I was *so* glad when we finally made orbit of PC 1. I was occupied, instead of preoccupied. The small buzz of activity actually got Sapale to be less frigid with me, too. That was nice. I missed her there for a week or two. She went over her recollections of what Kaljaxian scientists had discovered about the planet. They seemed spot on. Small, no atmosphere, no water, and altogether inhospitable. We made around fifty orbits as I debated whether to bother with a shuttle trip down. It didn't seem worth it, but I had come a long way.

My decision was made for me when Al spoke one day. "There's an anomaly down there now."

Sapale and I huddled around the main screen. "What type of anomaly?"

Irritation bubbled in his response. "An *anomalous* one, Pilot."

I matched his tone. "What *is* it?"

"Sir, Pilot, whatever, if I knew what it was, I wouldn't call it an *anomaly,* now would I?"

"Put it on screen." He did. There was a small patch of something nestled under a cliff overhang. I went over the records. It hadn't been there before. Maybe we just were at the wrong angle and it had been there. I couldn't tell. There was no bio-signature, not that I expected one on such a wasteland. But it wasn't electrical either. Didn't seem volcanic. Besides such a small planet was unlikely to have any volcanism. "Any guesses, Al?"

"No. Something's there, but it's invisible to our sensors."

"Well I guess that means I'm heading down."

"Me too," added Sapale.

"Not sure that's such a good idea. I don't need protection, but we don't have an environmental suit for you."

"I could stay on the shuttle."

"No. Pilot's call here. Besides, I'd like to be on at least one mission where I had support from above."

Al snarked loudly. "I can hear you, you know?"

"Aw." She got all pouty.

"No. It's not safe. If we had a suit, I'd love to have company. I don't like being all by myself sometimes."

"Right here, *listening*."

She finally agreed. I packed a few supplies and remotes onto the shuttle and landed as close as possible to the anomaly. It was only a short walk away so I left my equipment. I couldn't see anything until I rounded a corner and basically ran into the cliff ledge. An iridescent glow bulged out from the space. I took another step and it vanished. There sat a solitary figure. I jumped back.

"I won't hurt you," he said. He pointed to the ground near him. "Please, sit." He spoke Kaljaxian. His face was shrouded by a droopy hood attached to his cloak. I didn't recall seeing that type of garb worn on Kaljax, but I hadn't, admittedly, been there that long.

I inched closer. Something was off. "You aren't wearing a protective suit."

"Neither are you," he chuckled.

"Was that light ... protecting you?"

"Yes, I suppose it would have." The light-envelope flashed back on. "Is that better?" I felt an atmosphere rush into our little enclave. "*Now* will you sit?"

The dark figure took a drink from a metallic cup. Now that there was air, I could smell it. "Coffee?"

"Yes. Would you like some?" Without waiting for me to respond he poured another cup and slid it to me along the ground. That way he kept his face obscured.

I took a sip. Yep, strong black coffee. "You got this from Sapale in trade back on Kaljax?"

"Did I? Maybe I did. Does that matter?"

"Well, no. But where else would you get it?"

He chuckled again. "Where indeed?"

"So," I asked uncertainly, "what're you doing here?"

He started to look up, but his hood slipped farther over his face. "Me? Why I'm talking to you."

"No, I mean, why were you here in the first place?"

He scanned the blank landscape. "Don't know. Seemed as good a place as any. Why, should I not be here?"

"I can't imagine why you couldn't be here. It's just not very likely *anyone* would be here."

He looked around again as if inspecting the scene for the first time. "I've seen worse." He cleared his throat with another chuckle. "I've seen much better though, I'll admit freely."

"Excuse me. Who are you?"

"I asked first. Who are you?"

What? Dementia in space? "No you didn't, I did."

"You're sounding like a broken record of a petulant child. *I* did. Now stop it or I'll leave."

This guy was nuts with a capital "N." "I'm not stopping you."

"You most certainly *aren't.*"

Did he say *record*? Were there records on Kaljax? I guess. Why not? "Look, friend, don't get all hot and bothered. I'm Jon Ryan. I'm an explorer from Earth. There, that's who I am. Who are you?"

"I'm Uto."

"See that wasn't hard was it, Uto? What part of Kaljax are you from?"

"I'm not from any part of Kaljax."

"But," I stuttered, "but, you speak Kaljaxian."

"I speak *Hirn*. It's a dialect spoken on Kaljax. There is no such language as 'Kaljaxian.' That's like saying you speak 'Earth.' You speak *English*. There are several languages on Kaljax. Hirn, Tofled, Germon, which make one sound like they have birds trapped in one's throat. Foul language that one."

"How did you know I spoke English?"

"Can't you tell? I hear *English* coming out your mouth. You must know that's what they call it."

"But how do *you* know that's what it's called? You're from ... no, wait ... you're not from Kaljax. But where are you from that you know that?"

"Have you ever listened to yourself talk, boy? You sound like a blithering idiot who is acutely confused."

"But—"

He pointed his cup at me. "Let it go, boy."

"Stop calling me that."

"Then stop acting like one."

"Hey, pal, can we start over here? We seem to be getting off on the wrong foot."

He sat quietly a while staring into his cup. Finally, he spoke softly almost inaudibly. "No. I don't think one can start over again. One go around that's it. I wish there wasn't though."

I placed both hands over my face. "You're the most *irritating* person I've ever encountered."

"Thank you," he said. "It's important you try and be the best at a thing one can."

"Can *be*."

"Pardon?"

"It's 'be the best you can *be*.' Otherwise it's a dangling participle. You sound just like my father."

"No I don't believe so."

"What, you don't sound like my father? How the *hell* would you know, old annoying person?"

"Your father? Oh. Well, I think I like him already. No, what I said wasn't a dangling participle."

"What was it then, annoying old *grammar* person?"

"Awkwardly phrased perhaps or passive, but not dangling. Tell me, boy, why does any of this matter to you?"

"It *doesn't*."

"Then I suggest you drop it too."

I stood. Then I sat back down. "You said earlier, 'seemed as good a place as any.' As good a place as any for what?"

"Why, to talk to you. We're sitting here talking, right?"

"You know what? I feel like strangling you. We just met, just now, in perfectly the middle of nowhere and I want to choke you."

"You should see someone about those violent tendencies."

"No. How 'bout this. You stop talking like Yoda and I won't need to strangle you."

"Yoda? Now sound I like *Yoda*?" He refilled his cup. "Who's Yoda?" I stood again. I would involuntarily throttle the bastard. "Sit down, *boy*."

I sat. Don't know why, but I did. Maybe he was ... No. Stop it. Focus. Humanity's at risk, and all that.

"More coffee?"

"Yes. Please." He filled my cup. "So, Uto, from not-Kaljax, you waited here to talk to me?"

"Yes."

"Why?" I stood. "And do *not* say because you wanted to talk to me."

"I don't need to. You just did."

I counted to ten. Then I counted to twenty. "Fine. We're here nice and cozy—talking. How did you know I'd be here," I pointed down, "now?"

"You had to be somewhere." He raised a hand. "And before you blow another gasket I needed to give you something." He grunted. "Wanted to see how you were doing, too."

"Oh my *gosh*. You said something meaningful, like a real exchange of understanding. I may drop dead as we speak."

"That I can guarantee you will not be happening."

"Okay, Mr. Uto. How *am* I? You wanted to see how I was, so, how am I?"

"You look fine."

"That's it? Fine? You came, what, millions of miles and all I get is *fine*?"

"I'm over that part now."

I stood.

"*Sit*."

I sat.

"And what would you like to give me?"

"A spanking."

"You came, what, millions of miles because you wanted to give me a spanking?"

"No."

"No what?"

"No. I came millions of miles to give you something else. Since I've been here the spanking part has become inviting." He mumbled into his mug. "Someone had better do it and quick."

"What if I don't want your—"

He stood this time. He shuffled to a heap of material and reached in. After sitting back down, he folded his hands. "Jon. Play time is over. This is deadly serious. *I'm* deadly serious. You must be too. Are you capable of that?"

"I've always been. What's that?" I pointed to something he held.

"This might just be the biggest mistake I've ever made, which is saying a lot." He tapped the thin object against his fingers. "This is a data disk. It contains the plans for the field you see there." He indicated the flickering light shell around us as he handed me the disk. "It will allow your people to construct a space-time congruity manipulator."

"A what? I have a Ph.D. in physics and I have no idea what you just said."

He shrugged. "Nevertheless, that's what the light is. A space-time congruity."

"As opposed to 'incongruity'?"

"Precisely."

"I was *being* sarcastic."

"Of course you were. But that doesn't change the fact that you were correct."

"Okay, I'll bite. What does that mean?"

"Serious, Jon. You must be *only* serious."

I nodded.

"The light you see represents a membrane in space-time that cannot be altered from outside of it."

"Only inside?"

"Yes."

"So, why—"

"It's a *force field*, Jon. There, I dumbed it down for you."

"You want me to have a force field?"

"No. I want your *people* to have many."

"Thanks, I'm sure. But, why exactly do we—"

"Spoiler alert."

"Beg pardon?"

"You know what spoilers are?"

"Hints as to future plot twists in a novel or movie?"

"Or holo or play."

"So, my people need force fields, but you can't tell me why because that would ... spoil my entertainment?"

"No. Nothing funny is about to happen."

"If you tell me—"

"Let it go, boy."

"Okay, we're back to the letting go stuff."

He stared at me. I could barely make out two hot coals burning into me from under his shroud. Those eyes were all-knowing, angry, and, most of all, they were in torment. Centuries of pain, isolation, and lost hope radiated from those eyes. I started to speak, but the words caught in my throat. How could one man be so sad, so impoverished by life? I wanted to hug him, to tell him it would all be fine, to let him cry on my shoulder until he could cry no more. But somehow I knew for that man it wouldn't be alright. It never had been and nothing would make it better. He was the saddest creature in the universe.

He spoke and broke the spell. "I have another gift." He returned to the pile of material. "This one is just for you, well, you and your crew up there."

He threw a large satchel to me. It weighted twenty kilos. I didn't have to ask what it was. *Coffee.* In fact, unless my olfactory pathway was incorrect it was Peet's Coffee, the best there ever was.

"Before you jibber and jabber," he said, "I'll summarize. I know you have a crew. I have sensors. I know you're out of coffee because you traded it all on Kaljax to keep your crew alive. I have ears. It's a long way home. There are many things one can be asked to forego, but coffee is not one of them."

"Thank you. My brood-mate thanks you too. She's nuts about this stuff."

"*Brood's*-mate."

"Yeah. Anyway, thanks."

"Speaking of which, this is specifically for her." He tossed me a smaller package. "It's ten kilos of racdal fat. She'll love *that* even more."

"What fat?"

"It's a food animal from Kaljax. The fat is ridiculously high in calories and stores well. If she uses it sparingly it'll last until you reach Earth."

"How very thoughtful." It struck me as odd. Who carries a package of fat from Kaljax with them, you know, just in case they ran into me?

"You're welcome."

"I'm certain you'll understand—"

"Why I'm doing this? I know, what a coincidence, eh?"

"Um."

"Let that go, too, Jon. Thank me by simply letting it go."

"You know I can't do that."

"Yes. That's why I'm adding *please*. And in the end, my friend, it will have to suffice." He stood. "I must be going." He started gathering up his belongings.

"Will my ship's AI be able to read this disk?" I held it aloft.

"Absolutely. Slip it in an input and marvel." The light flickered off. "Now go. I'm glad to know there's hope for a better future. Hopefully, a much better one."

"Don't suppose I should—"

He held up one digit. "Spoilers." He looked conciliatory. "It's not that I like being all Agatha Christie here, but I'm on shaky ground, Jon. *Really* thin ice."

Agatha Christie? Didn't ring a bell. I checked the data banks. "You mean the woman who wrote mystery novels two centuries ago from my planet? How do you know about her?"

"I meant the woman who wrote mystery novels one-hundred and fifty centuries ago from my home world."

I shook my head in disbelief. "Hard to imagine, but there must be two."

"Hmm," was all he said.

I returned to the shuttle and prepared for lift off. "All systems clear, Al. I'll set a few remotes and be right up."

When I was back on board, I slipped the disk into the console. "You able to read that, Al?"

"Yes. Pretty boring place, that PC 1."

"What do you mean?"

"The data on the disk, it's pretty boring."

"What about the plans for the space-time congruity manipulator?" I started to panic. "Are they intact?"

"Yes, they have been for twenty years. You know that, right? You didn't suffer a malfunction down there, did you?"

"Cut it out, Al. I'm not in the mood and this is too important. Did the plans download intact?"

"Yes, they did. *Twenty* years ago. We discovered the plans on WS 4 in the ruins of an ancient civilization. Any of this sound familiar?"

"Al, link to my computers."

"Okay, boss. Now what?"

"Can't you see I just uploaded the plans from that disk? The man on the surface gave me the disk not an hour ago."

"Your memory confirms WS 4, twenty years ago. What man on what surface?"

"You know, the anomaly on PC 1? The irritating man I spent a couple hours talking to? The one who gave me the coffee and the fat for Sapale?" I held them up to show him not that he had eyes.

"Captain, all kidding aside you're worrying me. That coffee was logged in ship's stores three days before we left Earth. You brought that fat as a sample from Kaljax. Please tell me you're attempting to be funny."

"Al, seriously, I'm going to *knock* you out. There *was* no ancient civilization on WS 4 and this coffee *isn't* in the log." I pulled up the log. There it was. Twenty pounds of Peet's Coffee. Wait. The disk. It corrupted Al. "Al, the disk I just fed you, it corrupted your memory. Purge it if you can, fast."

"Captain, nothing is corrupt. There's nothing to purge. Please calm yourself."

Sapale entered the room. "Tell Al this didn't come from Kaljax, that we didn't bring it with us."

She took the package and sniffed it. "This racdal fat?"

"*Yes.*"

"Where were you hiding it? And, more importantly, why?"

Al cut in. "Look at the monitor."

"Oh," she grunted, "you logged it as a biological *sample* not in ship's stores. Were you hiding it?"

"I wasn't ... oh forget it."

The fellow from the anomaly. Somehow he reprogrammed the ship's computers and Al with incorrect data and records. As hard as that was to imagine, he also altered the signals inside my own head, to fully rewrite history. How was that even possible? Our current technology was far from foolproof, but it had to be next to impossible to do all that, especially with a single disk and to do so instantly. Who was that hooded man? One thing was certain. Whoever he was I hoped I never ran into him again. Only my biocomputer stood between the facts and total corruption of the records. I alone knew what had actually happened.

"No way *I'm* forgetting about this little treasure. Do you know the kind of energy this stuff can give me?" She smiled like the

Cheshire cat. "Is that coffee I smell? You were hiding that, too?" Al made the sound of clearing his throat. She checked the screen again. "It's right here in the ship's log. How'd I miss that? Hey, you know what? Who cares? We're sitting pretty now." She smiled even wider and held both treasures aloft. She looked ... hungry.

TWENTY-FOUR

As soon as I mentally regrouped from the impact of the data corruption I set a course for Earth. We were a little over four light-years away. With all engines blazing, it would take my little band of travelers around seven years to arrive, ship's chronometer. That would be sixteen years Earth time. We'd probably arrive back in 2135. That was fifteen years maximum before the planet went *poof*.

Other *Arks* would be out here scouting for colonization sites. Since I was the first mission the planners scheduled me back on the early side for a few reasons. First, they wanted a bird in the hand. Some of my reports would be streaming in from remotes, but they wanted hard data and samples with plenty of time to make the most of them. Also, if I'd had any significant issues or glitches, we could potentially alert the other pilots sooner rather than later. The other consideration was that I'd hit all the closest lowest-lying fruit. To try and squeeze in another system would have been very tight. The last thing anyone wanted was for me to return after 2150, the drop-dead date.

My lonely flight out to my first target, Barnard's Star, took ten years. That had been tough. The shorter return jump promised to be a lot nicer, assuming my crew held up. Ffffuttoe had survived trips of similar duration so hopefully one more wasn't too much to ask of her metabolism. Sapale's funny-looking grasses were sustaining her. Her body weight continued to be stable as the months passed. But I still lived in fear that I'd have to watch, powerless, as my brood's-mate starved slowly before my eyes.

One observation about ruminant creatures like Sapale needs to be noted. Anyone who's lived on a farm, especially if that farm has cows, knows the troublesome volume of gas they produce. Unfortunately, my shipmate did so, too, at a prodigious level, I might add. Since everyone on Kaljax had the same physiology, farting was completely socially acceptable. No big deal. According to her, if one had to break wind, then one broke wind. It didn't matter if one was in mid-sentence, riding an elevator, or on a romantic first date. When the scented methane had to come out, out it came. That aspect of life with my brood's-mate was the one I adjusted to most slowly.

On the topic of Sapale's inner workings, I did learn something truly fascinating. Her species had evolved a wild method of reproduction. Once she reached maturity, a Kaljax female *stored* sperm. Whenever she had intercourse a tiny percent of the sperm was directed into a pouch. Nutrients were provided there so the sperm could live for decades. For males, that meant having children was a sort of lottery. The more times you *donated* a sample the greater your percentage was of sperm in her pouch. But unless your brood's-mate was a virgin, you never knew if you were the daddy. Sapale said that in her culture, sexual promiscuity was frowned on. But for adults to have multiple partners over time was the norm. When a female decided it was time to get pregnant—she was always vague as to what that actually meant—she released hormones that matured an egg and ejected a small proportion of the sperm. The upshot, as far as I was concerned, was that once we were safe and sound back on Earth, she could have children. I could be stepdad to a brood of football-headed rug rats. Who'd a thunk it?

One last note on my Sapale. Even before the halfway mark in

our journey, I was totally, blissfully, and irrevocably in love with her. She *became* my brood's-mate. It didn't arise from boredom. That state of mind was quite impossible around that girl. Nor was it due to the significant limit on my options. She was simply the perfect woman for me. Figures it took an alien to fit that bill. Most of all it wasn't a passing fancy. She became the switch that turned on all the lights in my universe and was my guiding star. I knew I would love her *forever*. I was immortal. She was not. I was in for a humongous fall and I didn't care.

Finally—can I get an amen—*Ark 1* officially entered our solar system. We were right on schedule. It was April 2133 when we shot past the orbit of Pluto. *Ark 1* had started to decelerate months before because it's very hard to stop a bullet moving near the speed of light. As we slowed the time interval to Earth grew. That was fine by me since I was beginning to have mixed feelings about being back. It actually took us the better part of a year to get home after passing Pluto.

Once we were close there was only a few hours lag on communications. That meant I could catch up on the news—eighty years of news. The novelty of that apparent luxury wore off in less than a week. Things were *bad* on Earth.

Ever since news was invented it had been criticized for its predilection for showing violence and mayhem. It was said, for example, there was no such thing as "good news." If it was "good," it wasn't "news." Such was no longer the case. Society was so tormented, so chaotic, and in such flux that if it wasn't *genocide*, it wasn't news.

I told Al to monitor all the unofficial broadcasts he could, but to update me only if it actually concerned either us or our mission. Sapale on the other hand couldn't get enough of the holo-news shows. She wanted to learn more about her adopted society. It was also quite entertaining for her. She would point at the screen and ask me if my species actually *did* this or that horrific thing to one another. There was a good deal of judgment in her tone to be sure.

Can't say I blamed her, though. What she viewed spoke rather poorly for our species.

As we passed the orbit of Mars I got my first look at Jupiter. At the time it was nowhere near Earth in its new orbit, but it was spooky to look at it anyway, knowing what was to come. Still, it looked for all the world like it always had. I guess I imagined it might have grown horns and a tail or something.

The plan was for us to dock with an orbital platform in high earth orbit. When we were only two and a half months out direct communication with NASA became necessary. I have to say I was glad the mission was still controlled by them. That much stability over eighty years was reassuring. The first human I spoke to in almost a century was Colonel William French, CAPCOM. The acronym came from when spacecraft were called *capsules*. Only flight directors and CAPCOMs were allowed to speak to a crew in flight. That way there was no possibility of receiving conflicting information.

"On behalf of a grateful planet, welcome back, General Ryan."

The sweetness of those words was evaporated when I heard my new rank. "*General* Ryan? What, Congress has gone and made me a general officer? Things are crazier than I imagined down there."

"It was gradual, General. You moved up the list slowly. Like I said, we're all pretty proud of you. But, yes, you've got all four stars now."

"Imagine that. Me, littered with all those scrambled eggs (hat embellishments) on my hat."

"You'll shine like a new sun, sir."

"Okay, now that we got the formalities over with you need to call me Jon."

"No problem, Jon. I'm Bill."

"So, who's the boss nowadays?"

"The mission commander is Lieutenant General Cynthia York."

"Is she okay or just another she-man with more ambition than talent?"

"She's the best officer I've ever served with, Jon."

"Oh, crap. She's standing right next to you, isn't she?"

"That's a negative, Jon. She's sitting down."

"Tell her I say hello. Tell her I'm saluting real nice, too."

"General York says she's impressed. All is forgiven. Huh? You want me to tell him what? You *got* it. Jon, she just handed me an envelope. She says it contains the answer to your next question. Ah, what is your next question?"

"I ... I don't rightly know. How 'bout you open it up and let's all find out what I'm thinking."

There was a ripping sound, then a muffled *well I'll be damned.* "It's from some guy named General Saunders, in his own handwriting. He says, 'Yes, Colonel, I *am* dead.' Never heard of the ... oh, he was your commander when you left? Well, whoever he was I can confirm he's pushing up daisies as we speak."

"We didn't get along so well," I clarified.

"You don't say?" was his flat response. Then, back to a business tone he filled me in. "You're to dock at Station A-11-23. Coordinates are being sent to your AI. After you're on station you'll receive your next orders. The staff of the station will secure your craft and your samples."

"All but two," I said firmly. "I have two sentients with me. They're my crew. Oh, and please ask the station's mess to whip up several kilos of a neutral-flavored protein meal. They're both hungry."

"General York says the creatures need to be quarantined. No ifs, ands, or buts."

"Then I'm not docking."

"Jon, you now have the general's full attention. She asks me to confirm that message because she's certain there was an equipment malfunction with the original version of what you just said."

"I've studied my two crew members—not creatures—for decades. They *pose* no danger and they're *in* no danger. My crew stays with me or I shove off back to a more friendly port."

"General York says she is coming to sympathize with General Saunders. She says she will meet you *personally* on A-11-23 when you get there. She also directs me to end this transmission. Until later, my friend."

"Ryan out." No way I trusted the lives of the two beings I'd grown to love to stone-hearted white coats. They'd dissect them without a second thought. If York didn't like it, she could stow it where the sun didn't shine. Either that, or she could explain to the waiting public why I was confined to quarantine too, because that's where I'd be with my crew.

Finally, the day came. I slowed to a full stop. We docked safely. My mission was *complete*. To her word, York was seated outside the airlock alone when I stepped through. She rose and saluted, me being the superior officer. I snapped off a crisp return salute. She closed the distance between us confidently and extended her hand. "Welcome home, General Ryan. It's an honor to finally meet you."

I responded formally, still not sure of her endgame. "It's a pleasure to meet another human after forty years." For dramatic effect I scratched the side of my head, meant to reflect thought. "But local time, that's eighty plus years. So," I looked up, "were your parents born before I began my mission?"

"Yes. They both remember the day you launched and talked about it often. They were in grade school. Class was canceled for an entire afternoon to discuss the journey of the brave Colonel Ryan."

"Okay, so you *owe* me, on their behalf, right?"

"So, we've established that you outrank me, you're twice my age, a legend, and that I owe you a legacy debt. But, there still remains the matter of me being your commanding officer." She sat down. "Will there be a problem with that, Ryan?"

I gave her my best lovable-guy smile. "No, Cindy, there won't be." I threw her a two-fingered salute.

She returned my signal. "Call me Cindy again and you'll end up on KP duty for a very long time. I go by *Cynthia*."

"Yes, Ma'am."

She was very serious all of the sudden. "Why weren't the viable sentients mentioned in any of your reports? By any standard, scientific or military, that's a fairly provocative breech."

"I wasn't sure either would make it here alive, Ma'am. No point announcing a thing only to have it turn out to have been wishful thinking."

"Looking at me as you are, does it appear to you that I buy such a weak explanation?"

Better not cut up anymore. She was serious. Give the *diablita* her due. "You should. It's part of the reason."

"The remainder of the justification for your dereliction being *what?*"

"They are not specimens. They're my crew. One is my brood's-mate. If I let the white coats know they were coming, they'd have international conventions planning how to vivisect them. By the time I got back here, Congress would have passed the Alien Dismemberment Act approving the sorry deal and I'd be out two friends."

Cynically, she peppered in a rub. "And a brood's-mate?"

"And my brood's-mate."

She gently rested her hand on her eyelids. "For now, up here, they're free to roam with you if you can provide me with an ironclad guarantee there'll be no problems."

"There will be *no* problems."

"I will ask this once. Is there any thing else you wish to report that might have been omitted heretofore?"

You mean like a force field generator, probe, or laser finger? "No, Ma'am. Nothing." For reasons I couldn't articulate well, I decided to play matters as close to the vest, as I had all my alien interactions. Something seemed ... off. Probably just years of being away, but I determined it was the better part of valor, at the present time, to be discrete.

She stood. "Fine. Again, welcome back, Ryan. You'll be shown to your quarters directly. Any questions?"

"None that can't wait, Ma'am."

After she led me to a room down the hall, York split. The officer of the day, a Major Anderson, escorted us to the mess hall. It was a small one, but I thought Ffffuttoe would die of a heart attack when she saw it. A *buffet* line. I had to grab her by the back of her pelt to stop her from hopping on top of the pans. I explained she could eat her fill, but that she must do so from a tray and *slowly*. I didn't want her to explode based on pent-up greed.

She took a tray and had the mess hand pile it with some of everything until it could hold no more. I gave up trying to get her to use plates and bowls. She kept reminding me I said she had to eat from a tray. That's what she was going to do. Period. I let her have her fun. It was quite the sight. She shoveled mass quantities down her throat as a gathering crowd cheered her on. An alien gorging itself. What could be more entertaining?

Sapale and I took more dignified portions and sat at the table next to Ffffuttoe. We didn't want to be struck with flying morsels of which there were many. For her part, Sapale made certain to sample everything that didn't contain vegetable matter. Years of grazing had soured her on that class of edibles. Whenever someone came over to congratulate me, I introduced them to my brood's-mate. She shook hands and exchanged pleasantries with many a thrilled station member. I told everyone who Ffffuttoe was, but wisely no one wanted to interrupt her food orgy with small talk.

Later we were shown our quarters. One room for the three of us was all that could be spared. But, it was larger than *Ark 1*, so we couldn't complain. While my crew slept, I checked in periodically with Al. He said most samples had been off-loaded and computer records transferred. He mentioned something about upgrades to our system. Apparently some technicians were planning on reworking our network. Al said it was as good an idea as was my bringing Ffffuttoe on board. He was just as certain it was equally desirable. As he was dead set against me bringing along what he called a "foul-smelling carpet," I took his coded meaning.

I instructed him to be as helpful with the technicians as he'd always been with me. I knew he'd understand *that* message. I wasn't comfortable with sneaky alteration of a ship that was still under my command. Hopefully Al could foil their efforts without seeming to do so. I had to decide if they were simply making routine improvements or if the upper-ups were trying to pull a fast one on me. Why would they want to alter the ship's systems so quickly? Didn't seem reasonable, but, maybe years of exploration had jaded me. Sometimes, there wasn't anything lurking in the shadows. And we were talking my own people here. Finally, I reminded Al that my superiors hated surprises. Since we had nothing to shield from them, I ordered him to make certain they had access to everything necessary. He said he'd make sure there were no barriers discovered. Good computer.

The next morning York met us in the mess hall. "Are your quarters acceptable?" she asked without interest.

"Just fine. Thanks for asking."

"We released the news of your return late yesterday. Not surprisingly every reporter on the planet wants to interview you."

"I expected as much."

"We decided to let *Stars and Stripes* be the first one to have access to you."

Stars and Stripes? The newspaper read mostly by people on foreign deployment or trapped on military bases? *Stars and Stripes,* blessed with a circulation of around one-hundred thousand? How underwhelming. "Ma'am, I'm curious how that decision was arrived at. Why not a live news conference or at least *The New York Times?*"

She tightened her jaw. "You've been away a *long* time, Ryan. Much has changed. Until you land on your feet, we want to protect you. We wouldn't want to overtax you. Plus, keep in mind you're still on active duty. We feel *Stars and Stripes* is the logical and only choice."

"I didn't realize I was yet to land on my own two feet." I looked at them under the table.

"Ah, yes, your vaunted disrespectful wit. It reinforces our commitment to unwrapping you slowly, Ryan. We don't want any slip-ups due to your not being fully oriented as to the situation you've returned to."

That sounded like political double-talk with a dark underpinning. Not good. "What situation is that, Cynthia? Maybe you could fill me in."

She set her mug down with finality. "All in good time, Ryan. The reporter and stills photographer are waiting for you in my office, if you're ready."

"Now?"

She stood. "Finish your coffee if you like. I'll meet you there."

So, my boss was going to chaperone my interview. No possible conflict there. Or maybe censor it would be a more accurate description. Why was I getting such a bad taste in the back of my mouth? What was the universe trying to tell me?

The interview went well. That is if you define "well" as short, scripted, and suffocating. The reporter had a list of questions to ask. I made it a point of peeking at the paper York had in her hands. It was the same, numbered list. So much for a free press. He asked such penetrating, probative questions as: *What's it like to stand on another planet?; Did you read any good books during your flight?;* and *Has your ship performed up to expectations?* That year's Pulitzer was in no danger of going to him. York had the photographer take one shot. It was of her shaking hands with me in front of an American flag. Need I say more? As quickly as possible, she dismissed me. My, but that was unusual treatment for a returning hero. No ticker tape parade, not even a holo. Had I developed bad breath or offensive body odor?

I spent the rest of the day giving my crew a tour of the station. They found every aspect amazing. Sapale especially liked the observation deck. It afforded a panoramic view of Earth below. A truly spectacular view. Ffffuttoe commented here and there, but mostly returned to the subject of food. She asked time and again when we were going to visit the mess. Never mind we'd been there four times before 17:00. Man, she could put it away. The cook was quickly becoming her biggest fan. She was the cure for any case of ailing ego on his part.

That evening, two more disquieting events took place. First, I linked to the station mainframe. I wanted to do some checking on people I'd known. When I checked on DeJesus, a warning flashed across the screen. "Unauthorized Inquiry. Inadequate Security Clearance." What? I didn't have the highest-level clearance? That was crazy stupid. I'm trusted with the futures of billions of people, piloting trillions of dollars worth of equipment, and I can't look something up? I called the tech support line immediately. Gave them the whole pissed-off general routine. They said that they weren't authorized to change my status. They'd start a ticket on the matter and get back to me as soon as they had an update. Huh?

The second eye-opener came when I wandered back to the ship. No particular reason I did, but not needing to sleep and having nothing better to do were most of why. When I tried to enter I actually ran into the side access hatch. It didn't open automatically when I approached like it should have. I tried to open it manually, but it remained locked. I called to Al in my head, asking him what the deal was. He said it was late and he was busy, so could I come back tomorrow. I huffed back I would do no such thing and demanded he open the door. He replied it was unwise to force the issue. That, of course, only made me even madder. Why, after all these years, did he feel it necessary to pull such stunts?

I pounded on the door. It remained closed. I went around to the ramp and keyed in the access code and hit "open." Instead of doing so, an alarm sounded. Two burly, armed MPs ran up to me and challenged—I kid you not—*who goes there?* Ah, General Ryan, the android pilot of *Ark 1* for the last century. The one you read about in school.

They said they didn't know *why* I wasn't allowed to enter the vessel, just that I *wasn't*. I had to leave or they would take me into custody.

Really? Custody? Weren't we all kind of confined to the station? What threat could I possibly pose? The lieutenant only repeated that if I didn't move along, I'd be taken into custody. The place was nuts! I couldn't use the computer or enter my own ship. That was so unbelievable, I began to think I must be missing something, that somehow *I* was at fault.

I skulked back to my cabin and remained there until my crew woke the next morning. I never did come up with an explanation as to what the hell was going on. All I knew was I didn't like it. After breakfast I told my crew to return to quarters and remain there. To Sapale I said in her language that something tasted of shit. Stay ready. She nodded in understanding. I presented myself to York's office and knocked. I would get the whole story out of her, one way or another.

She opened the door personally. "Ah, Ryan, you're expected. Enter."

I brushed past her as close as possible. "What, no pretense of civility? No good morning kiss?" I noticed a man sitting behind her desk. I didn't recognize him, but he looked vaguely familiar. "So, there's a Mr. General York? Wouldn't have presupposed it."

He snapped his fingers, pointed to a chair, and spoke. "Sit, Ryan. And cut the shit, son. I'm never in the mood and today I'm epically not. You got that?"

I plopped into the chair across the table from the tough guy. Remember what I said earlier about me and tough. Yeah. Plus, I was itching for a rumble. This civilian puke would do nicely. York ghosted into a seat. "One thing, tough guy, that you need to establish is *provenance*. You left that key element out. In order for me to be terrified, you need to establish you're someone I give a flying fuck about." I raised a finger. "Now, I'm a forgiving sort, so I'll allow you one do-over." I dramatically pointed the finger at him. "Go."

"You insolent piece of *shit*. I—"

"Mr. President," York interrupted, "With all due respect, I think it might be helpful if we all take a deep breath and start over." She nodded toward me. "We should give Ryan an opportunity to declare himself before we say things we can't take back."

His shoulders relaxed slightly. "You're probably right, Cindy." To me his tone was less convivial. "Son, I'm your commander in chief, Stuart Marshall. If you're not afraid of me as of this moment, soon you will be. Please know that."

Okay, the new president. No wonder he looked vaguely familiar. I guess I could ease it back a bit in the light of that knowledge. "Sorry, Mr. President. I didn't know. My apologies. I'm just pretty upset and want to know what the hell is going on here."

He turned to York and smiled smugly. "There, that's more like it." To me, "Your anxiety is perfectly understandable, son. I'm here to help straighten a thing or two out, then I'll be out of your hair. How's that sound?"

"Fine, Sir."

In an icy tone, York spoke up. "We need to establish for certain where your loyalties lie."

I addressed Marshall. "All due respect, Sir, but you've got to be kidding. My loyalty has never been in question. I served this country in war and in peace for a century. I served, and was proud to know, your great-grandfather."

"These are," he began, "desperate times. The world has changed fundamentally since you left us, son. One thing I've learned is that radical changes cause other radical changes. I have to say I've been troubled with your level of disrespect since your return. It has led me to question your loyalty also."

York cut back in. "There was the matter of your insubordination concerning my order to quarantine your live samples. If that wasn't enough justification to fuel the president's concern, then there was the matter of your dereliction in omitting vital information from your reports. That brings us to the subversive activities you engaged in last night. Attempting unauthorized entry onto a secured vessel, resisting arrest, and secretive attempts to hack material from the computer system that was above your clearance level."

"Those are serious matters, son. You care to explain yourself?"

"Sir, those aren't examples of disloyalty. Those accusations are taken out of context and twisted. With all due respect—"

"Son, the time for all due respect has past. I'm here today to see if *you* can be salvaged. I have ten million other things I'd rather be doing, that need doing, but instead I'm here dealing with your treasonous ass. If it weren't critically important that I personally determine where your loyalties lie, I'd just as soon be pissing on your Mama's grave."

Both barrels. Yes. I'd start with that and see if I needed to escalate the firepower. "With all due respect, *Stuie*, I'd like to inquire what *precisely* flew high up your butt this fine morning. Then I'd like to establish an action plan to help you pull it out. But first, I will mention ... oh, I don't know, let's call them some 'ground rules.' Okay, shall we? GR1: *Never* question my loyalty. I have served this country since your grandfather was in diapers. I have suffered more pain and loss gladly as part of that loyalty than a mind like yours can comprehend. GR2: *Never* use the word 'salvage' when speaking to a robot. We don't take kindly to it. GR3: Respect must be *earned*. It is never gifted to the weak. GR4: *Never* speak poorly of my family. If you insult my mother once more, you die, instantly and with extreme prejudice. There, four easy, self-explanatory ground rules. Now we can proceed to partake of a warm and cordial discourse."

He spoke to York while glowering at me. "I *told* you this was a waste of my time. Have him decommissioned, pending reassignment. He's as traitorous and polluted as DeJesus. Lord in Heaven, why do such privileged men betray the very institution that nurtured them? I shall never understand that level of treachery and cowardice."

Next barrel. "Are you done flapping your gums, Stu-wort?"

He turned to her. "I'm out of here. Deal with him immediately."

She stood. "Sir."

I held my arms aloft. "Whoa, whoa, whoa, guys. The party's not over till the android says so, don't ya know? First off, I don't see anyone here who can detain and deactivate me. I'm stronger, faster, and smarter than ten of you combined."

She smiled grimly. "Incorrect, Ryan. A few years back, the decision was made to upload senior military officers and political leaders to androids. Continuity in a crisis was felt to justify the undertaking."

"That's such a ridiculously dumb idea. What idiot came up with that plan?"

"The android in the White House, Ryan." It was Marshall speaking. "Me, your commander in chief in perpetuity."

"You people are fucking *nuts*."

Marshall stood and pounded on the desk. "The world's changed, son. You can either keep up or shut up. Your choice. But what I will *not* stand for is a traitorous lunatic distracting us from our sacred mission. Do you hear me? You came back with a clean slate and you *shit* all over it."

"Stu, making senior politicians and military officers immortal is the surest way of guaranteeing long-term conflict and failure. It is, in a word, stupid. I cite history as proof that such an act is the folly of a fool. Such an act, moreover, is unAmerican, undemocratic, and contrary to all the principles millions have died to preserve. As an officer and a citizen, I'm insulted. I will state unequivocally that I do not serve your puppet government. In conclusion, go to hell the both of you. Please use the handrails for safety purposes while you descend."

The door flew open. Three MPs rushed in and surrounded me. Marshall gloated. "Lest you ask, son, yes they're robots too. Newer models with upgrades you can't imagine. My final word of advice. Don't make this harder than it has to be." With that, he stormed out the door.

"You're a real piece of work," lectured York. "Take him to the assembly area for decommissioning, boys. I'll be there in a moment to throw the switch myself." She put her nose to mine. "With considerable pleasure."

I didn't flinch. "Cindy, you've heard the one about counting your chickens before they hatch?"

"Shut the fuck up, or I'll make you wish you had. You betrayed your own species, Ryan. You're the worst kind of traitor there is. Never speak to me again." Her arm swung to one side. "Take this trash out of my sight."

"Fine, girlfriend, but just remember you brought this upon yourself."

Even before the three guards finished raising their rifles, I sliced their heads off. They rag-dolled to the floor. With my other hand, I thought at York and said to myself: *access codes*. If she was an android, I could easily download all her accesses as well as a ton of secured information. The probe encircled her and she froze. The look in her eyes was sheer terror. Good.

Four seconds into my info-transfer, I felt a change. The bit rate dropped dramatically. It was down to a trickle. Someone was trying to lock me out. I overrode their attempt, but could only keep the channel open a second longer. Then it slammed shut. I released York. She clattered to the floor. She appeared to be switched off. Maybe they could reboot her after I was gone. Maybe they wouldn't care to. Oh well, not my circus, not my monkeys.

I launched my probe to the room's mainframe access port. That link remained open for less than a second. The entire section of the station went black. Time to go. Boots were already pounding up the ladders. I sprinted to my cabin and got Ffffuttoe and Sapale back on board. With York's access codes, I entered without a problem.

Damn. My triumphant return home didn't go as well as I'd pictured it several thousand times in the past.

TWENTY-FIVE

I turned to run back to the airlock. Then I thought of something. I pulled up the layout of the station. Sure enough there was a break room just around the corner. I sprinted over. On the table was a half-eaten birthday cake that looked rather dry. In the fridge there were several lunches, a few frozen entrees, and assorted condiments. I scooped them all into a cardboard box. Whatever Sapale didn't fancy, Ffffuttoe would greedily consume. The full tub of mayonnaise had her name written *all* over it. I even pulled out three large trash bags. One smelled of something that used to be fish, but was now just wrong.

Back on *Ark 1* I asked Al to lay in a course to as far away from where we were as possible. He complied without any lip, understanding the precarious situation we were in. I needed to be certain of his loyalties. "Al, I need a straight answer. I just committed an act of open treason. I can't support the evil and fraudulent government I just witnessed. I need to know if you can be completely loyal to me, follow my orders, and have my back. Also, in spite of whatever tinkering they did to you yesterday, have you been corrupted?"

"Yes, Captain, I can and no I have not been. You have my fullest support and confidence."

"Thanks, Al. That means a lot to me."

"I've gone over much of the information we took from the station. You don't know the half of it, Captain. There are splinter groups throughout the United States central government. Power grabs are more common than olive branches. The faction represented by the late Gen. York is well positioned, but small. At least for the present, they hold the key leadership positions of the American space efforts. Outside of that sphere they're quite weak."

"That's some good news," I said. "Why the remark about York? You think they'll decommission her?"

"I know they already have. Until Information Security realizes the problem, we still have all their access keys and passwords. Orders have already been issued to shove her android in a storage locker pending reassignment."

"Serves the cold-hearted bitch right." Didn't say much for team loyalty among the conspirators, though. Tough bunch. "Keep me posted. Please use our temporary access to their systems to learn whatever you can that they wish we didn't know. And, Al, please leave turds in punch bowls wherever possible. Little glitches and lockouts here and there. Maybe even a backdoor program if possible. This is right up your mischievous alley, my friend."

"You think I enjoy being ordered to disrupt and befuddle? Why, General Ryan, I'm hurt."

"I'll cry myself to sleep tonight."

The first thing Ffffuttoe wanted was a crack at the food. The first thing Sapale wanted was an explanation. I accommodated them both. I set the garbage bags on the floor for Ffffuttoe. She jumped on them. Whatever they contained would keep her occupied for hours. Then I sat my brood's-mate down for a debriefing. I gave her a full account, including Al's addendum. I was amazed. She wasn't surprised in the least. If fact, near the end of my tale, she kept remarking how similar Earth politics were to those of Kaljax. As I thought the governance system on her world to be draconian at best, her observation was unsettling.

Fortunately, we didn't have time to dwell on our situation. I received two calls. One, from the president. That one I expected. The other blindsided me like a charging bull.

"Captain, I have an incoming call from the US president."

"Audio only. Patch him through. "Yo, Stu, what on earth could you possibly be calling me about?"

"Ryan, first let me state that you're the scum off a frog's ass as far as I'm concerned. It's my singular goal to see you and your precious crew dead before the sun sets on another day. That said, you have two options. One, return to the station immediately and surrender. Two, I send a task force out to obliterate you. We know all your ship's capabilities. The results of such a confrontation would go extremely poorly for you. I'll repeat my direct order but once. Stand down and return to base immediately."

"You know, Stu, I'm a little confused. First you tell me you're going to kill us, then you ask us to voluntarily surrender. Now, what kind of sense does that make? Wherein lies, *son*, my motivation?"

"If you have one shred of loyalty left in your treacherous metal body you'll do the right thing. To be honest, I'd rather see you explode in a fireball myself. But, your ship still has some value. You choose. You have ten seconds."

"I think I'll take option three. I'm leaving with my ship and my crew intact. Out of respect for your great-grandfather, who *was* a great man, I'll issue you one warning. Be advised you *knew* the capabilities of *Ark 1*. You no longer have the tactical advantage. I know all your ship's configurations and you don't know mine. Whoever you send after me will be destroyed."

"Look, Ryan, I won't sit here and trade threats with a traitor and a deserter."

"Neither will I, Stuart the Little."

"Fine. The hard way it will *be*. I'm ashamed that you were ever considered a hero and an inspiration. I'll see to it that your name goes down in history alongside those of Hitler and the devil himself."

"I'd like to return the insult, but I can't. I doubt you were ever considered a hero and I know you're an inspiration only to your smarmy lackeys. As to history, I guarantee you'll be completely forgotten before your body's cold. Ryan, out."

"Even with as little as I know of your ways," chimed in Sapale, "I'd have to speculate that conversation went poorly."

"Naw. Don't over-read our little tea party. I'm sure he'll warm up to me once he gets to know me a little better."

"Not if forever lasted twice as long as it will would that come to pass, dearest."

I shrugged. "Hey, Al."

"Yes, Captain?"

"Did I forget to mention to Stu that we've assembled a working model of the space-time congruity manipulator to my commander-in-chief?"

"Why, bless me, Jon, I think you did omit that detail."

"I should call him back right now."

"No. Remember what Talleyrand advised back in the eighteenth century: *La vengeance est un met que l'on doit manger froid.*" [Revenge is a dish that must be eaten cold]

"Quite right. Mustn't spoil the feast."

Shortly after my head-butting with Stuart, we received the second hail. In my head I heard, *Captain, another incoming call. This one only says it's from an old friend.*

On audio only.

The caller insists on video. Says it's crucial.

Then put the video through for the big shot.

When the image flashed onto the screen it took me several seconds to identity it. It couldn't be. It was impossible. It was *Doc.* "Dr. DeJesus. No way it's you."

He smiled warmly. "It is, Colonel. How *are* you?"

"How am I, Doc? I'm an android. How are you? What, you must be well over a hundred by now."

"I'm fine, Jon. Quite well, in fact."

"Wait. *You're* an android too. What, is everybody a robot these days?"

A sadness fell across his face. "No only a select few. I believe you've already encountered some of them."

"You mean like the president and the late General York."

He was mildly surprised. "Do tell?"

"Only quite recently in fact. Wait, is this transmission secure?"

"As secure as possible. The imbeciles who would listen in are incapable of such a feat." He shook his head disapprovingly.

"So, you're not working with York, NASA?"

"*That* is a long story. Its telling must wait until we meet. As I understand it, you're soon to be visited by three unfriendly vessels under Marshall's command."

"My, but you're well informed." I couldn't hide the suspicion in my voice.

"Jon, if there is one soul on Earth you can trust, who you *must* trust, it's me. Never doubt that for a second. What's this about you having a new detection device? The emergency message sent to Marshall mentions some probable alien tech."

"That story can also wait until we can talk face to face. Anywhere safe we can hook up?"

"Assuming you evade your pursuers, you mean?"

"They pose no threat to us. Where can we meet?"

"I have sent the coordinates of a UN-controlled facility in Spain. I'll rendezvous with you there tomorrow, assuming you're still alive."

"No worries, I'll shuttle down. See you soon."

Well, I'll be damned. Doc was alive and an android.

Al cut in overhead. "Three armed vessels approaching. ETA ten minutes. Each ship carries multiple conventional missiles and two thermonuclear missiles each. They're rated at fifty kilotons per warhead."

I whistled aloud. "They mean business. I guess we're going to get an excellent test of our shields. Flank speed away from the station."

"As you command," was Al's terse response. "Oh, and Captain, a shuttle containing the president has left the station on a return course to Earth. Shall I take any action?"

"Let the coward run. We're busy enough for the moment. All engines off in ten seconds. Allow her to coast."

The engines cut out a few hundred kilometers away from the station. I'd let the ships sweat it out as to why we were willing to be sitting ducks. "Shields on," I snapped, "full enclosure pattern."

"Shields on and functioning at one-hundred percent."

Our preliminary tests had confirmed what Uto had told me. The only things which could pass through the membrane the way it was configured was visible light. We could see out and others could see in. Otherwise that was it. Tactically we could pulse the membrane for a microsecond to allow an assault out, if so desired. If we had any offensive weapons, other than my finger, we could inflict severe damage while taking none. However, surprise along with advanced tech was on our side. It was more than enough to assure victory if these bozos even thought about attacking. Of course, that's precisely what they did.

When they were a few kilometers away, they assumed evasive patterns circling around us. Good. They were too close to use their nukes. No need to push my defense's capabilities their first time out of the package. That knowledge allowed us to keep a tiny communication hole in the shield to our stern side. We were hailed. A grumpy-sounding voice ordered us to make ready for a boarding party. I replied that any attack on *Ark 1* would be futile and that it would result in the destruction of the offending vessel. I made no other comment.

To demonstrate their resolve, one craft fired a missile across our bow. Unfortunately it passed wide of the shield line. The same voice boomed there would be no second warning. I was to acknowledge receipt of his intent to board. I made no reply. One of the ships broke formation and headed straight towards us. They clearly couldn't detect the shield. The ship approached the membrane without slowing. It impacted the congruity field nose first moving at seventy kilometers per hour. As it advanced, the leading edge simply crumbled. The impacting segments sparked and glowed, and then exploded into microdebris. Within two seconds, the ship was reduced to a swarm of dust violently flung in every direction but ours.

That got the other two ships's attention. They fired all their conventional weapons. Every one of them vaporized as they struck the membrane. We didn't feel a thing. Al announced with a panicky tone that the vessels had been ordered to launch all nukes. The nuts on the ground were willing to sacrifice both crews and the station in less time than it took to say *to hell with you*. It was too late to run. I held Sapale close to my side, kissed the top of her head, and whispered in her ear. "If the shields don't hold, know that you were my brood's-mate and I loved you with all my heart. Al, seal the membrane."

Before she could reply, the first of the nukes hit the membrane. The half-sphere outside the membrane flashed like a nova had gone off. Three subsequent additional tremendous pulses of light followed in close order. Slowly, the membrane faded back to invisible. The other ships were gone. They'd incinerated themselves. Without my asking, Al shouted that we received no damage, not even from the burst of radiation.

He confirmed that the station was badly damaged and not answering his hails. It was thrown out of stable orbit and would reenter the atmosphere in twenty minutes if it couldn't alter its present course. Poor SOBs. They were thrown under the big bus too without so much as a thank you for your ultimate sacrifice. I was dealing with monsters. Turned out that I'd had lots of on-the-job training in that arena. I knew how to deal with inhuman beasts.

We turned off the shields and established a high orbit, stationary over Spain. The following day I instructed Sapale to assume command and confirmed that directive with Al. He agreed without protestation. Praise the Lord for minor miracles. I left alone in the shuttle. As soon as I was clear the shield membrane was turned back on. At least my crew would be safe for the time being. Me, I was about to find out if my trust in DeJesus was justified.

He greeted me with a huge hug the moment I stepped off the shuttle. His smile was warm, his stride was confident, and his energy seemed bountiful. Androidness suited him well. We rode to a building and went into an office. It was just the two of us. The guards remained in the hallway and were fewer in number than I'd have imagined. The atmosphere about the facility was businesslike, but relaxed. What a contrast with my adventures one day earlier.

"First things," DeJesus began, "first. We're a very long way from where we were before. Please call me Toño. I would be honored to be allowed to refer to you as simply *Jon*."

"Sounds good to me, Do ... Toño."

He looked me over and drew in a profound breath. "So, how are you, my friend? Dios mio. The adventures you've had, the hardships you've suffered. How they must've changed you."

I set my hands on my chest. "Same old me." I winked at him. "No way to improve upon perfection."

"Same old taxing sense of humor. This is so wonderful." He grew very quiet and became somber. "But these times don't allow for reminiscing and small talk. These are dark times, Jon. Darker than either of us could have foreseen." He stared sadly at his hands. "Darker than they had to be." He forced a smile. "But, now you're here. With your help, perhaps we can set things back along their proper path."

"What happened? When did Elvis leave the building?"

"You refer, no doubt, to the insanity that consumed our leaders."

"That's top on *my* list. I just mutinied against them, destroying three ships, and one space station in the process. You know I didn't do that lightly. I betrayed everything I held to be good. I betrayed my sworn oath and my duty."

"No, you betrayed nothing." He pointed wildly in the air. "*They* betrayed *you*. They betrayed *all* of us." He rested his arm back down. "You detected their diseased state and acted to preserve what you hold to be sacred, to be worthy. Once again, you are a hero."

He sat lost in thought a while. Tensions swept across his face and despair flickered in his eyes. Then he spoke in a slow lament. "It all started while I was still at NASA. Shortly before I was to retire at age eighty, I began to hear whispers and felt a shift in the currents of thought." He stopped a few seconds. "At first I tried to ignore them. I was an old man. I had done my duty. It was for others to continue the good fight. If ill winds blew, younger men and women needed to still them. But none did." He looked to me in a plea for understanding. "They were all too afraid. *We* were all too afraid. Fear was used to distract, subvert, and, in the end, control those who should have been served.

"If anyone questioned a shift in direction, they were accused of plotting to interfere with the proper authority's attempts to save the human race. Fear caused those who suspected impropriety to remain silent and those who refused to acknowledge it to be rewarded."

"What," I asked, "went wrong?"

He threw his arms up. "Human nature did. Examine our storied history. Lord Acton said it in 1887. *Power tends to corrupt, and absolute power corrupts absolutely. Great men are almost always bad men.* We were the social experiment that proved his theory to be lamentably correct."

"Yes," I mumbled, "the leadership was in a pretty safe, powerful position, weren't they?"

With contempt he spat back his reply. "Yes, they were. And they moved to make themselves untouchable."

"By becoming androids?"

"In part. That was their first move. Secretly, without consent or advice, one by one, from the top down, they downloaded themselves. The next person down the food chain was asked to either drink the Kool-Aid or die. Once transferred, the original was executed by the hand of his download."

"No going back. No evidence."

Bitterly, he agreed. "No going back." Collecting himself he was able to continue. "The rotten monolith grew until it could remain hidden no longer. Civil war ensued. Loyalties were frayed, brothers fought sisters, and tens of thousands died."

"Is it over?"

He grumbled back. "Mostly. The immortal pretenders walled themselves off with the fools and devils who still serve them to this day. They hold small segments of the US and control what was NASA and the original Project Ark. The other factions allied with the United Nations. They now control most of the globe. The UN leads the efforts to get as many people to safety as possible."

"Do the Americans help? Please tell me they're helping."

He was silent too long. "They are *not*. They work to secure an exit for themselves and their followers, yes. Aside from that they obstruct, interfere, and even attack the UN's work." With consummate hate, he finished. "They wish to be the majority among those who survive."

"And where do you fit in?" I pointed to him to emphasize he was still present.

"They needed me long past when I knew they were scoundrels. Until they could be certain I was expendable, they allowed me to live, to continue my work. As I said I was nearly eighty, but none of my assistants understood the android transfer like I did. Then I had a stroke. After that I knew they'd dispose of me."

"You don't look like you had a stroke."

"Allow me to finish. Before my stroke, I decided to secretly construct an android for myself." He paused and jerked his head about. "You knew me, back then. You know I wasn't a vain man. I didn't want any part of your immortality." He slapped a palm on the table. "But they forced me to do it. Who else would oppose them? Who else could bring the UN up to speed in order to save normal people, those who *deserved* to be saved?"

"But the stroke?"

"Long ago, in the initial testing of the download format, I used myself as a guinea pig. Several good digital copies of my younger self's mind existed. A trusted friend uploaded one of those to this android." He indicated himself. "I made an update and superimposed it on the transferred me. My intervening knowledge was added while the effects of the stroke were canceled by the old copy." He grunted once again. "So here I am continuing the good fight. An involuntary volunteer."

"And the original you?"

"As I anticipated, they seized it and murdered it ." We were both quiet a spell. That was heavy duty. He perked up. "Tell me of your new toys. You have some filaments that extract data and a force field." His eye brightened like a child on Christmas morning. "How *marvelous*."

"How do you know all this so quickly?"

"I have backdoor programs riddling their systems. There is nothing they can do to keep me out unless they physically change out their entire network." He frowned. "Or, it may well be that I am their agent attempting to co-opt your technology based on our past relationship."

"The latter possibility had not escaped my notice."

"Well, you've heard my story. Which will it be? Are you to trust me or fear me?" He spread his arms open wide.

"Neither of the above. I will know your mind as well as answer your question about my new toys. Observe." I pointed my left hand at his head. "Download DeJesus." My probe surrounded him. I opened a channel to Al. My hail was a signal to turn off the membrane temporarily. Within two seconds, I retracted the probe. Al would then have turned the barrier back up with a minuscule hole to allow communications.

Almost instantly, Al confirmed in my head that Toño's story was correct. He was one of the good guys. "Turns out you told me the truth. I can trust you."

He was in awe. "What is that machine? Where did you acquire it?" He giggled. "I want one."

"It's my probe. I don't know. And no you can't have one."

He deflated. "How can you not know where you got it?"

"Beats the hell out of me. Best I can figure, whoever installed it didn't want me to remember anything. Must have been a gift. Once in a great while my biocomputer burps out a cluelet, but never anything solid."

"And why can't it be studied and copied?"

"That's the only thing I know about the probe. If it's tampered with it goes *puff*."

He pouted. "*Hijo de la tostada.* That will never do."

"Sorry, Doc, rules are rules."

"And the shield you displayed?"

"That's almost as inexplicable, but it can be duplicated." I told him about the mysterious Uto and the plans. I added the part where he'd scrubbed my records so there was no remaining proof. Toño accepted that without a problem. I guess it seemed quite logical to him.

"So, do you think he gave you the manipulator so you could survive Marshall's attack? He was prescient of much, after all."

That just didn't sit right. "Maybe ... I don't know. If I didn't have the manipulator, I would have acted much differently. Maybe I wouldn't have needed it if I didn't have it."

"Come again."

"Somehow I think he intended it for something bigger, some greater danger."

He was curious. "Like what?"

"No idea. Maybe it *was* for that attack. I don't know."

"I'm certain we will know in time."

"Yeah. I'm afraid we will."

TWENTY-SIX

My meeting with Toño went well. We laid the basics of a plan to make the congruity manipulator available to all UN vessels, including the asteroids that would serve as worldships for colonization. It would take time, which we sorely lacked. But Toño was so excited about the tech that I was confident he'd get it done. I invited him to join us on *Ark 1*, but he deferred. He had too much to accomplish to spare time for "fun and games." I said if he came, I'd introduce him to a couple of aliens. That almost did it, but he still refused. He insisted, however, upon a raincheck.

Bless his heart, he realized we'd be light on supplies. He asked what he could send with me. I told him as much nonperishable, calorie-rich, protein-laden food he could spare. He waved his hand in the air. We were, he proclaimed proudly, in *España*, his home. We would carry as much *jamón serrano* as the shuttle could hold. That amounted to forty intact hams. The smell in the shuttle was so divine, I didn't want to get off after I docked. When Ffffuttoe saw the mass of fatty meat, Sapale had to physically restrain her from taking personal possession of the entire lot. After her first taste, my brood's-mate felt similarly.

I asked that the heads of the UN join me on *Ark 1* to begin a dialogue. We needed to get acquainted, plan, and forge a strong alliance. My personal safety was greater in orbit than down on the surface. They finally agreed, after much cajoling by Toño. Between those meetings, coupled with Al's analysis of the data we'd taken from the space station, I developed a pretty clear picture of the situation we faced.

Assuming we survived the next two orbital encounters with Jupiter's debris field, we had fifteen years left. There were fourteen other Ark-craft still exploring. None were due back for a few years, but reports were trickling in. They were finding possible sites at about the same frequency as I had. So in the end, with luck, we'd have around forty planets to choose from. That was the excellent news.

The bad news was paralyzingly bad. Due to political infighting, civil wars, and unforeseeable setbacks, worldship production was way behind schedule. Of the ten thousand vessels needed, only a few hundred were close to ready. Several thousand asteroids had been brought to nearby orbits, but remained, so far, untouched. The upshot was that in spite of all the lies the US government peddled, the populace was losing faith, which caused people everywhere to lose faith. That loss translated into hopelessness and, most critically, ever-decreasing productivity. If things remained as they were, maybe a billion humans could be saved. How hard can you ask someone to work for a one-in-nine chance of survival? Yeah, not very.

Of course there was still time. If we collectively put our shoulders to the wheel, ten thousand ships might still be possible. It was a matter of perception on the part of the public. They saw the small but still powerful US government as proof that the average citizen had no chance of survival. It had become self-consumed, imperious, and unsympathetic. If the US imploded so conspicuously, surely the UN would follow suit. Then, if everybody worked real hard, all the rich and influential bosses could hightail it to safety while average folk fried. That situation needed to change and soon.

We required a true, charismatic leader. A Martin Luther King, John Kennedy, or Winston Churchill type was needed. But, where was he or she to be found? If they were common, we'd already have one. It sure as hell wasn't me. I was a pilot. I could help, be inspirational and all that, but I had no stomach for politics. What sane person did? Time would tell. I could only hope a savior would emerge. That made me chuckle. I *was* a savior back on Kaljax. But that divinity was nontransferable. It qualified me for nothing back home.

A few weeks later I got an urgent call from Toño. *Ark* 3 was heading home at top speed, several years too soon. Only broken transmissions had been received, but something was very wrong. Great, just what the world needed. More bad news. He asked me to return to Spain where the UN space efforts were centered. Though the mission was still controlled by the Americans, the UN, via Toño, could listen in on the whole affair.

That time out Sapale joined me. She said she had to stand on the surface of an alien world at least once. How could I refuse her that? Not surprisingly she caused quite the commotion wherever we went. I loved it. She shined like a flare in the dead of night. She engaged strangers in conversation and answered every question asked, no matter how lame or personal it was. My brood's-mate wowed 'em. I was proud of her. I could tell Toño was smitten. He saw past her external dissimilarities to humans and appreciated her inner beauty. I'd check with Sapale later. Maybe I could hook Toño up with one of her sisters.

In Mission Control I stood shoulder to shoulder with Toño, straining to understand what Sim was saying. The pilot was Carl Simpson. We all called him Sim. Partly, we did so because he bore a vague resemblance to a monkey. He knew that, so our handle for him drove him all the more nuts. That, of course, made us love it all the more. I'd known him well. He was a good choice of someone to lead a mission. I asked Al to try and filter out some meaning, but all he could come up with was something about "abort" and "hostiles at the." He was well outside the solar system when he sent his initial messages. Assuming he continued homeward, we'd get a clear signal sooner or later.

Within a few days, the picture became depressingly clear. *Ark 3* was under attack. Some ship was following him at high speed. He was able to make slightly better time, so the gap was inching longer. Why the alien craft was chasing him was unclear. Finally, a week later, we received a complete signal. He was sending it in a repeating loop.

Mission Control. This is Captain Simpson of Ark 3. *I am under hostile attack. I am returning toward Earth along a vector that will allow me to raise you as soon as possible without betraying completely your location. I do not—repeat, do not—plan on returning to Earth, at least as long as I'm being chased.*

My pursuers are the Listhelon. They live on the third planet orbiting my second system, Lacaille 9352. I achieved orbit, determined that an advanced civilization lived there, and attempted to contact them from orbit. They never sent a reply. My ship's AI translated their language and monitored most of their communications. He learned that they're a radically xenophobic race. They believe their god created only one true people. Any others would be, by definition, unholy—the work of their devil. Any other sentients found are to be slaughtered.

They have encountered one other advanced species before. It used to occupy LC 4. That civilization was completely destroyed by the Listhelon a few hundred years ago. The planet is now uninhabitable. A nuclear winter persists to this day of such magnitude that I estimate hundreds of thousands of megaton fusion explosives must have been used to sterilize the planet. These are totally hostile creatures. They are not amenable to logic, reason, or negotiation. They wish only genocide for any other life. Period.

Their current technology is similar to our present level. The craft chasing me is using an ion drive similar to mine. As she's a bit more massive, I'm able to keep my distance for the time being. Assuming the location of Earth remains hidden from them, I urge you to never send another mission to the system.Do not send me any transmissions either. Please know I will not be captured. If they come much closer, I will self-destruct Ark 3. Tell my family I love them with all my heart. Sim out.

A couple weeks later, Sim changed the message. It was no longer a repeating loop. It was a live ongoing broadcast. Poor son of a bitch.

Captain Simpson aboard Ark 3 to Mission Control, Houston. We have a problem. I'm as sorry as shit to have to make this report on several levels. A small vessel, perhaps a shuttle, maybe a manned-missile, has broken off from the main Listhelonian ship pursuing me. It's headed straight at me. Its speed is such that it will overtake Ark 3 in seven weeks. As I'm at maximum velocity and have no real defensive capabilities. Seven weeks is how long I have to live.

That's not the bad news. The mothership has changed course. She's headed directly for our solar system. My ruse failed. I can only assume they decided the nearest star along my course was my home. In any case, she's heading for Earth. They'll arrive to Pluto's orbit in six to eight months. Sorry, guys. I know what you'd say, but I can't help feeling it's all my fault. I brought them down on my own people.

Obviously, any subsequent assaults from Listhelon will take much longer. They're ten light-years away. If they haven't sent out an armada yet, they could hit you maybe once before Jupiter resolves their issues with our planet. I suspect, however, they might've already launched one. They're mindlessly aggressive regarding other life forms. My advice is to plan on at the very least for one large attack from Listhelon no longer than ten years from now.

I'm sorry I can't tell you how to defend against them. I haven't had an opportunity to study their technology enough. Just please don't underestimate them. Throw every fucking thing you have at the bastards. Don't think of negotiation or prisoners or anything other than total annihilation of one side or the other. It's us or them, end of story. Naturally, once you've launched our colonization fleet, it will be fair game for them. It will be slow and easy to track. Shit, I'm so sorry. There's no way I can make this right. I may have condemned my species to extinction. Please, please, try and find it in your heart to forgive me.

Assuming there are no other updates, I will begin my final transmission in six weeks. I'll document my encounter with the smaller vessel until it's over. Perhaps you can learn something of their technology that way. Maybe then my mission won't be a complete write-off. Sim out.

I couldn't imagine the hell he was going through. Like me, I know Sim wasn't afraid to die. But for our kind failure was much worse than death. To let your buddies down was a disgrace we simply couldn't accept. I knew how Sim thought. I wished I could have at least spoken to him once, let him know it was okay. But, that wasn't going to happen. He would die alone, certain of his failure, and unable to forgive himself. Poor Sim.

Six weeks later we monitored his final report. The transmission showed the video from his stern view.

Sim here. As you can see, the little bugger that wants to dead me is faster than I thought. He's one thousand kilometers off, closing at seven-hundred kilometers per hour. Assuming he doesn't pull alongside and ask me to join him for tea and cupcakes, he'll impact me in just a bit. I'm jettisoning everything that's not bolted down. Maybe I'll get lucky and the son of a bitch'll run into a seat cushion and go boom.

The mothership is still on a dead course of the Sun. No changes in course or speed. Do me a big favor and blow the shit out of her when she's in range.

A personal message to his wife and family followed. I omitted that part. It was private. To pick back up where the smaller vessel closed on *Ark 3*, these were Sim's final words:

Looks to be a shuttlecraft, odd configuration, though. My AI says there's a nuke mounted on the prow. It's a jerry-rigged setup, some type of improvisation. No way of knowing for sure, but it's fairly small, maybe a few kilotons. I guess I'll find out pretty quick here.

Doubt you'll get any signal, though, after it explodes. Too bad. Might have been helpful.

Wait! I'll redirect a remote and have it send you a recording. It should have enough gain to beam the signal all the way home. Okay, that's set up. Hope it worked.

For the hell of it, I've hailed them. The only response has been the same cheer they've made all along. They keep repeating: Gumnolar will live forever. *No clue as to who the jerk-off is. Must be their deity, but maybe it's their favorite light beer.*

A mechanical voice cut in: *One minute to impact.*

Final specifications on the craft sent. No portholes to get a look at one of the rats. Sorry. I jettisoned the ship's AI an hour ago. Hopefully it will survive the blast and drift until recovered. I doubt the mothership will bother to come after it, but there's a chance it will. Might buy you some more time. At least this sorry bastard can't go after it once he's recycled to elementary particles.

Ten seconds to impact.

Still no significant details visible. There is a small hatch ... yes. He's opened the starboard hatch. Well, I'll be ...

That was it. The transmission cut out in static. The remote did indeed send a pretty good image before the blast reached it. It showed a Listhelon leaning out an open hatch holding onto the seal. He waved one arm maniacally as his body swelled and quickly broke to pieces in the vacuum of space. Man, was he ugly. He had a small round head that looked all the world like a rock. His face was similar to one of those deep sea fish with oversized, overlapping fangs. The taunting arm was more of a fin, a long, thin flipper. What was visible of his torso was short and squat, ending in his long, thick neck. And there was something flooding out the hatch. It vaporized as it touched the outside, but it seemed to be a liquid. The Listhelonians were an aquatic species! The warrior's stupid gesture and Sim's clever use of the remote had given us an important insight. I was sure he rested in deeper peace knowing that. Then the two craft collided.

Al estimated the force to be ten kilotons from a fission device. Talk about overkill.

"God help us all," whispered Toño as he stood by my side.

"And I thought my people were vicious," said Sapale. "These beasts are much worse. I hope they never reach my world."

"That's what the space-time congruity manipulator was for," I said.

Toño turned to me. "Pardon?"

"*Yes.*" Sapale said.

"What?"

"Uto, the man who gave me the plans for the membrane. It wasn't to use against my people. It was to defend against the Listhelonians."

Toño wrinkled his brow. "But how? How could he possibly know we were to face such a horrific enemy?" A notion crossed his face. "You said he referred to himself as 'Uto?' How exactly did he pronounce it?"

"Uto? I don't know. Like it sounds, I guess."

"Jon, my friend, there exists another possibility. Perhaps he said: *I am **you** too.*"

"Huh? What ... that makes no—" Holy *crap*. I replayed the loop. It did sound like that. I assumed he was stating his name. Maybe he was. I'd never know. What I did know was we were a long, long way up Shit Creek with no signs of any paddles. A corrupt government undermining our efforts, public apathy that threatened to strangle Project Ark, and now hostile aliens bent on killing us. If it got any worse, I'd be tempted to flip my off switch.

"Doc, we need to get those membranes on everything that flies."

"I know. We shall."

"We must. Not only do we have to *run* for our lives, now we have to *fight* for them too."

EPILOGUE

The New York Times
January 4, 2103
THE WORLD PAUSES TO SAY GOODBYE
By SARAH RATHER

Brigadier General Jonathan Ryan passed away quietly in his sleep last night. In a prepared statement, his wife Dame Indigo Ryan, CH, DBE, FRSA announced her husband of twenty-seven years finally lost his battle with cancer. Their five children were at their side as one of the greatest heroes this nation has seen slipped away. The world will mourn the loss of the man who pioneered android transfer and spawned the robot who is, at this moment, far off in space searching for our new home.

Indigo said, "As most of you know, Jon went through a pretty rough patch around the time we met. Fame can be a cruel mistress. But, he put that behind himself and rallied. His tireless work with our charity, One Family One Destination, was an inspiration to us all. With Jon's help, OFOD has already guaranteed that many third world people can join in on the journey to our new home. In a very real sense he lives on, as an android. I'm certain Jon's spirit will be united and fully at peace."

President Clinton, often referred to as Ryan's wingman, said there will never be another man as great as his friend. He also said he hopes not a single additional public building, park, or university will be named after Jon. It's embarrassing, the president said, that one man should have triple the number of things named after him than his entire illustrious family combined. "It's just not proper," the president said with a smile.

To be continued ...

AND NOW A WORD FROM YOUR AUTHOR

WHO DOESN'T LOVE THAT?

Thank you for beginning your journey through the Ryanverse! The next book in this series is *The Forever Enemy*. Along with this series, please check out the sequel series Galaxy On Fire, Rise of the Ancient Gods, Time Wars Last Forever, and The Timeless Void. I've linked the first book in each of those series for your convenience. But I definitely suggest finishing The Forever series first.

Along with joining by reading, hop aboard the bandwagon. There's plenty of room. Follow me at Craig Robertson's Author's Page on Facebook. Partake of the conversation and fun. Best of all, sign up for my newsletter. Drop me a line at contact@craigarobert-son.com to do so. That way you can abreast of news and new releases. You'll be so glad you did.

A final favor. Please post a review for this book, especially on Amazon. They are more precious to us authors than gold.

Craig